MICHAEL R. JOHNSTON

THE WIDENING
GYRE

This is a **FLAME TREE PRESS** book

Text copyright © 2019 Michael R. Johnston

FLAME TREE PRESS
6 Melbray Mews, London, SW6 3NS, UK
flametreepress.com

Distribution and warehouse:
Baker & Taylor Publisher Services (BTPS)
30 Amberwood Parkway, Ashland, OH 44805
btpubservices.com

Thanks to the Flame Tree Press team, including:
Taylor Bentley, Frances Bodiam, Federica Ciaravella, Don D'Auria,
Chris Herbert, Matteo Middlemiss, Josie Mitchell, Mike Spender,
Cat Taylor, Maria Tissot, Nick Wells, Gillian Whitaker.

The cover is created by Flame Tree Studio with
thanks to Nik Keevil and Shutterstock.com.
The font families used are Avenir and Bembo.

Flame Tree Press is an imprint of Flame Tree Publishing Ltd
flametreepublishing.com

A copy of the CIP data for this book is available from the British Library
and the Library of Congress.

HB ISBN: 978-1-78758-145-6
PB ISBN: 978-1-78758-143-2
ebook ISBN: 978-1-78758-146-3
Also available in FLAME TREE AUDIO

Printed in the US at Bookmasters, Ashland, Ohio

MICHAEL R. JOHNSTON

THE WIDENING GYRE

FLAME TREE PRESS
London & New York

For Elli and Tegan,
who make everything more fun.

CHAPTER ONE

My ship was almost ready for jump when the HUD projected in my visual cortex notified me of a distress beacon about five light-minutes out; the code meant a human ship was being attacked by marauders.

I thought about ignoring it – the odds of actually receiving a given distress signal are so astronomically low that the ship in distress had to know getting help was a long shot. The chain drive's ability to bypass the laws of physics cuts in-system travel times down considerably, but it still takes hours and sometimes days to get from a jump point to the inner system. Space is plenty big and empty, and life's pretty cheap on the outskirts of the Empire. And Kintar was on the outskirts of the outskirts. The 'dockmaster' on Kintar – a position so rarely needed it was a part-time gig – had informed me I was the only ship to dock there in weeks.

And that was if the signal was even genuine in the first place. The last 'distress signal' I'd answered had turned out to be a marauder battle gang, and I'd lost a good cargo when I had to dump it and run from far too many ships to fight by myself. I'm good at combat, but I'm not *that* good.

On the other hand, the signal's transponder code identified the ship as human. And humans, as a species, were already in pretty short supply in the universe. If that signal was real, I'd be condemning them to death by ignoring it. A memory of a tiny, gnawed-on body bubbled up from the depths of my military service, and I clenched my jaw. The marauders aren't known for being kind to human prisoners.

And most importantly, if I left this ship to die, there was no way I could look any human in the eyes ever again.

I sighed as I took the jump system offline, locked in the distress call's bearing, and swung my ship around. I dropped out of chain drive just long enough to reorient the ship toward the signal. A little more than five minutes later, I dropped out of chain drive again, heading at full burn toward what looked like a complete clusterfuck. "Well, shit," I said.

Four marauder vessels were harrying a single freighter. Those odds were terrible, but I hadn't been in a fight for a while, and my trigger finger was getting itchy. My scanners were telling me these ships had seen better days, but the tactical computer's threat assessment made it clear this was still going to be a hard fight. Even though I was using military-grade combat and tactical implants, and even though I'd heavily modified my ship over the years to increase its effectiveness in combat relative to its class and weight, my controls and equipment were probably no better than those the marauders had. Bottom line, I was flying a freighter, albeit a souped-up one, and not a fighter. Even their third-rate castoff junkpiles were more dangerous, ton for ton, than my ship.

On the other hand, the marauders would see me as a trader with some guns. They had no idea who I was, or how much I'd upgraded my ship. If I was lucky, they'd see me as easy pickings until after I'd done some damage.

But all that was secondary. The signal had been real, and people were in danger. I was in this fight. "What the hell," I said aloud, "you've gotta die of something." I'd always maintained a running commentary with my copilots, even when it wasn't necessary, and after fifteen years flying alone, I still couldn't shake the habit. I activated my combat systems and went to work.

My NeuroNet's tactical implants flashed the information from my ship's sensors into my brain, appearing seamlessly in my vision. The trader was IDed as the *Maggie's Pride*. I chuckled at the coincidence and, even more glad I'd answered the call, opened a comms channel. "*Maggie's Pride*, this is Tajen Hunt on the *Lost Cause*. I'm on the job, Katherine, but any help you can give would be nice."

Her familiar voice came back almost instantly. "Tajen!" she cried with relief. "Weapons and propulsion are down," she said, dropping into the measured tones of someone who's been in combat before. "We're trying to get them back up, but you're on your own for now."

"No worries. I'll swat these gnats while you get your systems back up."

The marauder vessels were, as usual, using their transponders to broadcast 'psych-out names' in the Zhen language, intended to scare the crews of small trading vessels into making mistakes. It often worked on civilians who weren't used to combat, but it didn't work on me; this was going to be a very bad day for the marauders. Today's corpses in the making were *Death Dealer*, *You Die Now*, *People Taste Good*, and my personal favorite, *Fuck You*. I chuckled and activated my comms through my neural link. "Attention marauder scum," I said. "You have the exceedingly bad fortune to have fired on a friend of mine. You have ten seconds from this transmission's end to cease your attack and leave. Anyone still here at that moment is getting their ass handed to them."

Warning marauders off had never worked before, but I didn't really care; I was doing it to amuse myself. I had it on good authority that the marauders hated the trash talk human pilots loved to broadcast. I flipped the safeties off of my weapon system; my implants, synced to my ship's sensors and computer systems, prioritized targets and gave me targeting reticules for manual fire.

As my weapons came up to full power, the energy bleedoff caused my skin to tingle. The flow of data through my combat implants, as well as my measured breathing, focused my mind to a razor point. It was like I was back in the Zhen Imperial Star Force again, aiming my ship's weapons at the enemies of the Empire. I felt more alive than I had in some time. I locked onto the *You Die Now* and fired, the feeling of my finger tightening on the trigger satisfying out of all proportion. The bright yellow-white pulses of plasma fire stabbed out from my ship, impacting the *You Die Now*'s dorsal shield. The shield fluoresced with the first hit, got brighter as the firepower concentrated on the shield grew, then flared as the shield collapsed and plasma chewed through the hull and into the ship's guts. I got lucky; I'd hit their reactor core. The entire ship blossomed into a bright yellow ball of light as I flashed past, already locked onto another target. My eyes flicked to my comms for a second, and with a thought I opened a channel. "One down, three to go!" I yelled. "Who's next?"

My battle computer alerted me to two incoming missiles. My pulse quickened even as I launched decoys, but the missiles were too close, and only one was fooled into detonating early. "Smart missiles. Shit."

I quickly changed vector, angling for one of the marauder ships. My lips tightened against my teeth. I felt the skin around my eyes bunch as I focused all my attention on that ship, my brows furrowing and my jaw clenching.

I flew perilously close to the *Death Dealer*, firing plasma blasts into his shields the entire time, then changed vector to put him between my ship and the missile, briefly slamming into chain drive. Quick start-and-stops like that risked damaging the drive, but it worked. The missile lost me and slammed through the marauder's depleted shields, leaving them a dead hulk. "That's two, you degenerate morons," I said over the comms. "Give up yet?"

A glance at my plot showed the remaining ships closing in on me. *People Taste Good* was closest, firing plasma bursts that flared against my shields. "Ha!" I shouted, not caring that nobody was on my ship to hear me. "Those are military-grade shields, asshole! Good luck getting through 'em."

No sooner had I spoken than the ship bucked under me as I took a solid hit. I flicked my eyes to the corner of my HUD that showed shield status and saw the upper shield had collapsed and there was a new hole in my hull. "Well, of course it did," I muttered. Just for a second, I considered getting out of this mess and leaving *Maggie's Pride* to her fate, but even before the familiar memory of dead ships hanging over Jiraad came to my mind's eye, I knew I couldn't do it. That freighter was still out there alone, and I wasn't going to leave fellow humans to die – especially when the captain was a friend of mine. "I've never lost a ship yet," I said, my voice developing a quavering quality I didn't particularly like. I reached out and patted the console. "Let's not start today, okay, ship?"

My ship's tactical computer automatically shunted power from the ventral shields to the dorsal, giving me back a small amount of coverage. I accelerated hard, grunting as the G-forces overcame my mass field's ability to compensate for inertia. As I shot between the two marauders, ignoring fifteen different alarms going off in my ears and my brain, I hauled back on the stick, flipping the ship onto her back so I was flying backward at several hundred meters per second, and fired everything I had at *People Taste Good*. My plasma fire burned away her shields in time for my last missile to slam into her hull, blasting a large hole in it. There was a flash of light from within, but the ship just went dead in space, still traveling in the same direction. I checked the plot and found that *Fuck You* had activated her chain drive and was already too far away for me to catch. "Yeah, you better run!" I shouted, throttling up to fight my inertia and locking the autopilot onto the freighter I'd come to rescue.

I checked my damage reports. Luckily the marauders' ships had been in crap repair, because my own ship had been taxed to the breaking point by that fight. My systems were still in one piece, but I was out of missiles, and the damage had caused my fusion reactor to come perilously close to redlining. I shuddered when I saw that report; had the automatic dampener systems not kicked in just in time, my ship would have become a momentary miniature star. Just imagining it caused goose bumps all along my spine. I was going to have nightmares for weeks. Worst of all, that hit on my topside had burned through the hull and damaged my chain drive's impeller system. That was a repair I couldn't manage out here, even if I'd had the parts.

"*Skalk*," I cursed in Kelvak. It's my favorite language to curse in – there is nothing as satisfying as the harsh consonants and default imperatives of the primary Kelvaki language. I set my ship to return to the *Maggie's Pride*. While the autopilot took me back, I considered my situation.

The loss of the chain drive was a problem. The chain drive system exploits a fluke of quantum physics to allow speeds up to around ninety-five per cent of the speed of light with no irritating relativistic effects. This far out on the edges of Kintar space, with my C-drive shot, I was going to get to know relativity quite well. There was no way I was going to get to the nearest repair station in Kintar's inner system in anything less than six months' subjective time, and that would be at least four years to everyone else. I had enough food and water – between emergency rations and recycling, I had enough for a year, if I was careful.

On the other hand, I had to count myself as lucky. Had the

attackers been from one of the wealthier, more put-together marauder clans, I would have been dead.

The autopilot brought my ship close in to the *Pride*, and I cut thrust and held station off their starboard side. Just in case Katherine Lawson, formerly a soldier of the Zhen Imperial Space Force, had turned more mercenary than she used to be, I locked weapons onto the *Maggie's Pride*, took a deep breath, and lounged back in my chair, the very picture of not giving a shit.

"Katherine," I said in a sardonic tone, "just so you know, I took a huge risk to help you. Anyone still alive over there, or did I completely waste my time?"

Katherine's face appeared, translucent, in my field of vision. "Tajen," she greeted me with a smile, "I guess *I* owe *you* now."

I grinned back. "Indeed you do," I said, releasing the targeting lock on their ship. "What's your situation over there, Katherine? Everybody in one piece?"

She seemed to deflate. "We're alive, but we took a lot of damage to our sensor suite. We're blind over here. All we've got are mass sensors."

"Can you repair it?"

She rolled her eyes. "If I had the parts, but we don't. I keep telling my quartermaster to get spares into stock, and he keeps telling me we can't afford them." She seemed annoyed, and if I remembered her personality as well as I thought I did, it was entirely at herself.

"I am quite familiar with that problem," I said. "What parts do you need? Maybe we can make a deal. Which, in this situation, means I'll give you whatever you need."

She sent me a text file with a list of parts.

I compared them to the ship's manifest. "Sorry, I haven't got any of those," I said. I looked around my cockpit, chewing the corners of my lips. "Look," I said, "my chain drive is out. I haven't got the spares to fix it. You willing to take me to Kintar, so I can get a transport ship out here?"

"I wish I could. But as I said, our sensors are out. C-drive is working, but without sensors we're not going anywhere. We could set off our beacon again."

"Hell no," I said. "We're already risking the marauders coming back with more ships the longer we sit out here. Let's not make it easy." A stray thought led me to check my scanners, and I said, "Do you have functional spacesuits? Looks like one of the marauder ships is still mostly in one piece. Maybe they had something we can use."

"Good idea," she said. "We've got enough suits, but my crew's busy trying to keep us from losing any more systems. I'll come with you."

★   ★   ★

An hour later, Katherine was sitting beside me in the copilot's chair as I brought the *Lost Cause* to matching velocity off the port side of a marauder vessel that was still mostly intact. There was a gaping hole in their hull, and no signs of life on my scanners, but I was reading a power source within. "Well, there's something still working over there," I said.

"Yeah," she said, her face glued to the sensors, "but I'm not sure it's going to be useful. I'm reading a lot of excess radiation in there."

"Dangerous?"

Her brows furrowed, her eyes flicking as she tracked the data. "Probably not," she said at last. "They're running a Skan:to J75 reactor, they put off zeta radiation, but not too much. I'm not reading anything out of the ordinary." She shrugged. "Probably should have brought my medical guy along, but he's pretty slow. We should be all right, though – I'm not getting any danger warnings."

"Still, let's make it quick," I said. "We're moving pretty fast. We don't want to get too far away from your ship." I swung out of my chair and followed her to the starboard airlock. I grabbed a small bundle off the airlock wall and, holding it to my chest, sent an activation signal from my NeuroNet. The bundle began to unfold itself around me, the nano-machines that made up the device forming themselves into an armored spacesuit and linking wirelessly into my NeuroNet's command and information lines. I paused the process before the helmet formed, and it settled into a collar at my neckline.

"Nice," Katherine said. "A full nano-suit. No wonder you can't afford starship parts." Her own suit was less high-tech, and had to be put on the old-fashioned slow way, by climbing into it limb by limb.

I shrugged. "Seems you're missing some parts too, Captain. What's *your* excuse?"

She sighed. "We've had some bad runs recently, and our ship costs a lot to maintain. We can't all fly *Kitkitlan*-class ships." She affected an impish look I remembered well. "Some of us have *crews* to maintain."

"I like flying alone. Less people to piss me off."

She stopped, her helmet in her hand, and looked at me. "That doesn't sound like you."

I could feel the skin on my head tighten. "How so?"

"Well, when we served together, I remember you being a pretty social guy. As I recall, you spent a lot of time in the crew lounge when you were off-duty. You still play the fiddle?"

"No," I said. "Not in years."

"I thought you loved that old music. You used to say it was the most important thing left of Earth."

"Things change," I said.

She took the hint and changed the subject, gesturing to my nano-suit. "When I mustered out, they confiscated everything they'd issued me, including reducing my NeuroNet's hardware access to civilian systems only. I guess there are some benefits to being the 'Hero of Elkari'."

I shrugged, not really comfortable with that particular sobriquet. "It also helps to have — well, not 'friends', but 'people who owed me favors' among the Zhen officer and medical corps. I called in the favors."

"Some favor. I haven't seen one of those since I left the military."

"And now you have," I said.

She looked at me. "Did I do something wrong?"

"What? No."

"Then why are you suddenly so…blank? I mean, don't get me wrong, I know we're not buddies, but we always got along, and the few times I've worked with you, you seemed friendlier. If you don't mind telling a fellow ex-soldier…what's eating you?"

I sighed and instructed my NeuroNet to send a link request to hers, requesting comms access. She accepted the link, and an icon showing her health status – heartbeat and body temperature, as well as a comms carrier signal identifier – appeared in my view. "It's… it's nothing. I just lost a good job by coming to your rescue."

"I'll try to make it up to you if I can."

"Hey, you know me better than that," I said. "I'm glad I helped. Just wish I hadn't lost my C-drive in the process."

As she put her helmet on, the back of it closing gently over her head, I mentally commanded my suit to close, and it flowed up my neck and over my head, wrapping me snugly in its embrace. I'd always felt safe in this suit despite its apparent thinness. From the outside, the suit looked matte black from head to toe, but from the inside I could see as if nothing was covering my eyes at all. To help Katherine keep track of me in the black of space, I activated blue beacon patches on my shoulders.

Once both of us were securely suited up, I cycled the airlock and hooked us to the marauder ship. We pushed off together and drifted through space toward the other ship, landing on the deck at the same time and immediately pulling our sidearms. We'd both activated mass fields in our suits, simulating gravity and allowing us to walk close to normally in the zero-gravity environment.

As I turned toward the cockpit, a flash of plasma hit the wall to my right. My eyes flicked toward the spacesuited figure who'd fired from the cockpit even as I fired my pistol, catching the alien in the faceplate. The alien clawed at the plate as the plasma burned through and it lost air, quickly falling still. I checked: it had the four radial arms and legs of a Hun, and was trapped in melted safety harness straps. No wonder it had missed; there was no way it could have hit me from those angles.

While I'd been busy with the Hun, Katherine had turned the other way and made sure we weren't ambushed. "Clear," she said. I repeated it.

As we turned to each other, Katherine pointed toward engineering. "Let's go that way first," she said. "More chance of something useful in the engine bay."

I couldn't help but smile as I followed her. "Nice work on the landing," I said.

"What, you forget I was a soldier too?"

"No, just…it's been fifteen years since I was in. And what's it been since that job in Muljat, six years? I haven't worked with many pros since then. It's nice."

We were communicating now solely through our implants. The system could technically just pick up our thoughts, but I could see through her faceplate that she was subvocalizing, just as I was. I'd known people who were able to communicate without any physical movement at all, but I'd never mastered that trick. For some reason, even though I could activate most of the NeuroNet's functions nonverbally, whenever I was communicating, my lips and tongue would move in an abbreviated manner, as if I was whispering to myself. It kind of drove me nuts, to be honest. I'd even started doing it when I was reading. Seeing someone else do it made me feel a little less foolish.

On the bulkhead of the corridor opposite the ship's mess, one of the marauders had spent considerable effort painting a star system map. There were eight circles, with an asteroid belt between the fourth and fifth planetary orbits. It was a mess. "What the fuck is this?"

Katherine snorted. "I know, I've seen better work from toddlers."

Most of the planets were simple splotches of color, but the third had been painted in minute detail. I looked closer. "This part's not half bad, actually. It's— Wait a second. Is that Earth?"

Katherine leaned in. "Looks like it." She squinted. "That's odd," she said. "Look at that orbit line. There are words around Earth. In *English*."

"Seriously?"

"Yep. It says 'The Great Lie'."

"What the hell does *that* mean?"

She shrugged, but said nothing.

"*Skak:tun* marauders," I said. "You know, I've tried talking to them a dozen times. It never ends well. They're freaking nuts."

We continued to search the wreckage, looking for anything we could use. Katherine was businesslike, moving with purpose, but keeping her eyes open for surprises. "You ever run into others from the *Shokala*?" I asked.

"Not really. You?"

I grimaced. "Just once. He was so incompetent he nearly got me killed."

"*Shar*," she cursed. "Please tell me who that was so I don't end up working with him."

"You probably know him," I said. "Guy named Jeremy Quince."

She groaned. "Oh hell," she said. "Tell me that moron is dead now."

I grinned. "No, but don't worry, he's stopped freelancing. Runs a minor resupply and repair depot out in the Enka Expanse. He's a class-one jackass, but his scope of influence is fairly small."

"Good. Bastard nearly got me killed several times over. Worst copilot I ever had. The day they transferred him was the happiest day of my life." She shrugged again. "It's always nice when idiots find their niche." Her voice dropped back into a professional tone. "How's your radiation meter? Mine's giving me weird readings."

I checked the meter in my HUD and frowned. The radiation was high, but more than that, the wavelengths of the radiation seemed off, and the suit was having trouble identifying the radiation's source. "That...doesn't seem right. Hold on." I reset the program and checked it again. "Same reading," I said. I carefully made my way toward the engine room, and stopped when the meter began flashing at me. "Not good. Looks like they were using a substandard reactor system." As I took another step, the words WARNING: SEVERE RADIATION HAZARD flashed in the middle of my HUD, and I stopped, backing up. "Can't go that way. Rad warning went nuts."

"X-ray readings don't seem that high."

I drilled down into the readings, asking my sensor net – the sensors implanted into my body as well as those that were part of the nanite machinery that made up the suit – for an analysis. It came through in a few seconds, and I swore. "X-ray readings are within normal – but it isn't just standard radiation. Looks like the reactor shielding cracked, and the reactor's spewing high concentrations of neutron radiation. It's spreading, but we've got a few minutes before it reaches us."

"Our suits should protect against that." Both our suits combined anti-radiation material and energy shields, powered by the suits' miniature power plants.

I checked the meter again. "Not at these levels. We go through there and it'll get through our shields. Looks like he was running his reactor well over the red line. Hold on, let me send a probe in; we'll see if there's anything there we can put through decon and use." I held out my hand, and a small shape separated from my suit's material and floated into the contaminated area. I shared the datafeed with Katherine, allowing her to see what the probe was sending me.

The engine room was a mess. The reactor looked to be held together by wishes and hope. Parts that had nothing to do with reactors had been bashed together to keep it working. "No wonder it's spewing radiation," Katherine said.

"Damned marauders. How did they survive this?"

"I don't think they did," she said. "Looks like it was working to contain the radiation until this battle. Look to the left."

I looked where she indicated, and saw a body floating beside the port bulkhead. It was vaguely human in shape, but the arms and legs were longer in proportion to the torso than human limbs. "It's a Tchakk," I said, directing the probe to look closer at the body. "Its suit is still functioning. Looks like you were right: the radiation killed it."

On the wall beside it, something had been scrawled in the odd angular writing of the Tchakk. Katherine sighed. "My Tchakka is limited to 'Please don't eat my mom' and a few other stupid things I learned in secondary ed. Get a picture of that; we can run it through my translation matrix."

"No need," I said slowly. "I speak Tchakka. It says 'The dogs have killed me. Death to the dogs and their lying masters.'"

Her helmet turned toward me. "What?" She sounded like she didn't believe the translation. A moment later she said, "I was hoping you were showing off but full of crap. But that translation checks out. What the hell does that even mean?"

I shrugged. "If 'the dogs' is us, then I guess our 'masters' would be the Zhen."

"Not how I'd characterize our relationship to them."

I shrugged again. "There's some truth there, maybe. They run the Empire."

She snorted in disdain, and I grinned at her. "You're from Terra, aren't you?"

"Yeah."

I nodded. I'd seen her attitude before in people from the only human-majority world in the Empire. "You'd see it differently, then. Fewer Zhen there sticking their noses into your business, I bet."

"Zhen's different?"

"Yeah. You can't throw a stick without hitting someone who thinks we're the idiot children of the Empire."

She frowned. "Still. Dogs and masters?"

I shrugged. "It was probably insane and half-dead. That radiation was way beyond Tchakk tolerances."

"As ravings of a half-dead alien go, I guess that one's pretty bland."

I shut down the probe and gestured around the cabin. "Anything we can salvage in here?"

"Let's find out." She dug around in the consoles we could reach for several minutes before sagging in defeat. "Nothing. Everything is either jury-rigged within an inch of its life or just destroyed by the fight." She sounded disgusted. "This trip was a waste of time. *Shit.*"

We left the wreckage and returned to my ship. Katherine slumped in the copilot's seat of the *Lost Cause*, her helmet hanging from the back. "We're blind, and your chain drive is toast. My chain drive won't fit in your ship. And I can't use your systems, because *they* won't fit into *my* ship."

I smiled at her. "That's about right."

"I'd just abandon my ship and pay you to take us all back — it'd strain your systems, but it could work even without your chain drive. But I've got a cargo I'm not willing to leave. The loss would destroy me."

"At worst, you could get back here in a little less than a year. Odds of someone finding it are pretty slim."

"Are you forgetting the guy who got away? As you reminded me, they could come back at any moment. Then they'll get my cargo *and* my ship. You really want to let that happen after you got your own ship shot up saving mine?"

"You're welcome, by the way."

"Thank you," she said. "Though I did say that earlier."

I frowned at her. "No, you didn't."

"Yes, I did."

"Didn't."

"Did."

We looked at each other and started laughing. "If only we could find a way to use your chain drive on my— Oh." I sat forward, thinking, and gave her a manic grin. "Oh, that could work—"

"What?" she asked warily.

"Hold on to your hat," I said. "I've got an idea."

★　　★　　★

"When you said you had an idea, I didn't think it would be this stupid," Katherine said.

It had taken us several hours to link up our ships. My grappling system, originally designed to move large cargo pods or small asteroids, was now gripping her ship in several strategic locations, and her entire drive system was slaved to my flight controls. My ship would be the brains of the flight, while hers provided the muscle. My implants, working with my ship's computer system, would hopefully be enough to keep us synced, firing the maneuvering thrusters in perfect tandem. If it worked, we'd both get back to the inner Kintar System in one piece, with Katherine's cargo intact. If it didn't, both ships would be in pieces strewn across this star system. We were risking our ships, our lives, and the lives of her crew.

No pressure.

"What, you don't think you can make it work?"

"Of *course* I can make it work," she said, looking at me like I'd insulted her. "Anyway, I've got to get on the drive links, so I'll let you get to it." She threw me a jaunty wave and headed back toward the airlock.

"What about the control systems?" I called after her.

"In the cockpit!" she called over her shoulder.

"I *know* they're in the cockpit," I muttered. "It's my *kark*ing ship." I made my way to the cockpit and, as I ducked through the doorway, stopped cold.

A man's legs, along with about half his bare torso, were protruding out of the electronics hatch in the middle of the cockpit. "Shit!" whoever it was said, apparently to himself, as that access space was too small to have anyone else in it.

"Who the hell are you and what are you doing to my ship?" I barked.

His legs jerked, and he began kicking them as he backed out of the access hatch. As he worked his way free, it began to dawn on me that he was incredibly close to my type. He finally worked his head free. "Hey," he said with a disarming smile that removed 'all doubt that he was *exactly* my type. Which didn't make it okay that he'd been in my electronics without my permission, but at the same time, he was clearly one of Katherine's crew, and I was suddenly having trouble breathing right, so I just glared at him instead of ripping his face off.

I'd been in space a *long* time.

I shook it off. "Who the hell are you?"

"I'm Liam," he said. "And to answer your second question, I'm working on linking the control systems of our two ships."

Liam held out his hand to me, and I couldn't help but notice the muscles of his bare arms and chest. I could feel my heartbeat pounding in my chest as I took the proffered hand and met his eyes. He was movie-star handsome, with close-cropped dark hair and eyes I could easily lose myself in. "'Lo," he said.

I smiled for a moment. "Hi," I said. "Because you're Katherine's, I'll let it slide, but it's usually a good idea to get permission before messing with someone else's ship." I was talking too fast. Dammit.

"Yeah, sorry," he said, looking sheepish. "Kath said we're on a tight deadline, so I figured I should get straight to work. Bad call, won't happen again." He gave me an impish look. "I'm not Katherine's, though."

Before I could say anything, he was diving back into the hatch. "You've got some weird setups down here," he called. "What's this nonsense in junction A-7/B about?"

"The extra connections?"

"Yeah."

My face warmed. "It's about me being pretty much an amateur with that system. Field repair went pear-shaped; that was the best I could do. Works okay, though."

"I can fix it if you want. Take me about ten minutes."

"Oh, hell yes," I said, trying to peer around his legs to see what he was doing. "It drops power on me at the most ridiculous times."

"Looks like it could cut your weapons out if you do a high-gee maneuver."

"It does, sometimes. Total lack of power in my guns."

He craned his neck to grin at me and, with a waggle in his brow, said, "I can fix that too."

I abruptly stood up and turned to the nav computer. "I'll get started on our course while you do that," I said.

He chuckled, and my face got hot again. I shook my head, took a deep breath, and began plotting our course, doing my best to ignore him.

★　　★　　★

When every connection had been checked at least half a dozen times, Katherine called me from her ship and gave me the green light.

"About time," I said.

"Thank me when we don't blow up," she said.

I grinned at her image and reached for the flight controls. I took in a deep breath, held it, and started the normal-space thrusters. With a minimal amount of oh-shit-I'm-gonna-die vibration in the ships, we slowly built speed. When a few experimental course changes went through without a hitch, I crossed my fingers – my mother had said it was a good luck charm; I'd never believed in that sort of thing, but what the hell, right – held my breath, and initiated the chain drive. As the drive cycled up to full power, I closed my eyes.

I opened them when I realized we hadn't exploded.

In fact, we were doing fine. There was a minor vibration I didn't like, but it wasn't anything I hadn't experienced before hauling oversized cargo pods, so I counted it as a win. After several more minutes of not exploding, I whooped in delight.

Katherine, on her own ship, smiled at the video pickup. "Told you I could make it work," she said.

"I'll admit it, you're amazing."

"So I've been told," she said. "All right, I need to eat. I'll monitor the drive. Let me know if a problem starts to show up; I'll do the same."

I nodded and signed off.

It would take about four days to get to our destination. A lot of that would be pretty safe, relatively speaking. As long as my 'Net was logged into the system, I could do whatever I wanted. My personal oversight was only really needed during course changes, when the linkages between the two ships would be stressed, but I pretty much lived in the cockpit for those four days. To kill the time, I played hologames and talked with Katherine over the comms. While we were on separate ships, our NeuroNet link made it look and feel like we were sitting in my cockpit together.

I wasn't sure why I was bothering. I knew that once we reached the station, we'd go our own ways again. But it was nice to talk to someone. And she was very easy to talk to.

When we'd used up all the reminiscing about the 'good old days' in the Space Force, we'd begun to ask each other more personal questions. Apparently it was her turn now. "So, *Tajen*. Is that from one of the Terran nations?"

"No, it's not an Earth name. There's a superstition in my family that naming a kid with a true name from Old Earth is bad luck. Most of us have names adapted from the literature the Lost brought with them or from the aliens in this part of space. My brother and I thought it was stupid. He named his kid with an Earth name. Dad wasn't happy."

"So where'd Tajen come from?"

"It's adapted from a Kelvaki name."

"What's it mean?"

I sighed. "Please don't ask."

"You don't like it?"

"I've always thought it was awfully pretentious, but...it's my name, you know? My turn – who is Maggie?"

"My mother." There was a pause, as if she was considering her words. "The name's sarcastic, really. She didn't want me to be a trader captain, said it would lead me to a bad end. So I did it anyway, and named my ship to annoy her."

"She ever come around?"

"Eventually, yeah. Said it was a waste of my life, but that I was doing 'okay' anyway."

"Sounds like a character."

"She was. She's gone now."

"Sorry to hear that. What was it she wanted you to do?"

What came over the comms sounded suspiciously like a snort. "She wanted me to join the family business and become a lawyer."

"Not your cup of tea, I take it?"

"Spending my life on a planet, chained to a desk? No thank you."

I glanced at the clock. "I've been awake far too many hours," I said. "I should probably sleep."

"Go ahead," she said. "I'll get someone here to keep an eye on the drives."

I nodded. "Good night," I said, and signed off. I slept, trusting my implants to wake me if anything catastrophic happened.

★   ★   ★

I was up and halfway from my bunk to the cockpit before I even registered the alarms blaring. My eyes roamed the board as I strapped in, assimilating what I saw with the information coming over my tactical implants. "Shit," I said, "shit shit shit shit shit!"

"Tajen!" came Katherine's voice. "What the hell is going on?"

"A lot of shit!" I called over the comms. "We're losing the chain drive!"

"No shit!" she said. "Drop us out!"

I tried to slow us down, but nothing changed. I swore and hit the drive cutoff, but the only effect was more shuddering. I scanned the sensor feed. "Not working," I said. "Can you cut the power?"

"We're trying, but—"

Liam's voice broke in. "No good! The radiation from the drive is too high. We can't get close enough!"

"Katherine, you need to evacuate."

"What? Hell no, I've got cargo!"

"Katherine, your chain drive is nearing the red line. If it goes, we're all dead. If you can't shut the drive down, your only choice is evac. Now get your ass off that ship or I swear to God I will cut you loose."

"Gods *damn* it!" she yelled. Half a minute later, my implants notified me that two escape pods had ejected from the *Maggie's Pride.* "We're clear!"

I hit the emergency release control for the cargo claw. The control lines linking my controls to the *Maggie's Pride* were broken by explosive clamps Katherine had rigged in case of an emergency, and then the entire cargo grappling claw was ejected from my ship, taking the other ship with it.

My ship jerked back to normal speeds when the displacement field left us behind, throwing me against my restraints. I fought the controls, trying to avoid the ship shaking itself apart. Being dropped from chain drive in such a way was hell on the ship, but it beat exploding, which would be happening to the drive any—

A bright star flared in the sky, far enough away that I didn't need to worry about wreckage. I scanned for the pods. Their automated systems had kept them near each other, but I'd have to catch and dock with each one separately to get the crew off.

The first one had two men in it that I'd seen on Katherine's ship, but hadn't met. The first was a male version of Katherine, with light brown skin and messy black hair. I grasped his hand and helped him out of the pod. He smiled at me. "You're related to Katherine, aren't you?" I said.

He nodded, hands on his knees, breathing deeply to shake off the rough ride he'd just been through. "Her twin brother," he panted. "Takeshi."

"Welcome aboard."

The second man was older, with deep creases in his face. He seemed to be about sixty, putting him into the beginning of middle age. Taking my hand and crawling out of the pod, he nodded. "Hail and well met," he said.

"This is Ben Denali," Takeshi said. "He has an annoying habit of not getting shaken up by rides like that."

Ben grinned. "Not my fault I'm not a fearful git," he said, patting Takeshi's shoulder. "We can't all be winners."

"Fuck you, old man," Takeshi said.

"Welcome aboard, both of you," I said, redirecting them. I motioned for them to follow me to the cockpit. I slid into the pilot's couch. "Let's get the others," I said. I brought us in to the other pod, but it didn't respond to my docking computer's instructions. "Crap."

"Problem?" Ben said.

"Bit of one," I said. "Pod's being difficult. We're gonna need to go in on manual."

"That's not dangerous, is it?" Takeshi asked, his eyes widening.

"Nah, not really. I mean, if I fuck it up, it could get worse. But I can do it."

I brought the ship in close, flipping to place the airlock facing the pod's. My lips pursed while I contemplated my approach. I finessed the controls, bringing the ship in close while matching the pod's spin. Once we got close enough for the airlocks' systems to lock onto each other, the two came together with a clang. "Done," I said. "Let's get 'em out."

Katherine was first. She took Takeshi's hand and pulled herself out of the pod, a bit wobbly due to the ride. She looked downcast. "I'm sorry," she said to Takeshi and Ben.

Takeshi took her into his arms. "Hey, hey," he said. "We knew it was risky."

Ben nodded. "We all knew what we were getting into. We voted on trying his—" he motioned to me, "—plan. Losing the ship? It's not on you."

"But our—"

"We'll figure something out," Ben said reassuringly.

They were busy, so I retreated to the cockpit and got us back underway. Without a chain drive, it would take months to get to the closest repair bay; we didn't have time to waste.

I'd barely settled into the pilot's seat when the alarms went off in my skull. "*Kark*," I muttered as I silenced them. "I hate to be the bearer of more bad news," I called over my shoulder, "but we've got more problems incoming."

Katherine and her brother squeezed in behind me. "Marauders coming back?" she asked.

"Not sure," I said. "Big ship, though."

"What can we do?"

"At this point," I said with a sigh, "we can think good thoughts."

"Already there," she said.

"We're getting a hail," I said. "That's a good sign; marauders would just start firing." I put the hail on the ship's speakers. "This is Tajen Hunt of the *Lost Cause*. Identify yourself."

"This is the *Glorious Endeavor*. We monitored an explosion nearby. Do you require assistance?" The voice was unmistakably Zhen. I relaxed; while the Zhen weren't perfect, I'd never heard of one allied with marauders.

"Indeed we do, *Endeavor*. We lost our chain drive and require a ride to Kintar Station for my ship and passengers."

"Stand by," the voice said. Several minutes later, the signal returned. "We will offer transport, *Lost Cause*. Stand by to dock with our vessel."

★　　★　　★

"Are you kidding?"

"No," said the Zhen captain. "You are asking me to transport your ship, as well as five humans, to the inner system. It is a short distance, but it still requires energy. Oxygen. Food. These things cost money. You must pay."

"I don't object to paying," I said. "But that price is ridiculous!"

"Nevertheless, that is the price," he said. "If you would prefer, you can all get back in your ship and travel at sublight to Kintar Station. It should take you only six months to make the journey."

He had us, and he knew it. I looked to Katherine; she shrugged. We'd already pooled what we had available. I sent the sum to his reader. With a smile as warm as a grave, he gestured to a Tchakk crewman, who led us to our assigned quarters: a single cabin with four beds, a small table with two built-in chairs, an infotainment screen, and a couch.

"Looks like someone's going to have to share," Liam said with a salacious grin.

I quickly sat on the couch. "I'll take this," I said. No one argued.

Takeshi looked around the room and grabbed the control for the screen. As he scanned the available content, he sighed. "Nothing on here but Zhen entertainment," he said.

"What's the projected travel time to Kintar?" I asked.

He looked it up. "Two days."

"Hell."

Katherine snorted in agreement. "Well, settle in, folks."

★　　★　　★

The journey was unpleasant. Let's leave it at that.

Once docked at Kintar, I arranged for a repair tech to give me an estimate on the *Lost Cause*'s systems, made plans to meet with Katherine and her crew for dinner – their insistence; they wanted to thank me, they said – and went straight to the Ragged Angel, a bar on the cheaper – read: human – side of the station. Right about the time I started to relax, my NeuroNet alerted me to an incoming call. I sighed and looked up and to the right, at the routing code that floated in my visual field. The message was from someone on Zhen:da, and the caller— "No fucking way," I said out loud.

It was from my brother, and it was marked urgent.

I stared at the blinking icon. My heart beat faster and the skin on my scalp tingled. I suddenly didn't want to answer it. After fifteen years, an urgent message couldn't possibly be anything good. But it was my brother, so I called up the message.

An image of Daav appeared in the air in front of me. Before it began to play, I flicked my eyes to the barstool on my right and sent a mental command. The small image became a life-sized, fully realistic rendering of my brother, standing beside me. The stool simultaneously lit up green to signal to others I was taking a call in that space. I took a deep breath, waited a moment, let it out, and thought the command to begin playback.

"Tajen," the hologram began, "I need you."

I pulled up my comms system and prepared to call my mechanic while the playback continued. "I know it's been a long time, and we'll talk about that when we *have* time, but...." He stopped talking, closed his eyes a moment, and continued. "I've found something, Tajen. I don't want to say what on an open channel, but it's big – big enough that I'm getting attention I don't want. I'm being followed, and I'm pretty sure my office was bugged. Maybe my house too." He took a deep breath. "I'm scared, Tajen. Please come. And...." He ducked his head, licked his lips, and looked directly into the pickup – which meant directly into my eyes. "Bring a crew for the *Dream of Earth*. We're going to need her." The hologram flickered out, and I immediately called the mechanic.

The portly human appeared to be standing where Daav had been a moment before. His reedy voice called out, "Tajen, I was about to call—"

"How much, and how long?" I said. "Sorry, Bil, but I'm pressed for time."

"Sorry to hear that," he said. "But okay. Fifty thousand *dekka*, and a month."

"Are you kidding?"

"Hey," he said defensively, "class four C-drives ain't cheap, and you want it done right, it takes time!"

"I need to be on Zhen yesterday."

"Well, a month is the best I can do. Take a transport, do your business. The *Cause* will be ready when you get back."

I sighed. "I also don't have fifty thousand."

He grimaced. "Well, there we have a problem."

I saw Katherine and her crew file in, and smiled as an idea hit me. "I'll get back to you shortly," I said, and cut the feed. I waved them down and the four of them joined me.

"How'd things work out with your client?" I asked.

They exchanged glances, and I wished I hadn't asked. "Not well," Katherine said. "The cargo was expensive, and the penalty on top was awful. And, before you ask," she said, holding up a hand, "my insurance deductible alone nearly cleaned me out. Paying the *Glorious Endeavor*'s fees finished the job."

"Ouch. Got any backups?" Smart traders often tried to protect themselves by spreading their accounts around.

"I did – but there's not a lot left in them."

I nodded. "So, you're screwed."

She pursed her lips. "Yes, and thank you so *much* for putting it that way." She sat in silence, for a moment, then said softly, "This too shall pass."

The words were English, from Old Earth, but among the humans of the Zhen Empire, they'd taken on a special meaning. It usually translated as 'Fuck the Zhen,' said in public as a way to vent our frustration without risking Zhen displeasure. I smiled and raised a glass. "You speak English?"

"Mom insisted. Said too many people had fought to make it legal again for me to ignore it."

I smiled. "My mom felt the same way. Anyway, I'm a little better off than your group. My ship is going to cost far more than I can afford to fix, but I still have enough credits to get you all to my other ship."

"You can afford another ship?" Liam asked, his eyebrows climbing toward his hairline.

"I *own* another ship. Well, I own half of it."

"Who owns the other half?" Takeshi cut in.

"My brother." I took a deep breath. "Look, without getting into the fine details, I haven't seen him in a while, but he's contacted me with a job, and told me to hire a crew. In one of those incredible coincidences the universe is known to throw at us from time to time, I happen to need four crew."

"Really?" Katherine asked, a smile tugging at the right side of her face.

"No, not really," I said with a shrug. "I need three, but the ship can carry more than that, and I see no reason to tempt fate. As it is, it'll take weeks to get to Zhen:da, and I don't want to waste any more time. That said, I'm not real clear on what you all do. I gather Katherine is the captain, and a damned fine engineer, but other than that...." I spread my hands, palms up.

Katherine gestured to her brother. "Takeshi is the ship's cook. Liam—"

"Hey now," Takeshi interrupted. He turned to me. "I'm not just 'a cook', I'm a full-on chef. Used to run a restaurant on Terra, got bored and joined up with Katherine. I guarantee you no ship that isn't a full-time, first-class passenger carrier will have food as good as I can make." He turned to Katherine. "*Now* you can continue."

"Thank you," she said drily. "Liam's our security officer-slash-cargo handler. Ben here is a fully certified doctor, which comes in pretty handy."

I looked at Ben. "Forgive my saying so, but you're pretty old for a spacehand."

Ben looked me in the eye, not speaking for several heartbeats, then simply said, "That a problem?"

"No," I said, choosing to drop it. "I guess not. Let's talk money."

CHAPTER TWO

Slipspace is a funny thing. It makes interstellar journeys possible by vastly cutting down the time it takes to get from one star to another, but the jump isn't instantaneous. It can take anywhere from a few minutes to a few months. The time in transit depends on several factors – distance is only one of them. Anyway, over the three weeks we were in transit from Kintar to Zhen:da, I got to know the crew.

It was late in ship-night, and my new crew and I were chatting over the remains of our meal. There had been a few Zhen in earlier, and we'd waited for a table for over an hour as one of the Zhen groups sat around talking after having paid their bill, so we were taking our time in clearing out.

"Wait a minute," drawled Liam, as he draped himself over his chair. "Are you seriously claiming that Kelvaki music is actually *tolerable*?" He shook his head sadly. "I hate to say it, Captain, but no true Scotsman could ever actually believe that." He raised his glass, and my gaze locked for a moment on his bare bicep before I self-consciously forced myself to meet his eyes.

'No true Scotsman' was one of Liam's favorite expressions. Like me, the tall, dark-haired man was an enthusiast of ancient Scottish heritage, which included a love of whisky, ancient music, and ridiculous hyperbole. He didn't have the ancient Scots accent, of course, but apparently he'd learned it from old movies, and from time to time he'd drop into faking it. I, as a habitual imitator of accents, had picked it up, much to the annoyance of Takeshi.

"You can't hold me as a 'true Scotsman', Liam. I was born on another planet, after all. As were you."

"Yes, but the blood runs true, my friend," he said in his affected brogue. "The blood runs true."

"Aye, that i'does."

"Gods of my ancestors," Takeshi cried, and turned to Katherine.

"Now there are *two* of them! What were you thinking?"

Katherine winked at her brother. "Hey, how was I to know these two idiots would bond so fast?"

Takeshi shoved his messy hair out of his eyes and turned to Ben imploringly. "Ben, surely you can stop them?"

"I could," Ben said in his deep voice, pausing to take a sip of his whisky, "but I think they're funny as hell."

"You can't stop me, old man!" Liam cried, pointing at Ben in challenge.

"The fact that I don't get up and give you a good beating should not be taken as evidence that I am unable to do so," Ben replied. I smiled at him. Despite the foot I'd put in my mouth when we first met, Ben and I had been friendly on the trip so far, and as we'd be living together for a while, I wanted to stay on his good side.

The others continued talking as I pulled out my slate and began to call up information. I fell into a work trance until I felt pressure on my shoulder. I glanced left and nearly bumped Liam in the head when he leaned over to look at my screen. "What's that?" he asked.

Normally, I'd be irritated at someone getting in my space like that, but I'd already realized I had an issue with Liam. The man was just too cute, and too engaging, for me to get irritated by a little shoulder touching.

I was going to have to be very careful with this one.

"I'm looking over the specs for the ship, and comparing them to the service records my dad left behind," I said. "Figuring out what needs to be done to get her spaceworthy. She's been sitting in dry dock for years."

"You don't think your brother's done it already?"

I snorted. "Daav's a history professor, not a spacer. I'd be surprised if he even knows where the reactor is."

"So what are we working with?" He glanced at Katherine, but other than a smile for him, she didn't join us. She and I had already discussed the ship's needs earlier. I slid the slate so it was between us. "She's *Taka*-class," I said, a little proudly. "Heavily modified over the last century by my family. She's got modern avionics, good shields, and point-defense systems."

"I haven't seen a *Taka*. Aren't they warships?"

"Sort of. They were heavily armed light freighters. They've been replaced by the *Weyani*-class in the manufacturer's lineup, but they're still good ships – and unlike most of the ships available in the Empire, they were designed for humans from the keel up, so there's no stretching for controls just out of reach. She's got less cargo space than a pure freighter, but she can hold her own in a fight better than the *Lost Cause*, especially after all the modifications my father and grandfather made."

"Why was your ship called the *Lost Cause*? Seems unusual for a guy like you."

"A 'guy like me'?"

He waved his hand in the air. "You know, handsome war hero," he said with a waggled eyebrow, "setting out on his own, and he names his ship the *Lost Cause*? Seems weird to me."

I blushed. "I was angry."

"And?"

I gave him the look my mother had always called 'the Hunt death stare'. "That's all."

I could see in his eyes that he knew that was bullshit, but he apparently decided on the better part of valor and changed his tack. "What's the Hunt family starship called, anyway?"

"*Dream of Earth*."

Liam sat up and looked at me like I'd grown an extra head. "You're a Dreamer?" He shook his head. "Did *not* see that coming."

Humanity's place in the Empire started with the *Far Star*, a colony ship sent out from Earth with a million people in cold sleep on a hundreds-of-years-long journey. Something happened to the ship – a meteorite strike, an explosion, we don't know, really – that killed three-quarters of the sleeping colonists. The ship drifted until it was found by a Zhen patrol ship on the outer reaches of the Empire a few centuries later, its power reserves nearly depleted. In exchange for what the Zhen had given us – a planet to call home and a new lease on life – the human survivors had agreed to become a client state of the Empire. *Dreamers* was the label given to humans who felt that we'd lost something as a species when we made that bargain. Dreamers tended to spend significant chunks of their lives uselessly searching through the remnants of the *Far Star*'s data stores for the location of Earth. Many hoped to be the one to find it.

Every few decades, some fool claimed to have found the route. After all, the person who found it would be the celebrity of the millennium and a hero. More importantly to some, they'd be wealthy beyond reason. But none of the claims had ever panned out. Dreamers and drifters searched their whole lives, but nobody had ever found it, and over the centuries, Dreamers had dwindled, reduced to a largely derided group that few wanted to claim membership in. Still, the lure of Earth remained strong for many.

I frowned. "I've never liked that label. Makes it sound like I spend my days daydreaming about Earth. I don't. I'm not on some fruitless crusade to find Earth. But...yeah, I guess I am one of them."

Ben nodded from across the table and I realized he'd been listening to us all along. "Me too."

Liam turned to Ben, sputtering. "How did I not know that?"

Ben grinned. "Because you're a dumbass."

Liam threw a napkin at him. "But what's the point? I mean, yeah, I'd love to see Earth. But it's gone. Nobody's been able to find it for literally hundreds of years. I think the chance of anyone actually going there is pretty much in the negative at this point."

"That's no reason to stop dreaming," Ben said. "To stop believing."

"But dreaming of *what*, exactly? Nobody alive has ever been to Earth. It's been almost a thousand years since the colony left. And assuming there's anyone still alive there, our languages and cultures are bound to have shifted on both sides. Even if we found it, we'd effectively be refugees, not long-lost brothers and sisters. What's the point?"

Ben took a breath as he considered his answer. "Every Dreamer is different. For some, it's about feeling the same wind on our faces that our ancestors felt, being warmed by the same sun, swimming in the same waters. It's where our species began, and where we belong. For me...." He paused, and smiled. "The reason you never knew I'm one of them is that I don't advertise it. I don't talk about Earth, or finding it, because I don't think anyone here ever will.

It's centuries in practically any direction from the place the *Far Star* was found. We're not even sure the vector she was on was the one she started from.

"But Earth is where we're from. We're humans. We're not Zhen, or Tradd, or Tchakk, or Kelvaki. We can learn their ways, their tongues, how they think…but we'll never be them, and nothing can change that. We come from proud people who lived, worked, and died on a tiny little ball of rock light-years from where we are now, and we must never forget that. We must never forget our culture, or our languages."

"What happens if we do?"

"We become a lost people, homeless and unable to ever reclaim what we were."

Takeshi leaned forward. "Fewer people speak human languages every year. There's just no reason to learn them, really. It seems pretty inevitable that we're going to forget Earth as anything more than a legend nobody knows much about."

"I hope not," Ben said.

Liam spoke up again. "You keep saying Earth's important. But don't you think we'd have had other colony worlds? We're descended from a colony. Even if the Accident had never happened, we'd have grown up far from Earth."

Ben waved that off. "Course we would have. But Earth would have been a known quantity. We might have been able to go back there. Earth will always be home to our species, even if we never set foot on it. With it gone, our people lack something we need, a place to ground ourselves."

"I'll drink to that," I said, and raised my glass. "Dreamers may want to go to Earth, Liam, but even more, they want a place where we can be something more than the Zhen's bootlickers."

Katherine had stayed out of the conversation up to now, but at that, she leaned toward me. "'Bootlickers'? Isn't that laying it on a bit thick?"

"No. It isn't." I leaned closer to the middle of the table and lowered my voice. "I served in the military because I believed at the time that if I worked hard enough and rose through the ranks, the Zhen would respect me. If I served well, maybe it would help humans rise in their estimation." I sighed. "It didn't take long for that delusion to pass. No matter how good I was, I was still human. Still less than a Zhen. Hell, they gave me command of a squadron and I *still* didn't measure up in their eyes. And once I failed at Jiraad...." I snorted. "Well, it was either resign my commission or get assigned to some ridiculous patrol on the edge of the Empire. I decided I'd rather feel like I was in charge of my own life. Out here, when I'm not in port, I feel free in a way I can never feel on a planet in the Zhen Empire."

Liam shook his head. "I don't get it," he said. "I know they can be a pain in the ass, but they saved our people. They earned a little condescending superiority." He winked. "But you're still cute."

I grimaced at the compliment, waving it off with a casual motion. "On that note," I said, rising, "good night." I made my way back to my cabin and threw myself on my bunk.

I tried to sleep, but I couldn't stop thinking about Daav. I hoped he was all right.

★　　★　　★

"What happens when we drop into orbit?" Katherine asked at breakfast.

We'd decided to meet alone to discuss logistics. I could see Liam, Ben, and Takeshi at another table, talking animatedly. I smiled at Liam's antics, then realized Katherine was across the table smirking at me and schooled my expression.

"Are we going to have a problem there?" she asked.

"No," I said. "I'm the captain. I don't dally with crew."

"We're not military, Tajen. Nothing against it, as long as you treat him right."

"Still not a good idea."

She tilted her head at me. "Not a good idea to have a meaningless sex romp, no," she said. "Not that Liam would say no to you. But that would be a *bad idea*," she said, placing the perfect emphasis on the words to let me know what she'd think of it. "But if something real developed...well, that wouldn't be the end of the world."

I thought about it for a second, then caught myself before the smile showed. That wasn't going to happen. "Won't be an issue," I said tersely. "He's crew."

She sighed. "I think you might have misunderstood my intent here."

"No," I said. "I didn't. But he's part of my crew."

"Your ship," she said. "I assume your brother will be XO?" We'd covered pay in our original negotiations, but we hadn't discussed crew jobs beyond each crewman's specialty and backup jobs.

"Not a chance," I said. "My brother is a smart guy, but he knows precisely shit about running a starship." I leveled my gaze at her. "No, I want you in that role."

"Me? Why?"

"You don't think you're a good choice?"

"Oh," she said slyly, "I'm a fantastic choice. But I want to know why you agree with me."

"Okay," I said. "First off, because you're military-trained, like I am. I need someone with the right training."

"Liam's got that training too. He was ground forces, but he knows how to operate with someone like you."

I smiled. "I'm sure he does," I said, "but I need someone who isn't going to keep knocking me off center."

"He's not *that* good-looking," she laughed.

I just looked at her, a neutral expression on my face, until she admitted with a look that yes, he was that good-looking. Then she pursed her lips and stared at me, her head cocked, for several long moments. I got the feeling she was weighing me.

"How're we going to work?"

"I'm in command of the ship, but most of the time it'll work like this: In combat, I'm in full command, and we work it just like a navy ship. Assuming you all stay with me after Daav's business is done, you'll have the most say in business decisions, because quite frankly, I stink at that part." She laughed, and I continued. "Anything in the middle ground, we discuss and make the decision together – assuming we have time."

"What happens if you and I can't come to an agreement?"

"Then the rest of the crew votes."

She raised an eyebrow at me. "You don't think they'll side with me?"

I shrugged. "They're not stupid. If they side with you, there's probably a good reason."

"Okay," she said. "I think that works." She sat up straighter. "Now, what happens when we get to Zhen:da?"

"I make contact with Daav, while you get the crew and the gear we brought with us to the ship. Once I have the codes for the docking bay, I'll transfer them to you so you can get in and start settling in."

"Sounds good. We'll—" She was interrupted by the ship's announcement chime.

"Attention passengers. We are entering orbit of Zhen:da. We will be docking with Shrakan Station in two hours. Local station time is second *ahn*."

Station time was synced with local time in the capital and Virginia City, so it was mid-morning. Katherine nodded. "We'll get rooms on Shrakan and wait for your call," she said.

As soon as the ship linked with the station, the two computers began to interface, and my NeuroNet updated with a message to call home. It was marked *Urgent*.

"*Kark*, Daav. Slow down," I said to myself as I instructed my 'Net to make the call.

Instead of Daav, a young woman appeared. She was a young kid – a teenager, really. She was cute, and vaguely familiar, with red hair, green eyes, and freckles. I realized who it was just as she said, "Uncle."

"Kiri, is your dad home?"

Her face started to crumple, but she took a deep breath. "Dad's dead."

I felt cold. "What?"

She took a deep breath. "He's dead. Flyer crash."

"When?"

"Last week," she replied. "He told me he'd sent you a message, and he'd be back in a few days. He was on his way home when his flyer crashed on the cliffs."

"I'll be down on the next shuttle," I said.

"Don't be ridiculous; take the elevator."

"Kiri, that's—"

"I'm okay, Tajen. Contact me when you reach the surface." She disconnected, leaving me gaping at the screen.

★   ★   ★

No matter what Kiri said, I wasn't going to spend three days coming down the ribbon, so I paid for a shuttle flight to the surface. Once dirtside, I rented an airspeeder and headed out toward Virginia City.

The city was the first human presence in the Empire, built on a peninsula the Zhen had given over to humanity in the first years after the Rescue. Even after humans had been granted our own world, many had decided to stay, despite the widespread prejudice of those days, to take advantage of the opportunities available on the Imperial capital world. A side effect of our assimilation was that the oldest building in Virginia had been built by an advanced civilization in full command of its technology. Unlike what I'd seen of Old Earth cities in our database, Virginia was a pristine paradise of beautiful, soaring skyscrapers integrated with huge open parks, with none of the trash or grime of cities described in the old literature that had survived the Rescue.

I hated it.

Don't get me wrong. It's not like I wanted it covered in grime and graffiti. But I've never been completely comfortable under open skies; at heart, I'm a spacer. Since the moment Dad first took me on board the *Dream of Earth*, space has been my home and comfort. Daav was the opposite. Starships made him uncomfortable, but he loved Virginia. He once said the only thing more beautiful than Virginia was the ice sculptures of Scalti Prime, and he couldn't stand the cold there. The tropical heat of Virginia was more his style.

I smiled at that, and then I remembered, and the smile dropped. Daav was never again going to complain about the cold, or anything else. He was never going to say anything to me. My brother was dead.

Dead. The word hung there, in my mind's eye, glittering with diamond-edged regret. We hadn't spoken in nearly fifteen years, since his wife's funeral. He had a daughter to raise alone, and I had my guilt, so we didn't put much effort into contacting each other. Occasionally there'd be a message, usually entirely about Kiri, to which I never replied. I sent regular messages to Kiri, and got some in return, but I never saw her in person after the funeral.

Now I could never say all the things I'd wanted to. I could never apologize. All my fantasies of making things right between us, of balancing the scales, were over. All those probabilities had now collapsed into a future in which I would never see Daav again, never hear him lecture me about human history, never...yeah, you get the idea.

I kept thinking back to the message he'd sent. *I need you*, he'd said. *I've found something.* I wondered what he could have found that was so important he'd contact me after fifteen years of silence, and that would need a ship and a crew. It had to be something to do with his research. Last I'd known, he was studying the history of humans — not a popular field even among humans, considering it mostly meant trying to reconstruct ancient Earth stories from the fragmented and corrupted data the *Far Star* had left when the Zhen found it.

And who had been following him? And why? None of this made a lick of sense.

I might have descended into a lot of that kind of thinking, but the Hunt family home was near. I brought the flyer in to land on the house's pad. The house was situated on the rough coast at the extreme eastern edge of the city, an area known as Highcliff, because the original colonists were the least imaginative humans in history. What the hell, it's better than 'New San Francisco', which local legend said the original builders out here wanted. It was high enough that the spray was well below, but the patio allowed a perfect view of the open ocean and the waves crashing on the rocks.

As I shut down the flyer's engines, Kiri stepped out of the house. The wind was intense, and my hair whipped about as I approached her, while hers was restrained in a tight braid at the back of her head. I was nervous. Although Kiri meant a lot to me, and I'd doted on her when she was born, it had been a long time, and I'd hardly been a good uncle, even accounting for the distance. A few quick letters when I'd had a spare moment and too much to drink. I had sent a few messages early on, but when I got no replies, I stopped trying. Daav didn't want to hear from me, and I'd learned to be okay with that…or so I told myself.

I took a deep breath and let it out as she approached. When she was a few feet away, I spoke up. "Kiri. It's…good to see you. I mean, the situation…sucks. But…." I trailed off. *Idiot*, I thought. "Hi," I said.

She smiled and said, "Hello, Uncle."

I started to open my arms to give her a hug, but she turned and walked away, and I was left standing on the landing pad blinking. I'd known things would be weird. How could they not be? But I hadn't expected her to react quite like that.

I was trying to interact with the Kiri of my memories, the bubbly baby girl I'd bounced on my knees and whose nose I'd nibbled on while she giggled. I was trying to pick up where I'd left off fifteen years ago.

But that wasn't going to happen, and I'd been a fool to ever think it might. Kiri was seventeen years old. She'd finished her schooling and the social learning two years ago. She was an adult, one with a life that had nothing at all to do with me. And that made me feel even more alone than I already did.

I stood there a moment, collecting myself, and followed her in.

The house was pretty much like I remembered it. Daav had never really been good with décor; his wife had taken care of that stuff, and when she'd died, he'd done little more than repair things. I saw he'd replaced a few pieces, but overall it looked much as it had when I'd left.

Kiri led me to the living room and gestured toward one of the couches in the house's conversation area. She gestured me to a seat on the sofa. When she sidled by me, I moved over to make room for her, but she sat in the chair at the end of the table.

Daav and I had loved this area when we were kids. We'd sat here and pretended we were two of our parents' fancy friends, a starship pilot or a professor or reporter, and mimicked the conversations they'd had when their friends came to the house.

We sat awkwardly for a few moments. I wanted to say something, but nothing seemed right. "Are you okay?" I asked.

Her eyes burned into me. "My dad is dead, 'Uncle'," she said, the quotes obvious in her voice. "Given that, I'm fine."

"I—"

"Where have you been?" she asked. Before I could answer, she jumped up, crossing to the bookshelves on the far wall. "Fifteen years, Tajen. *Fifteen years.*"

"I know."

She glared at me. "When my dad said he called you, I couldn't believe it. He'd barely mentioned you my whole life. I've been telling him for years to call you, and he wouldn't. Suddenly, he tells me he's calling you home, because he needs you."

"For what?"

"I wish I knew," she said, acid dripping from her tongue. "But he kept this project secret up until he called you. Then, a few days later, he dies? Great timing, Dad."

I honestly couldn't tell if she was angry at me, or her dad, or what. I sat there, wishing I knew what to say. Finally, I asked, "What caused the crash?"

Kiri gestured, and something in her NeuroNet transferred to the table's holoprojector. A series of windows opened above the table. As she sat down again, they shifted angles so we could both see them. Three of them had local newsfeed stories, one had what appeared to be an official communiqué from the municipal authorities, and the last one was a view of a flyer, presumably taken from a nearby public camera, now frozen in flight. "According to the *Sekt*," she said, referring to the Zhen planetary security service, "his flyer went down in the Mashala Valley. Equipment failure."

My brows furrowed. "I know I've been gone a long time, but your dad always gave me crap for not performing regular maintenance. He should have known something was wrong in his flyer." I gestured at the screen with the flight data. "May I?" She gestured to go ahead, and I reached out and tapped the part of the hologram that would advance it.

The screen showed the flyer going straight and true over the valley floor, then suddenly diving for the deck. I frowned. "That doesn't make sense."

"What doesn't?"

"If it was a mechanical failure, it wouldn't have dived so quickly. Flyers don't just fall out of the air if something breaks — not without a pretty obvious cause. There's nothing there. It looks like he just dove, and couldn't pull out."

"Maybe the software malfunctioned?"

I thought. "Maybe, but I've literally never heard of that happening outside of vids. Have they looked at the flight recorder yet?"

"I've heard nothing."

I rose. "Let's go find out."

★   ★   ★

"What do you mean, you don't have it?"

The Zhen technician looked at me. "I mean I don't have it. Is there something wrong with your hearing, human? Or do you not understand the concept?"

I took a deep breath. "Do you know who does have it?"

"I am sure I do not care."

I calmly brushed my coat aside and rested my hand on the dagger I wore there. The tech's breath caught as her eyes followed the motion. The *ten:shal*, embossed with the Imperial Seal, marked me as a Hero of the Empire, one of the highest honors any citizen, human or Zhen, could achieve. There were only seven of us currently living in the Empire. I was allowed to wear the dagger anywhere, even in places where weapons were not allowed. In addition to marking my status, it had a cachet that could occasionally make things easier.

She tilted her head to the side, a gesture that meant she was going to give me some information she probably shouldn't. "The flight recorder was taken by the *Sekt* investigator."

"Did you get a name?"

"No," she said. "But…."

"Yes?"

"He was a Zhen:ko."

Crap.

The average Zhen is about eight feet tall, mottled green, reptilian, and quite muscular. But the Zhen:ko are a full foot taller, red, and far, far more dangerous. They have maintained their stature and color for hundreds of years, breeding only within their own caste. As the ruling caste of the Empire, they are free to act in any manner they wish with absolute immunity from prosecution. Treason is the only crime for their kind.

If a Zhen:ko took the recorder, it meant there was more going on than I'd realized.

"Thank you," I said, moving my hand from the dagger. I signaled to Kiri to follow. As we left the office, I said to her, "You know what that means?"

"It means we're fucked, right?"

"Right."

CHAPTER THREE

I wanted that flight recorder, but first I had to figure out where it had been taken. I was trying to work out how to find it when Kiri informed me we had to attend the reading of her father's will.

"Now?" I asked.

"Is there a better time?" she asked, an eyebrow rising. "Appointment's this afternoon. I made it before you got here."

I nodded and she went off to do – well, I'm not sure what. I watched her go, my brow furrowing. I wanted to say something, but I couldn't figure out what.

The ride to the lawyer's office was silent. I watched the city go by, and occasionally daydreamed about crashing into the buildings below.

Once we landed, we were ushered into a well-appointed office. A short, punctilious man in an old-fashioned suit came forward and took Kiri's hand. "Kiri, welcome," he said. He turned to me, oblivious to my jealousy of his easy manner with my niece. "It is good to meet you, Mr. Hunt." He gestured us to seats near his desk and shook our hands as we sat. The desk was *carak* wood, carved and inlaid with the ornate patterns that marked the legal profession among the Zhen.

"Pleased to meet you as well," I said. "But I'm curious why this meeting couldn't be held via virtuality conference?"

He smiled. "My firm does not, as a rule, do business through the slipnet."

"I see. How long have you represented my brother's interests?"

"About ten years, now," he said. "While we've never met, sir, I want you to know that I represent the family. This makes me Kiri's lawyer and, should you need it, yours – your brother left a sizable retainer for the firm to ensure our continued service."

"I doubt he intended you to represent me. He was rather

adamant that I was no longer a member of his family."

He frowned. "Yes, well, that shall become clear soon."

"I see."

He smiled. "No, I don't think you do. But no matter. Shall we begin?"

"Of course."

"Kiri knows this, Mr. Hunt, but because you're new here, I'll explain that we here at Lathram and Smith eschew many of the modern conveniences of life in the Empire. We keep client files on non-networked media, for example, and load them physically when we need them."

"Okay," I said, not sure where this was going.

"This does not, however, mean that we are low-tech around here. For example, your brother recorded his last will as a standard Senselink file." He slotted the chip into his computer and pushed a button.

An icon began blinking in my field of vision, alerting me that a nearby computer was attempting to connect to my NeuroNet. I allowed the connection, and Daav appeared in the room, standing beside Lathram's desk. He looked much as I'd last seen him: plain brown hair, brown eyes, plain face. He appeared to be across the table, facing Kiri and me, with Lathram sitting beside him. "Kiri, Tajen. There's so much I would like to say, and no more time. I'm sorry." Daav turned to me, the sophisticated VR routines adjusting things to maintain the illusion he was here. "Tajen. Before anything more is said, we need to establish your identity. Mr. Lathram."

Lathram pulled out a blaster and pointed it levelly at me.

"What the *shrak*?" I asked, jumping up.

"Sit down, Mr. Hunt."

"Like hell!" I said.

"Uh…Mr. Lathram?"

Lathram didn't look away from me, but spoke softly to Kiri. "Yes, Miss Hunt?"

"What's going on?" She sounded scared.

"Only what your father wanted." He stepped forward and, holding the gun steadily on me, held a DNA test stick to my mouth. I opened my mouth and took it in, getting it good and wet.

He withdrew it and slotted it into a computer. When the readout appeared, he glanced at it. To the hologram, he said, "Continue code one."

The hologram hadn't looked at Lathram, but now it sat on his desk, its eyes on me. "Tajen, who was responsible for the deaths at Jiraad?"

I stood there like an idiot until I saw Lathram's hand tighten on his blaster. "I was," I said.

The hologram shook its head. "That is not the correct answer." My blood ran cold as the hologram looked at me, a soft smile forming. "But it is what my brother would say. Mr. Lathram, put the gun away," the hologram said, and Lathram's blaster disappeared. As Kiri and I sighed in relief, I sat down, and Daav's hologhost continued. "Good. Sorry about the DNA test, Tajen. But I've had some weird things happening lately, so I need to be sure you're the right person. On to business. To my brother, Tajen," he said, his voice taking on the quality of Official Business, "I leave one quarter of my shares in the *Dream of Earth*. I am leaving Kiri the remaining interest in the vessel. Combined with his own shares, this will give my brother control over the ship and business until such time as Kiri is ready to be a full partner. When that happens, I *ask* Tajen to transfer that one quarter interest back to her, should she want it, or to buy her out, if that's her choice. Teach her well, Tajen.

"I also leave to Tajen the contents of this datasolid," he said as Lathram placed a small device in front of me. "Please upload the contents before leaving this office, then give the chip to Mr. Lathram for disposal. I'll wait." The hologram froze.

I blinked and shrugged, directing my NeuroNet to interface with the device. It offered a file for upload, and I approved the transfer to my own implanted storage medium. Once it transferred, I tried to open it, and couldn't. I frowned at Lathram. "The file won't open."

Lathram took the device from the desk and placed it in a small bracket, then took out a small holdout blaster and fired at the chip, which exploded. "This is a bit theatrical, I admit," he said, holding the blaster up, "but your brother felt this would make you understand how important the file is. The contents of the file will

THE WIDENING GYRE • 43

be revealed to you at the proper time and place." To the hologram he said, "Datasolid destroyed."

The hologram continued, "I also leave to Tajen one last item: the rock we passed back and forth all those years. It's sitting on a desk in my office, Tajen – please collect it before you leave Zhen.

"The remaining assets in my name are to be liquidated and the cash value to be given to Kiri. Mr. Lathram has already handled the details." As he said this, Lathram handed Kiri a credit stick. "The house is to be vacated within forty-eight hours. That is all. This is my last will and testament." Date information flashed, and the hologram faded.

Kiri and I sat in silence for a few minutes, before she broke it with a frustrated cry. "What the hell? He's selling the house?"

Lathram cleared his throat, clearly embarrassed. "He felt you would understand…in…well, I'm sure you're already tired of hearing this, but…in time."

"Why?" I asked. "That house has been in our family for over a hundred years. Why rip Kiri from it now?"

He looked slightly pained. "I don't actually know. He told me only enough to make sure his will was carried out. But he felt you would both understand tonight." He handed me a blank sheet of paper; as I touched it, words began to fill the page. "This explains the process, but the gist is that you he wanted you to spend tonight in the house, at least. You'll have forty-eight hours from this morning, and then I'm afraid I will have to take possession." He looked at Kiri. "I'm sorry."

"No, it's fine," she said. "If I'm going to go to space, I don't need to take much, and I don't have many things, anyway. Dad taught me to keep my possessions minimal." She turned to me. "Well, Tajen? Shall we return to the house?"

I nodded, and we left the office, united in our silence, if nothing else.

At the building's landing pad, Kiri used her comms system to hail a skycab. I gave the address to the cab's computer and sat back, watching Kiri as the cab rose into the air. "Virginia's changed a bit," I said.

"Well, you've been gone for fifteen years."

What could I say to that? I sat in silence for a while.

"I'm sorry," she said eventually. "I'm not trying to be rude."

"I didn't imagine you were," I said.

"It's just…you've been gone for *fifteen years*. What can I say that won't sound hurtful and rude? 'Hey, Uncle Tajen, miss me?' 'Hey, at least you saved on presents!'"

"What?" I asked, taken aback by the venom in her tone.

She looked a little embarrassed. "Sorry! Sorry, it's just…when I was a kid, I used to tell everyone that my uncle was a spacer, and they always thought I'd get a bunch of cool stuff, and I was always so embarrassed that you never sent me anything."

"But I did."

"What?"

"I sent presents for you every birthday and every Landfall, as well as messages, until about four years ago. You never responded even when I asked you to, so I assumed you didn't want to hear from me and stopped sending them."

She stared at me. "I never got them. You said you sent messages?"

"Yes, both text and visual. They came on chips with the presents. You didn't have a NeuroNet back then."

"I never got those either." She stared out the window. "Son of a biscuit," she said abruptly.

I snorted, amused.

She didn't look pleased. "What's so damned funny about that?"

"Nothing, sorry. It's that phrase. Did your dad say that?"

"No, it's just something I always say. Dad didn't like it, for some reason."

I smiled. "Because you got it from me."

"What?"

"When you were a baby, I said it if you were around. You must have caught on to it."

She smiled, and leaned back against the seats. "I can't believe he did so much to keep you out of my life. We talked about you, recently, and he *said* he wanted me to talk to you. But I figured *you* didn't want to talk to *me*."

"Can't fault you for that."

"But why block messages, especially when his will basically dropped me in your lap?"

"Yeah, about that."

"What?" she asked guardedly.

I took a breath. "Look, I'd love to take you, if you want to go, but...if you don't, I can buy you out of your shares of the ship early."

"No," she said. "I...whatever Dad wanted, I want to see it through. He must have had a reason."

"I guess he must've."

"But what do you think it was?"

I shrugged. "Dunno, kiddo. We'll figure it out, I guess." I didn't say what I knew – Daav had had good reason to kick me out of his life. But there was time for that later. I'd just gotten to meet my niece for the first time since that night all those years ago. I was damned if I was going to throw it away already by telling her the truth.

★   ★   ★

The cab put us down on the landing pad just in time to catch a spectacular sunset. Even my dedicated spacer attitude had to admit that the beautiful expanse of orange-reds before me was well worth coming down into the gravity well for.

As we leaned on the railing and watched the sea, the skycab took off and headed back downtown. Kiri glanced sidelong at me and asked, "So what's so important about a rock that Dad left it to you?"

I grinned. "It isn't the rock itself, it's the memories. Long story. The short version is that he and I traded that rock back and forth for almost twenty years, and now he's essentially told me he won."

She cocked her head at me. "I'm going to want the long version someday."

"Maybe, youngling. When you're ready."

She rolled her eyes. "C'mon, let's go get your rock."

As we approached the door, it recognized her and clicked open. At the same time, my NeuroNet notified me that the house 'Net had recognized me and I was cleared for all access points. As we entered, I asked Kiri, "Office still in the same room?"

"Yep."

Kiri preceded me into the office. I entered behind her, and metal doors slammed into place over the door and windows. My NeuroNet informed me it had lost connection to the local slipnet node. I spun to the door and tried to open it. "What the hell? Kiri?"

"Beats me. I don't know what triggered the alarm. Hold on, there's a code panel—"

"Behind this picture," I said, flipping the relevant photo out from the wall. I entered the code I remembered, but nothing happened. "Did your dad change the code?"

"How would I know?" she said, pushing me out of the way. "I didn't know it when you were last here." She entered a code – and again, nothing happened.

I was about to try blasting the door when a file blossomed into my view. It interfaced with the house's dedicated slipnet architecture, and my NeuroNet gave me a request for a virtual conference. Puzzled, I accepted the request.

Daav appeared in the middle of the room, causing Kiri to jump back with a yelp. "Tajen," he said. "I recorded this from a flyer, on my way home. The *Dream of Earth* is waiting for you. She's fully stocked and ready to get underway. But I need you.

"I'm being watched. I'm not sure who's keeping tabs on me, but this…I can't let it end up with just anyone, not if what I've begun to suspect is true."

He waved his hands in a dismissive gesture and said, "I know what you're thinking – I've always been big on wild theories that turned out to be nonsense. And you're right. But this…this is insanity if it's true. It could change everything. I was going through some old files, and the links led me to some stuff in the Imperial archives. It didn't make sense, but I followed the links and—"

He shook his head and took a deep breath. "Tajen, I found the route to Earth."

I was stunned. *Bullshit*, I thought. *Earth has been lost for centuries. People have been searching for over seven hundred years.*

Daav's voice from the grave continued. "Well – I found most of it, at any rate. All but the last jump. My plan is to follow the route to that point. I'm pretty sure the last jump can be figured out from what's in the files and a star reading from there. I know it sounds crazy, but I'm certain this is real.

"But I think someone knows what I know. I've…there've been threats, brother. From, I'm pretty sure, Imperial agents. I just got another one. I'm headed home to get Kiri, and then I'm going to call you and get away from this planet. I need you. I'm leaving this message just in case the worst happens. In that case, you'll be directed to this room, to see this message. The rock was just to get you in the room.

"The coordinates for each jump are in the *Dream of Earth*'s navicomp. Follow it, brother. Kiri ought to be able to work out the last jump given the information in the files and whatever you find along the way. Don't trust any Zhen in this, please." Daav looked away from the camera a moment, then looked back. "Tajen, if I'm right about what's coming, then I might not get a chance to say this in person. I'm sorry. Sorry for kicking you out, sorry for keeping you out. I was wrong, brother. Please forgive me." The file ended.

I stood in the office, staring at Kiri, each of us absorbing what had just happened. The metal shutters retracted.

Kiri spoke first. "Shit."

"Yeah."

★   ★   ★

After that bombshell, we decided to have a drink. Then 'a drink' became 'all the alcohol in the house'. We talked, mostly me telling stories about Daav and me, late into the night, until finally Kiri fell asleep on the couch in the small hours of the morning. Half-drunk, I covered her with a blanket and then took a walk around the house, cataloging in my mind the milestones of my youth – the room Daav and I had trashed when we tried to make a pet of a wild *shkill*, an animal that we didn't realize would spray a vile substance to mark its territory. My bedroom, where my friend Jacob and I had discovered we shared the same attraction, and where he'd broken my heart a year later. Memories surfaced as I walked; most, from the time before I'd received my NeuroNet, were hazy with time, but one in particular was from the last time I'd stood in the kitchen with Daav, the night of his wife's funeral. Thanks to my implants, that memory was perfect and pristine.

I'd explained how Jiraad had happened – how I'd screwed up, and his wife had been killed. He'd been angry, blaming me for her death, and had kicked me out.

He'd begun by throwing things at me, screaming in incoherent rage. I remember hearing Kiri, upstairs, start crying, woken by her father's anger. He'd stopped and collected himself, glanced up the stairs, and then looked back at me, his eyes shining with rage and hate. Then he'd said the words I had never expected a member of my own family to say to me: "Get out, Tajen. I never want to see you here again." He'd turned his back on me, gone to Kiri. I'd gathered my bag and left, not even bothering to call a cab until I'd walked down the road.

I hadn't been back since that night. I had my guilt over his wife's death – over the deaths of almost three million people, most of them human, a species that had already been in short supply – and he had his anger. The two couldn't mix.

Remembering all that broke the dam I'd built to hold back the pain of losing my family. I sank to the floor, sobbing for the brother, and the happiness, I had lost all those years ago.

CHAPTER FOUR

When I woke up the next morning, groggy and draped over a bed in a guest room that had once been mine, my NeuroNet informed me that I had a message from Kaaniv, a Zhen soldier and the closest thing to a friend I had among the Zhen – for whatever that's worth. I took a deep breath and played the message.

"Tajen, why didn't you tell me you were on Zhen? I had to discover it myself? I have reserved a table at Korta's. Meet me for lunch, let us say, sixth *ahn*."

I groaned. Korta's catered exclusively to Zhen; while they didn't forbid humans – they were far too 'classy' for that – no human would want to eat there, no matter how adventurous they were. The last time I'd tried to eat food prepared in the traditional Zhen style, I'd spent half the night regretting it. But to decline the invitation would be a grave insult, and it's never a good idea to anger a Zhen who seems to like you. One never knows when one will need their help. I'd have to go. I rolled out of bed and shrugged to myself. Kaaniv was a decent enough sort, and it would be a pleasant diversion, aside from the food. My NeuroNet's time display read that it was now halfway through the fifth *ahn*. More than enough time to get a shower, then. I tottered out to the living room, where I found Kiri at work with a computer. "Kiri, I need to go into the capital to meet someone. I'll be back by the eighth *ahn*, okay?"

"Sure," she said distractedly.

"We'll head up to the ship when I get back."

"I'll be ready. Just loading the files I want to take with me."

"Great." I started to walk away, then turned back. "I have to meet him at Korta's. Have a bucket and an indigestion tablet ready for me, would you?"

She made a face and nodded. "Good luck waiting till you get back," she said.

I showered and dressed, then went out to meet the aircar I'd ordered. On the way into the heart of the Zhen capital city, I mentally prepared myself to don 'the Mask', the practiced ability to withstand the heaps of shit I was accustomed to receiving from Zhen.

On paper, humans were citizens of the Empire. However, we were also a client species, and by the rules of Zhen society, we counted as less important, less deserving of respect, than a Zhen. Even the Tradd tended to treat us poorly, and they were fellow clients.

To be fair, there were many Zhen who felt differently, and treated humans as equals – Kaaniv being one example. There was even a minority political party in the *Talnera*, the elected officials that advised the Twenty, that advocated for ending humanity's client period early, though they never got much traction. We'd officially become full members of the Empire in another twelve hundred years, but if you asked me, it'd be a long while after that before the Zhen stopped seeing us as their inferiors.

The cab dropped me off on the landing balcony of Korta's. I looked out over the city for a moment, then entered the restaurant. The host was a Zhen, dressed in a leather warrior costume out of the *chikar* period, about ten thousand years ago. It was a period widely regarded by the Zhen as the beginning of their culture, but by humans as an age of complete barbarism, with near-endless war and constantly shifting national boundaries. He turned to me, his crest quivering, rose to his full height, and growled a question at his Tradd assistant.

I fought the urge to roll my eyes. He was speaking *Zhensakko*, an older dialect that hadn't been widely spoken in hundreds of years. Most humans don't speak it, nor do most Zhen, except for a few backwaters. When I was in the service, we were required, in the name of 'tradition', to learn it in the Academy. Clearly, he didn't expect me to be able to speak it. It didn't translate to English well, but roughly, it meant, 'What is the prey doing here?'

Yeah. Creepy, right? It gets worse – there used to be a primate-like species that competed with the Zhen, back in their dark ages. There aren't any left. According to Zhen legend, they were delicious. The Zhen don't eat sentients now, of course, but some of the darker legends say the Zhen got spaceflight when one of the tribes ate a first contact team from another species. I tell myself it's not true. It's certainly not what the official history says, but history is written by the living, as they say, and the dead don't argue. So, I don't know.

Korta's is a theme restaurant. It serves food from the *chikar* period, which is mostly raw – or in some cases, still living – meat. Because of course it is. Zhen food in this day and age is cooked, because somewhere between then and when they found the *Far Star*, they'd discovered the benefits of cooking your food. Korta's was meant for a certain kind of Zhen – one who loved 'the Old Ways', which was usually said with a particular relish that revealed a lot about the speaker – and it often attracted those who were inclined to wonder why humans were tolerated. After all, we were smelly, ugly, stunted little things. We were a blight on the mighty Zhen Empire.

I knew better, but I'd had a bad few days and I wasn't ready to let this go. I stepped up to the Zhen, nearly a head taller than me, a snarl on my lips, and spoke to him in the same dialect and mode he'd used. "I am not *food*, you *da lhak*. I have hunted in the stars, while you cowered in the mud of Shinnkokor," naming the tiny, and rather poor, backwater he was from, judging by his clipped speech, which had a probably undeserved reputation for producing deeply stupid Zhen. I glanced at the Tradd, and said, "You smell like it. I take it you're close?" The Tradd squeaked in horror as the Zhen's crest flared atop his skull. "Back off," I continued, "before I rip off your *kffar* and use it for bait."

The remark about the Tradd wasn't very nice to the Tradd, and I felt a little bad about it. But if there's one species the Zhen think lower than humans, it's the Tradd. The little guys had been uplifted by the Zhen a couple thousand years ago, and they were mostly servants. Zhen psychology is weird – while they think humans are below them, they at least respect us for getting ourselves into space, like they did – certain legends notwithstanding – and they dislike, or at least claim to dislike, the almost godlike reverence with which the Tradd look at them.

The Zhen began to puff himself up, and I placed a hand casually on my dagger, moving my coat to reveal it. His eyes widened as he saw the gesture; among Zhen, placing one's hand on a weapon during a confrontation is Just Not Done unless you're willing to fight right there and then.

Before he could do anything, another Zhen's hand closed on his shoulder. The host turned to see who had touched him, and his crest flattened with his immediate fear reaction as he realized who had grabbed him.

Kaaniv smiled. "Considering the insult you offered my guest first, you will stand down, yes?"

"Of course, Honored One." The host turned to me. "My apologies..."

"Tajen Hunt," I supplied, and smiled as his eyes changed again. Of course he already knew my name; he'd known when he saw the *ten:shal*; I'm the only human who's been awarded one so far. While among humans I'm mostly known as the guy who lost Jiraad, among the Zhen I have a different reputation. As he began to stutter out his apology, I brushed past him and went to Kaaniv's table, climbing up into the slightly oversized seat that had been placed for me with a practiced ease and dignity.

Kaaniv returned to the table a moment later, and sat, his chest rumbling with laughter. "That was an interesting insult, Tajen," he said.

"He deserved it."

"No doubt," he sighed. "However, I will have some work to do to prevent that from coming back to haunt you. I suppose some things never change." I shrugged my indifference as our waiter arrived, and Kaaniv ordered a pile of raw meat − a pretty average meal for a Zhen.

I ordered a simple meal of seasonal fruit, and even that was likely to make me sick, due to biochemical differences between Zhen and humans − it was pretty unlikely that Korta's would stock human-safe fruits.

I took a sip of the water placed before me, taking a moment to let my NeuroNet use the implants in my jaw to analyze the water and declare it poison-free before swallowing. Old habits. "So," I said, "it seems you're still in Intelligence. I assume you saw my name on the recent arrivals list?"

He made a noncommittal grunt and shrugged.

"Still attached to the Fleet?"

He grinned, and the hair on the back of my neck rose. The sigh and the shrug were human gestures, something he affected to communicate with me. But that wide a 'smile' was no part of an affectation; he'd dropped back into Zhen emotional displays. For a Zhen, that was a threat display. He wasn't showing amusement; he was telling me that this was no mere 'catching up' lunch between friends. As soon as I saw his razor-sharp teeth, a few things clicked into place in my brain.

He'd asked me to meet him for lunch at a restaurant that sold only Zhen food. He knew I didn't like the place, or the cuisine. It was a calculated choice, subtle enough not to insult me by the rules of Zhen society, but clearly reinforcing his dominance as a Zhen despite our friendship. And he'd found out I was on Zhen:da within a standard day of my arrival. Even for a second-class citizen in an Empire with a healthy internal security service, that was pretty unusual. They were watching me.

"How long have I been under surveillance, Kaaniv?"

He did me the honor of not trying to deny it, making a gesture of acknowledgement as he activated the table's privacy field. "For a while now."

"Why?"

"The Imperial Security Service does not explain itself. Even to you, *shoka*."

The term meant 'honored one', and was Kaaniv's way of telling me that while this was business, we were still friends. I didn't believe him; I'm sometimes blind, but I'm not stupid. Daav had said I shouldn't trust Zhen, and my problems with Daav aside, he wasn't prone to paranoia. I should have remembered that before I came to this meeting. "What's going on, Kaaniv?"

"We want your brother's files," he said, in the same tone one might say the sun was up at midday. "I have been asked to request them from you."

"Why is Imperial Security interested in my brother's files?"

He simply stared at me. "We want his files, Tajen."

"What files?"

He fixed me with the 'hunter's stare', his eyes fixed on me, his body completely still but for an unconscious hunching of the shoulders, as if preparing to attack. "All of them."

Fortunately I'd long ago gotten used to this particular display; I have a habit of pissing Zhen off. I shrugged and shook my head. "I don't get it, Kaaniv. My brother was a historian. What could he possibly have that would be important to you?"

Kaaniv switched into the superior imperative mode of speech. "Tajen. Do not play the fool with me. I was there, at Elkari. I know how well – and how fast – you think. I know what your brother was chasing, and so do you. It is dangerous."

"To whom?"

He flashed a series of images to my NeuroNet, overriding my ability to refuse the files – an unnerving ability only Imperial Intelligence officers had. The images were surveillance images of Katherine, Liam, Takeshi, Ben...and Kiri.

I glared at him. "A threat?"

He shrugged and gestured *certainty*. "A statement." Zhen often flavored their conversation with NeuroNet signals that added emotional shading to their words, used when tone of voice needed to be controlled. It had originally been a series of physical gestures, both with the hands and the crest. Over the centuries of NeuroNet use in the Empire, there had come to exist a set of accepted and widely used signals, sometimes used in concert with the physical gestures, sometimes not. While it wasn't a widespread practice among humans, I'd learned to do it when talking to Zhen. I gestured *irritation*.

"And here I thought you just wanted to catch up."

"I did. But my superiors had other desires." He gestured *resignation*. "We tried to explain the flaws in his reasoning to your brother. We tried to explain that his research was not what he thought it was, that it would lead him to a place that could endanger the Empire." He paused as the waiter put a plate of raw and bloody meat in front of him. He speared a piece with his claw. "Unfortunately, he would not listen." He plucked the meat off the claw with his teeth, and licked the claw clean. "Do not follow in your brother's footsteps. Do as he could not, and live a long life."

A blossom of cold fire bloomed in my gut as his meaning crystallized. "What did you just say to me?" I asked him, my voice cold and low.

He sighed, another affectation. "Your brother would not place the needs of the Empire over the dream of a human homeworld." He took a few moments to eat some more meat, and I fought the urge to leap over the table at him. "It was decided that perhaps the Hero of Elkari," he said, gesturing to me with a bloody claw, "would be more amenable to the needs of the Empire."

I could barely speak through the rage I was feeling. "You sit here, your claws dripping with blood, and you tell me this? You killed my brother?"

"No, Tajen. No!" I was about to sigh with relief, but then the son of a bitch had to be honest with me. "Not I. I could not do such a thing to you." He shrugged. "Another agent did it. I could do nothing to stop it, the directive came directly from the One."

I fought to maintain control. In this moment, rash action would only get me killed; Kaaniv had the rank and the power to make that happen, and I knew now that I could not trust him, that all his talk of human equality had been a sham. I managed to keep my face still, but when Kaaniv's eyes flicked to my right arm, I realized my hand was grasping the hilt of my blaster with a white-knuckled grip. "You mean you *would* not stop it."

"It is the same thing, when one serves the Twenty and the One."

"No," I spat. "It is not." The Twenty and the One were the ruling council of the Empire, drawn from the ruling caste. Of course, they were all Zhen; more specifically, they were all Zhen:ko. They had ultimate authority, and Kaaniv's branch of the service answered directly to them. I had three choices here. I could draw my gun and fire it into his face, kill an old 'friend' in retaliation for the actions of others, and then die. I could do as he asked, hand over everything I knew to the Zhen and move on with my life, stuck in their shadow forever. Or I could get on the path Daav had laid out for me, and follow it to whatever it was the Zhen didn't want anyone to see.

Honestly, there was no real choice. I peeled my hand from the gun and sighed. "You owe me your life, as I recall."

He looked apprehensive. "Yes, I remember." I'd saved his life in the Battle of Elkari, and Zhen take that pretty seriously by human standards.

"Give me a day."

He looked at me, and I could see he was both disappointed that I wasn't going to acquiesce to the Empire's demands, and excited at the prospect of the hunt. "I will give you your day," he said nonchalantly, as the main course arrived. "But if you don't turn over the files, I will hunt you down and kill you myself." His hands moved in a gesture of *regretful duty*, but his crest unconsciously quivered in the gesture meaning *eager anticipation*. I rose from the table and gave him a slight bow, ignoring the sick feeling in my stomach.

As I turned to leave, the waiter, about to place my lunch before me, asked, "What should I do with your food, sir?"

"Shove it up your ass," I said, brushing past him. "Or, better yet, his."

As I exited the dining room, the host from earlier stepped into my path. "You have not paid for your meal, sir."

I gestured back at Kaaniv. "Put it on his tab. I'm his guest."

He sneered at me, an unnerving expression on a Zhen. "Typical," he spat. "The human leaves the Zhen to clean up his mess."

My gun was in my hand – and in his face – before I even thought about it. "You know what, asshole? I have had enough of your shit. In fact, I think I've had about as much shit from your entire species as I can take, ever. Now, go sit down before I decide this lobby would look better with your brains all over it, okay?"

He moved. As he sat, I looked at the other Zhen in the room. "Anyone else want to piss me off? No? Good." I glanced back at Kaaniv, who was standing beside his table. He made a great show of sitting down and resuming his meal, sparing the sun hanging outside the windows a meaningful glance, reminding me that I was on a time limit. I holstered my blaster and kicked the old-fashioned door open as I reached it. On the landing strip outside, I jumped on a nearby skimmer and used one of those NeuroNet capabilities I wasn't supposed to have anymore to bypass the ID system and start it up as I grabbed the control yoke. I took off, angling toward the Virginia Peninsula, pushing the skimmer to the limits.

★   ★   ★

While I raced through the skies over the capital city, headed for the Virginia Peninsula, I tried to think about something other than my brother being killed by the Empire I had served.

I'd never been under any illusions about the state of the human race under the Empire. We weren't living in any kind of Golden Age, here. We were legally paid less than Zhen, we couldn't live anywhere on Zhen:da other than the one small, overcrowded peninsula we'd been assigned, and our one colony world was heavily taxed and barely self-supporting.

But I'd always believed we were safe. The Empire took a lot out of us, and it asked a heavy price for our survival, but it protected us. Actual violence against us was illegal – sure, it still happened, but the perpetrators were caught, and punished. Usually, anyway.

Riots happened, from time to time. Idealists who didn't like the deal their ancestors had made for a place to call home, demonstrating in the streets demanding the Empire pass laws to pay us better, lower our taxes, the like. But they were rare.

The military was the way out, for those of us who could hack it. I'd gone in, and refused to join Dad's business, because I wanted out. Dad did okay, but I didn't want to scrounge and scramble for a living. So I'd gone into the military, and done my best to succeed there.

And it had worked. I'd become a genuine Hero of the Empire, granted the right to bear arms in public, granted a leeway that few humans ever got.

Mind you, it wasn't perfect. It hadn't saved me from getting my ship impounded, and while the dagger that marked my social status had certainly kept me from the worst effects of Zhen superiority, it hadn't saved me from all of it.

But I had been the Empire's man. Even after I left the service, after Jiraad, I was still loyal. I still believed that the human race was better off under the Zhen than out on our own. There were far too few of us to try ourselves against a hostile universe without their support. In human dives across the Empire, I'd argued in favor of the Zhen, sometimes as our benefactor, sometimes as a necessary evil, but always in favor of not rocking the boat, not going against the bargain our ancestors had made. Before that, I'd allowed the Empire to use me as an example, holding me up as a symbol of humanity's growth toward a larger, more central role in the Empire.

And despite my service, they had killed my brother without a qualm. Because he said 'no' to their request to let go of our own homeworld. So now I had a decision to make: what was I going to do about it?

What I wanted was to go completely *shal'kran*, the path of revenge. Get some armament, and shoot my way toward the One, see how far I got. It would be satisfying on some level – but monumentally stupid. I'd never get anywhere near the One, and then Kiri would be left alone.

Or I could follow Daav's path, see where it led. It was probably as much of a death sentence as going on a rampage was, but at least there was a chance.

I couldn't just ask Kiri to come along, though. Or my new crew, for that matter. I wasn't in the military, and I didn't have total power over them. We'd need to discuss it, and decide what to do together. But I knew what direction I wanted. That was a start.

I banked around a slow-moving barge and sent a message to Kiri. "Kiri, I'm on my way. We're leaving as soon as I get there, whether you're ready or not. I'll explain later." Then I switched to Katherine's comms. "Katherine, Kiri and I will be coming up on the next shuttle. The ship is in docking bay D-1. Meet us there. Have your bags packed and be ready to hit space as soon as possible. We'll have some things to discuss as soon as we're out of Zhen:da's sky." She confirmed nonverbally. My mouth tightening in concentration, I gunned the engine as hard as I could, making a beeline for the house, hoping I could trust

Kaaniv this one last time. I knew that the next time we met, one of us was going to die.

I was going to make damned certain it wasn't me.

★   ★   ★

As I came in for the final approach to the house, I realized I was going too fast to land in one piece. So I didn't bother. I slammed the skimmer down onto the pavement, scraping my way across the landing pad, leaving parts strewn across the ground and stopping only when the bike slammed broadside into the balustrade.

What the hell, we weren't going to own the place anymore.

Kiri came running out of the door. "Are you insane?" she yelled.

Just to mess with her, I ignored my racing heart and responded calmly. "Quite possibly. Are you ready?"

Nonplussed, she said, "You said to be. So I am." She gestured to the rented aircar. "All packed."

"Good. I'll be right back," I said.

"What's the problem?"

"Later. Wait here."

She nodded, and I went into the house, going straight to my room. I grabbed my bag and went to the office, pulled a small silver disk from my bag and placed it on the computer's central memory store. I sent a code to the disk, which began beeping softly, lights along the rim glowing in a diminishing sequence. It was a small explosive, designed to destroy the house computer beyond repair and recovery.

I left the house at a quick trot, and gestured Kiri into the aircar. After I'd climbed in, I started the engine and lifted as fast as the car would go, throwing it into full throttle as I did. The engine screamed in protest, but the car held together. While we climbed, my NeuroNet informed me that the bomb had gone off. A few seconds later, the shockwave hit us, and I fought to control the aircar. As it settled down, I glanced at the rearview screen and saw the burning wreckage of the house.

Kiri was beside me, gaping at me.

"What?" I asked.

"What the *skalk* do you mean, 'what'?" she said.

"I'll explain later," I said. "It's a lot, and I don't want to have to say it more than once. Your dad...." I shook off the tears that were threatening to start again. "Later."

Something in my voice and my expression must have told her to wait like I asked, because she nodded. But she turned to look at the burning wreckage that had been her only home, and she kept watching it until she couldn't see it anymore.

We landed at the groundside spaceport and got on the first shuttle we could. As far as I could tell, nobody was paying any attention to us; I guessed Kaaniv could be trusted after all. To a point, anyway.

Once we arrived on-station, I led Kiri straight to the *Dream*'s docking bay. We ran into the others just inside the bay. "This is my niece, Kiri," I said, gesturing toward her. "She's part owner of the ship, so she's coming. We'll figure out how she fits into the crew structure as we go, okay?"

Liam nodded, but the others looked to Katherine. She looked at me for a moment, measuring, and nodded. She grinned. "What, we're going to say no? Welcome aboard, Kiri." She turned to me. "Now, in the name of all the Holies of Old Earth, would you please explain what's going on?"

"Not until we're away," I said.

I opened the door when we were still several meters off, and the others stood aside as I walked aboard — it's human tradition that nobody boards before the ship's owner. When we'd boarded, I told the ship to add the crew as authorized personnel, and systems began powering up around us.

I checked the ship's manifest and smiled. "Looks like Daav did a good job prepping her." I dropped my bags.

Kiri said, "You sound surprised."

"I am. He was a terrible ship-wrangler when we were growing up. Could never keep it all straight."

She shrugged. "I guess people change."

I nodded and smiled at her, but she didn't return the smile. I turned away before she could see my reaction to that. Katherine saw, and her eyes softened when they met mine. I shook myself.

"Kiri, assign everyone quarters and verify the manifest is accurate," I said, sending it to her. "Your dad was smart, but let's not take any chances." She turned to leave, but I stopped her. "I'm in the captain's cabin, Katherine in XO's, you guys settle the rest amongst yourselves. They're all pretty much the same."

She rolled her eyes. "I'm not an idiot, Tajen," she called after me. I turned and headed for the bridge.

When I entered the ship's small bridge, the displays came to life. Most were hard displays, projected by the computer onto a haptic control surface that arced around the front of the pilot's couch, but some were illusory, placed into my field of view by my implants. When I sat in the pilot's couch, it automatically turned to the control console as the system began to link with my NeuroNet. I began to re-familiarized myself with the *Dream of Earth*'s control setup. I found myself irritated by the placement of some of the displays, and dragged them into positions more suited to my preferences. "Much better," I said to myself. I'd probably end up tailoring the system more later, but we were in a hurry, so I did the minimum necessary at this moment.

I fired up the comms system. "Station control, this is vessel *Dream of Earth*, requesting departure clearance." This was one point where Kaaniv could totally screw me if he didn't live up to his word. I didn't really think that would happen, though; he was a hunter at heart, and if he stopped me now, there'd be no hunt at all.

"Vessel *Dream of Earth*," came a human voice, "you are cleared for departure. We are sending exit vector. Confirm receipt."

The vector information showed up on my traffic control display. "Receipt of vector instructions confirmed. Undocking in thirty seconds." I cut the connection and switched to intraship. "Attention all hands: we will be undocking and getting the hell out of here in thirty seconds."

When the time was up, I hit the release on the docking clamps. I used the maneuvering thrusters to get lined up on the vector station control had given me. As soon as the tactical system indicated it was clear of ships I accelerated, going to full power the moment the ship cleared the station.. The inertial dampers strained under the acceleration, and I was pressed back into the seat. Station control began protesting my speed, and probably my parentage; I don't know — I wasn't listening. I shut down comms and ignored them. "Not coming back here for a while anyway," I said to Katherine. She just raised her eyebrows at me and shook her head.

When we reached the edge of the station's interdict field, I activated the chain drive, and the moon hanging off our starboard side vanished instantly into the distance as we reached an apparent velocity of thousands of kilometers per second. A few minutes of that and I cut thrust, lined up on a randomly chosen vector, and jumped back into chain drive.

Thirty minutes of this routine later, I brought us to a stop. We were past the hyperspace jump limit. We'd be safe out here; anything approaching would be seen before it got close, and the odds of anything coming out this way were pretty unlikely unless they were tracking us. I set the sensor net to the maximum passive-only range. My job done for the moment, I activated the ship's PA system and said, "All crew, please report to the lounge. We've got some things to talk about."

★   ★   ★

"Earth? You've got to be kidding me. Do you know how many people have claimed they found Earth?" Takeshi asked.

"Yes," I said calmly.

Kiri added, not really very helpfully, "Twenty-two thousand, four hundred and ten over the last eight hundred years."

"And how many found it?"

"One."

"Right!" Takeshi asked. "Only one—" He looked at Kiri quizzically. "Who found it?"

"My father."

He threw up his hands and turned away.

"Look," I said, "I know it sounds crazy. Daav wasn't exactly immune to being taken in by conspiracy theories. No offense, Kiri."

She grinned. "None taken, it's completely true."

I smiled at her. "But my brother wasn't stupid. And yeah, he might have been wrong. But if he was, then why did the Zhen kill him for it, and why did Kaaniv warn me off following his clues?"

"Did they?" Katherine asked.

"I told you, Kaaniv—"

She interrupted me. "Yes, I know, but it's possible there are other reasons for that. Maybe there's something dangerous out there. Maybe it's true that he might have made something out there notice us. Maybe it really *was* for the good of the Empire?"

I nodded. "Maybe it was. But you know what? I don't care." I looked at Kiri, and I saw my brother in her eyes. I swallowed the lump that was threatening to overwhelm me and turned back to the others. "Look, Kaaniv admitted that the Zhen killed my brother because he wouldn't listen. He wouldn't do what they wanted. I'm supposed to be a karking Hero of the Empire," I said, touching the dagger on my belt, "and they *still* killed my brother. Well, I am sick and tired of them treating us like we don't matter. I'm tired of being second class. So if *they* don't want us to know what's out there, then I damned well want to know what it is they're hiding." I looked at each of them. "Maybe Earth is out there, maybe it isn't. But they killed my brother, and I need to know why."

Katherine said, "Look, I'm sympathetic. And I don't like being treated like I'm garbage either. But we *are* relatively new to the Empire, and the Zhen *did* save us. I'm not sure bucking the people who've been protecting us for nearly a thousand years is a good idea, and there's plenty of profit to be had hauling goods. I say no."

I sighed, was silent a moment, and finally nodded. "Well, I didn't think we'd use them so soon, but we did set up rules for this." She nodded at me, and I turned to the others. "We're asking you all to vote: do we go looking for whatever it is my brother found out there, or do we go back to being safe, anonymous humans in an empire that thinks of us as less than the dirt they walk on?"

Kiri immediately said, "I'm with you."

"Wait a minute," Takeshi said. "Point of order."

"Here we go," Ben said with a grin. To me, he said, "Takeshi's a self-trained parliamentarian. He'll argue anything."

"Very funny, Ben," Takeshi said, "but this is actually pretty important if we're going to work together."

"Go ahead," I said. I noticed Katherine nod approvingly at me, but I pretended I'd missed it. Besides, I had a good idea where Takeshi was going to go, and he was right.

"Look, no offense," Takeshi said to Kiri, "but we've all signed on to an agreement about how the ship runs. Now we find out you're part owner – but we don't know where you fit into the crew. Can you break ties? Do you have more of a vote than Katherine? What is it you do on board? I need answers to all that before I can give a crap what you say."

I started to say something, but Kiri held up her hand before I got more than a syllable out. "He's right, Tajen. We need to figure that out." To the others, she said, "My uncle filled me in on the basics of your contract. I know that even though he owns most of the ship, he's got no more or less of a voice than anyone else, except in certain circumstances. Katherine, as cocaptain, is the same. So all I ask is the same deal – when the crew votes, I get one vote, same as you. That's it."

"What about when I decide to transfer all your shares of the ship to you?" I asked.

"I don't see why anything would change," she said. Katherine nodded.

"How do we know you won't always just side with Tajen?" Takeshi asked.

She glanced at me. "Have you met him? I promise you, that's not going to be an issue."

Ben spoke up. "What's your job?"

She looked around the room. "Any of you computer specialists?"

Katherine said, "I'm the closest thing we've ever had to that, but I'm only as qualified as the next engineer. Probably less, to be honest. I'm more into hardware than software."

Kiri said, "Then, if there are no objections, that can be my job. My dad insisted I learn to use the sensor suites on this ship, and I'm rated as an expert on standard computer tech. Hell, I could probably build better computer systems than this ship has."

Takeshi thought about it a moment and tipped his head in assent. "Good enough for me." The others concurred, and he clapped his hands once. "So, you agree with Tajen. Not terribly surprising, given the circumstances. Anyone else?"

Ben nodded. "I grew up on Zhen:da. I have been treated like dirt for way too long. As my third great-grandfather was fond of saying, 'Fuck 'em.' Let's do it."

Katherine and Takeshi looked at each other.

Takeshi frowned. "I don't know. I just...." He shrugged. "No."

Everyone turned to Liam. If he voted with me, then it was done. If he voted with Katherine and Takeshi, then we were in a stalemate. I wasn't sure how we'd handle that; we hadn't set up anything formal on that score. It hadn't seemed necessary at the time.

Just as it occurred to me that that had been a stupid oversight, Liam spoke. "You know that if we do this, we'll probably end up dead."

I looked at him and nodded reluctantly.

"And even if we don't," he said to the others, "Kaaniv will still be hunting Tajen. So, basically we're voting on whether we remain a crew or not."

"Yes," I said. "The question is really 'How much danger do you want to be in?'"

He answered me with a grin. "Who wants to live forever? I say we go."

I nodded. "You gotta die of something." He flashed a smile at me, but there was something in his eyes that made me look away, to Katherine and Takeshi. "Are you okay with this?"

"Well," Katherine drawled, "it isn't what I would have chosen. But I can hardly sign a deal that lets the crew vote and then complain when it doesn't go my way." She looked at her brother, and then back to me. "We're with you, Tajen. Wherever it takes us."

Takeshi added, "But I reserve the right to say I told you so when it all goes to shit."

"Feel free," I said. "It'll drown out my inner voice saying the same thing." He grinned and threw me a passable salute.

I returned to the bridge and checked the scopes. We were still alone in the deep dark. I spun up the jump drives and input the course I had worked out using the first coordinates on Daav's list as the target. As soon as the drives showed green on the status board, I made the jump into slipspace.

The great thing about slipspace is that there's nothing to hit. Well, almost nothing. Stars, and a few artificial phenomena, can cast mass shadows into slipspace. Hitting one of those mass shadows would dump us back in realspace, at best – and at worst, it had been known to tear ships apart. So my course took known hazards into account. If this journey led us into anything not on the charts, we'd probably end up dead – but the early parts of Daav's route were in known space, so I set the ship in motion and relaxed.

Kiri joined me a short time later. "Where we headed?" she asked.

"Akhia Station."

She frowned. "Never heard of that one."

"It's on the edges of Zhen space. It's owned by an old friend of mine, Dierka. He's Kelvaki. He runs the place in a backwater system. There isn't much out that way, so it makes a convenient trading station for spacers – especially moving not entirely legal goods to and from Kelvaki space."

"Is it safe?"

I shrugged. "Well, no. But according to the file your dad left, he hid some of the information we need in a file cache on Akhia Station."

"I wonder why he chose that place?"

"Out of the way, not a Zhen station, owned by someone he knew – and whom I trust. Lots of reasons, really. And Akhia is a place you can get pretty much anything you need, for a price. If he wanted information kept safe, it's a good place."

She sat quietly for a while, watching the oddly beautiful, yet disconcerting, colors of slipspace slide across the glasteel viewport. She didn't look at me, which was convenient, as I was staring at her. She was clearly bothered about something.

"What's eating you?"

She blinked and turned to me. "What?"

"You look like you've got something to talk about."

"No." She sat silently for a few seconds, then said, "Yes. But I can't."

"Why not?"

She turned in the seat to face me. "Because we're not there yet."

"'There'?"

She sighed. "We're not...." She gave up and made a frustrated sound.

"We're not family," I said.

"Right. I mean, I'm sorry. We are, but we're not. It's been fifteen years. I need more time. But I need to talk to someone. Maybe someone I shouldn't know better than I do would be a good idea."

"We've got a crew. Take your pick."

She blinked a few more times, then smiled. "Good point. Maybe I can talk to Liam." She looked at me wickedly. "And perhaps more?"

I adopted a neutral expression and tone. "Whatever helps."

She snorted. "Don't worry, Tajen. I won't steal your guy."

"He's not my guy, for *shrak*'s sake."

She grinned knowingly. "Ah, so you *are* interested." She left the bridge before I could tell her to mind her elders. So I shouted it down the corridor after her.

Her reply was unprintable.

★   ★   ★

Later that night, I was sitting in the crew lounge with a whisky and an open bottle in front of me. I'd barely touched my glass, but the smell alone was comforting. It was 0300, shiptime, and I was alone, the lights out, staring out a small viewport at those ridiculous colors.

My solitude was shattered when Liam sat beside me, plopped a small glass on the table, and poured himself a couple fingers of whisky. He picked it up, saluted me with it, and sipped. He sat silently a few more minutes, and then said calmly, "Kiri loves you, you know."

"She doesn't even know me."

He shrugged. "Doesn't matter. The universe sorts itself like that. Blood calls to blood."

I blinked. "Didn't figure you for a Universalist."

"Well, why not? I don't think you can be a spacer and not see some of the Universalist ideas have some merit."

I waved a hand out the viewport in general. "I agree with some of the basics. All life is worthy, all beings deserve basic respect. No problem." I leaned back and looked frankly at him. "But an energy field that connects us all is a little far for me to stretch."

He chuckled and finished off his whisky. "Nobody ever gets that one right. Someone took Universalist writings and an old movie and conflated them." He poured himself another glass and leaned back, holding it before him, watching the light play through the amber liquid. "It isn't so much a real thing. It's an idea, a metaphor, for the interconnectedness of life."

"Once we leave the worlds where we evolved, I'm not sure I can buy that we're connected to much."

"That seems an odd thing to say, given who you are."

"What do you mean?"

He leaned forward. "You're one of the first humans to command a task force. And yeah, it ended badly over Jiraad, but you're also the Hero of Elkari. The Elkari colonists would have been wiped out if you hadn't been there. And an Elkarian scientist saved my life by developing the treatment for Wilkins' Syndrome."

I whistled. The disease was named after the first colonist who contracted it. The bacterium that caused it was harmless to Zhen, but deadly to humans. Nobody'd known about it until Henry Wilkins, a human employee sent to the colony, contracted the disease.

"You had Wilkins'? That must have been rough."

"You've no idea. Every nerve in my body burned. Anyway, the guy who treated it was on Elkari when you destroyed the Tabran task force."

I frowned. "I wasn't the only commander in Elkari space that day. I didn't defeat them on my own."

"Oh, shut up. Even the Zhen commanders on scene credited you with the battle plan. Can you think how much that cost them, to praise a human?"

I conceded the point with a wave of my drink.

"Anyway, as I was saying before you decided to interrupt me, you saved him, he saved me. You and I are connected. *Quod Erat Demonstrandum*, my friend."

"Nothing's been proven at all," I said, rolling my eyes.

He smiled as he stood. "You keep believing that." He walked

out the door. A second later, he leaned around the door and said, "We're connected!" Then he was gone.

Absolute crap, I thought. I shook my head and cleaned the glasses. But I couldn't help but smile.

CHAPTER FIVE

The mad chaos of slipspace faded into mundane reality as my ship exited the Margali System jump point. Using the maneuvering thrusters, I sideslipped my ship out of the jump zone and paused to get my bearings, my eyes flicking over my viewport even as my mind focused, on a subconscious level, on the data being shunted from the ship's computer and sensors to me via my implant. Margali was supposed to be a safe system for independent traders, but the last time I'd paid attention to a reputation like that, I'd nearly gotten shot up by the marauders who just happened to be in-system that day.

It took only a moment to lock navigation onto Akhia Station's beacon. A quick mental impulse opened comms. "Akhia Depot, this is *Dream of Earth* requesting docking clearance."

A gravelly voice answered, clearly non-human. "No can do, *Dream of Earth*. We're full up just now. No berths available."

I snorted. "Dierka, you piece of shit, sell that crap somewhere else. From where I'm sitting, you've got ten empty berths. Now give me clearance or you'll get another one blasted into your reactor core."

Laughter – a horrible sound, from a Kelvaki – came from the comms. It was like ten thousand men stomping on puppies. "Okay, okay! For you, honored *draka*, I'll make an exception. You're cleared for docking port Beta Eight."

I cut in the main thruster, maneuvering slowly in toward the station. Dierka's beacon showed my ship where I was to dock, and once I got into place for the approach, I activated the computer-controlled auto-docking sequence and sat back, my hands still on the controls, ready to cut the autopilot out and take over on a moment's notice. I guess Dierka had maintained his station's computer better than the last time I was here; docking was as smooth as I could ask.

Katherine, sitting in the copilot's seat, cocked an eye at me. "Odd friendship you have there. Sure you can trust him?"

"Dierka?" I snorted. "He's an old friend. Early in my time with the Imperial Navy, I was loaned to the Kelvaki, and served with his unit. We fought in an early battle in the Third Marauder War. Of the entire *k'chokk* – twenty-seven Kelvaki soldiers and me – only he and I survived. I came out of it mostly sane, but Dierka kind of lost it."

She furrowed her brows. "Aren't Kelvaki units often made of brood-siblings?"

I nodded. "Yeah. Half of the soldiers who died were his brothers and sisters."

"I'm surprised he didn't go *tonkaat*."

Kiri, who'd entered just as Katherine said that, frowned. "What's *tonkaat*?"

I grimaced. "It's a ritual suicide. Under Kelvaki law, it's considered one of the supreme rights of any Kelvaki of age. It isn't common now, but it happens, usually in cases where the Kelvaki has lost his or her family, social position, or their sanity."

"That's horrible," Kiri said.

I shrugged. "To humans, sure. To the Kelvaki, not so much. He might have killed himself if he'd been alone – but he had me with him, and to commit suicide would have left me to fend for myself behind enemy lines." The docking complete, I got up and led them out to the airlock. As it cycled, I continued. "By the time we got out, he'd lost any desire for death. But he also lost his respect for the military hierarchy. Resigned his commission as soon as he could, used his hazard pay, and the death-price for his brood-mates, to buy Akhia Depot." I stopped talking as the outer door opened and we exited to the arrival desk – in addition to the usual intake workers, Dierka was waiting.

Katherine and Kiri both gasped. I smiled; it was a common reaction to Kelvaki if you'd never seen one in person, and most Kelvaki not in their military tended to stay in their own systems. Dierka was a pretty typical example of the breed: eight feet of rough-skinned muscle, topped with a wide-mouthed face fully a foot across, lined with rows of teeth that reminded me of pictures of sharks from Earth. The Zhen were reptilian too, but where the Zhen were tall and sleek, the Kelvaki were even taller and wider. He was nearly four feet from one shoulder to another, and his arms were huge, ending in four-fingered hands. I knew that each finger held a retractable claw, with another halfway up the forearm that had evolved into a bone spike.

"*Tcho'ka!*" he cried. "Come with me, don't stop for this nonsense. The usual rubes we check. You? You, I know, will not hurt me. Come through, come through!" He gestured us to follow him and started stomping his way back to the admin offices.

"Kiri, stay with the ship," I said. She looked disappointed, but didn't argue, as she stepped back through the airlock and cycled it shut. While Katherine and I followed Dierka, she looked at me quizzically. "I don't speak Kelvaki. *Tcho'ka?*"

"You don't even have a translator prog?"

"Don't evade the question, pilot."

I sighed, feeling my face get warm. "It's an old nickname. It's pretty much equal parts a play on my name, a Kelvaki joke, and a comment on how I live. Dierka thinks I'm looking for my life. Don't ask me, it's a Kelvaki thing."

"I don't need to ask," she said drily. "Sounds apt to me."

I would have said something smart, but Dierka thumped my shoulder so hard I staggered through his office door before plopping into a human-sized chair in front of his desk. "Ow, Dierka. Thought I told you to stop doing that?"

Dierka peered at me. "And you thought I would honor your request, why?"

"Good point," I said, rubbing my shoulder.

"So! What are you here for?" Kelvaki aren't like humans in a lot of ways, and sometimes it can be hard to deal with the cultural differences. However, this one I've always appreciated – they always get right to the point. Small talk, to a Kelvaki, is a kind of torture. If they ask about the weather, they really want to know what you think. If they want to rip your face off, they say so – or they just do it. So I knew better than to approach the subject obliquely.

"My brother hid some data somewhere on your station before he died. I need the data."

"Something dangerous?"

"Not in and of itself. It's a just a data file, but it has information the Empire killed him for."

Dierka's earflaps closed, a sign of irritation. "He hid something like that on my station? Without telling me?"

I shrugged. "He needed somewhere to stash it that wouldn't be suspected – and would be outside the Empire. He knew we were friends." I hesitated. "And, Dierka – I'm sorry, but we're being hunted. I don't think they can trace us, but I can't be certain. And you know how information flows. No matter how careful we are, someone's going to put something out there that leads him here."

"How much time do you think you have?"

"We left Zhen:ko via a random vector. I'd say we have at least a couple of weeks. More if you lock down comms for a few days, but not much."

He affected a human-style shrug. "I suppose I can live with that. Do you know where Daav hid your file?"

"No idea."

"Then how will you find it?"

"I've got a pretty good comptech on my crew, she'll find it." Only after I said that did I realize I hadn't called her my niece.

Dierka gave me a long look. "If it were anyone else, I would sooner allow my innards to be eaten by *k'tellh* worms. But you, honored *draka*, you I will allow to poke your crewman's nose into my station."

"Thanks, pal. Should only take a couple of hours."

★　★　★

It took three days.

Daav hadn't just hidden the file, he'd completely buried it in the station's system files.

"It's worse than that," Kiri snapped at me. "The file, which is huge, is distributed in parts throughout the system, and it's been integrated into the station code to run everything from the power grid to the food processors to the life support. Dad didn't just stash the file, he rewrote the code around it and made it a part of the station's operating system."

"That doesn't sound easy."

"It isn't. Honestly, I didn't even know my dad was that good with programming." She shrugged. "Maybe he hired someone, or maybe he was better than I knew."

"Why go to that kind of trouble?"

"My guess is that it would make it impossible for Dierka's people to spot the file in a system check – it's distributed so widely that it reads like it's part of the system. I only found it because I had an example of what to look for."

"So how do we get it out?" Katherine asked.

"Carefully. *Very* carefully," Kiri said. "I wanted to just copy all the bits, compile them, then erase them from the system. But they've all got copy protection woven around them – we can't just delete them without causing problems all over the station, some of them pretty deadly. Basically, I have to rewrite the station code while my computer extracts the information we need and puts it back together."

"Can't you just copy the relevant file parts and leave the code alone?"

"Sure – if you don't mind the Zhen finding the information when they follow us here. And you know they will."

I remembered Kaaniv's face and the certainty in his eyes that he would follow. "You're not wrong," I said. I sighed and clapped Kiri on the shoulder. "Get to it."

As I left the room, I heard her ask Katherine, "'Get to it'? Is he clear on how hard this will be?" I paused to hear Katherine's reply.

"He's clear. He's also clear that you're the only person he trusts who can do it. So get to it."

Katherine wasn't wrong. In the few weeks since we left Zhen:ko, I'd realized Kiri was the smartest person I'd ever met, at least when it came to computers. And at this point, I trusted myself, my niece, and my crew, nobody else. I wasn't even sure I trusted Dierka.

But it wasn't enough that I trusted Kiri. As her uncle, I should go beyond *trusting* her. She was family. But I just didn't feel that pull like I felt I should. *What's wrong with me?* I wondered, as I made my way back to the ship.

My childhood had been pretty normal; we hadn't had a large family, but we were close. I felt very close to my parents, at least until

I'd decided to go into the Imperial Forces, and Daav and I had been incredibly close until after Jiraad.

I hadn't seen Kiri since that night in Daav's kitchen. As I entered through the ship's airlock and turned toward my cabin, I asked myself under my breath, "How do you develop a relationship with your niece when you haven't seen her, even on a vidscreen, in fifteen years?"

"Well, boss," a voice said practically in my ear, "you could try talking to her."

Startled, I jumped to the side. I was reaching for my gun before I noticed it was Takeshi, and I stopped the motion. "Sorry," I said. "You scared the crap out of me!"

He chuckled and motioned me to follow him into the galley. "Sit," he said, pointing to a stool.

"Nah, I need to—"

"*Sit*," he said pointedly. Something in his voice made me listen to him, and I sat on the stool, bemused. Takeshi placed a bowl on the worktable and started pulling ingredients from his cabinets. "So, did I ever tell you about the time Katherine came home from training?"

"Uh...no?"

"Didn't think so," he said with a smile. He began mixing things while he spoke, and I found myself almost hypnotically watching him. "So anyway, I was just beginning secondary school when Katherine joined up with the Space Force. Then she got sent out to Elkari, and I didn't see her for six years. When she came back, I'd graduated from secondary and was doing my culinary training." He turned the dough he'd created out onto the workspace and began working it with his hands. After a few minutes, he pulled the dough in two pieces and gave me one of them. "Here, knead this," he said.

"I have no idea what that means."

He rolled his eyes and showed me. "Just do what I'm doing," he said, and I began following his example, pressing and stretching the dough with the heel of my hand, rotating it, and doing it again.

"Anyway," he continued, "Katherine and I were both in hell when she came home."

"Why?"

"Well, at that point she'd been gone for six years. We sent vids back and forth, but a distance had grown between us. We'd become different people, and we didn't know how to connect anymore."

"You're obviously close now. How'd you get over it?"

"We just…didn't let it stop us."

I kneaded my dough for a little bit. "What does that mean in practice?"

He sighed. "It means we just talked. We pretended there wasn't a yawning chasm between us, and eventually, there just…wasn't."

"It can't be that easy."

He smiled. "I never said it was easy. But it worked." He took the dough from me and shaped it into loaves as I washed my hands in the sink. "Talk to her, boss," he said. "Doesn't have to be a big deal. Ask her how her day went, tell her about yours. Make small talk."

"I'm not good at small talk," I said.

"Understatement of the century. Try anyway."

"Yeah, okay," I said. I rose and moved to leave the galley, then turned back at the door. "Don't you have machines to knead the dough?" I asked.

"Sure. But doing it by hand is more therapeutic."

I cocked my head at him. "Do you have formal training as a therapist nobody told me about?"

"Nah," he said with a wave of his hand. "I'm just really good at listening. I was a great bartender."

"You're a good guy, Takeshi. Thanks." I left the galley. On the way to my quarters, I thought about what he'd said, and I decided I ought to try it out. So I turned around and went back to Kiri, first stopping in the galley for some tea – which Takeshi had already made, and handed me without being asked. "Smart-ass," I growled at his ridiculous grin.

I found her hard at work, hunched over the computer, her eyes tracing back and forth over words I couldn't see, her hands moving in the air as she worked with her simulated haptic interface.

"Hey," I said, placing the tea near her hand.

"Thanks?" she said, making the word seem like a question.

"I just wanted to say, you're doing good," I said. "So…how do you like Dierka?"

"He's nice," she said. "Um, look, Tajen. This is pretty delicate work, and if you want it done right I need to concentrate."

I felt my expression close up, and I rose. *Dammit.* "Sorry," I said, making for the door.

"Tajen, wait!" she said.

I turned back to her. "What?" I snapped.

She blinked at me for a moment, then said quietly, "Never mind."

I knew I'd screwed up. I knew I should apologize, and tell her I was just feeling stupid. Instead, I just turned around and walked away, pretending not to hear the frustrated noise she made.

Well, there's always tomorrow, I thought. *There's always something new to screw up.*

★ ★ ★

Three days later, we had the file. I was in the command area of the station, saying my goodbyes to Dierka, when alarms began going off. One of Dierka's subordinates, a Tchakk, waved his secondary arms wildly. "Commander," he called to Dierka, "multiple ships arriving in-system."

Dierka stalked over to the sensor display. "What vector?"

I followed, confused, as the sensor operator replied, "All around us, Commander. They appear to be setting up a blockade pattern."

"Damn," I said. "I thought we'd have more time."

He grunted. "I'm not the most popular with the Empire. This could be unrelated to your presence. In fact—" He was interrupted by a burst of sound from the communications system, a signal that the system was being overridden by external means.

"Attention Akhia Station. This is Fleet Commander Solaar Den'sho. We are here for Tajen Hunt and his crew. Remand them into our custody immediately. Refusal will result in bombardment of the station. You have ten minutes from the end of this communication to signal your compliance. Message ends."

The breath left me in a slow gesture of defeat. I knew Den'sho; I'd served under him. Like most of Clan Solaar, he had been born and raised to two traditions: military service and absolute loyalty to the Empire. He was also a terrible liar, so he'd cultivated a persona of absolute truthfulness in all his dealings. If he said he was going to attack in ten minutes, that's precisely what he was going to do. I raised a hand to Dierka's elbow. "Dierka, signal him that we're surrendering."

"What?"

"I know him, Dierka. Surrender."

Dierka nodded, then reached over and opened a channel. "This is station owner Dierka. This station is not in Imperial space, Fleet Commander. You have no authority here."

"Dierka!" I said. "I told you to surrender!"

Dierka looked at me. "Yes, you did. However, I am under no requirement to follow your orders."

The voice that returned was solid and confident. "This fleet is all the authority I require. You have nine minutes."

"Dierka," I said, "he's not bluffing. He'll do exactly as he says."

He grunted. "Doesn't matter." He switched channels and spoke once more. "Attention. This station is about to come under fire from a Zhen task force. I am issuing a general evacuation order." He turned back to me and raised his voice over the alarms now blaring. "There. Now you can undock and get away in the confusion."

"This is going to cost you. Why take the risk?"

He shook his head at me. "Because I adopted you into my family, stupid." He clasped my shoulder and pushed me toward the door. "Now go."

As I turned to leave, I noticed his comms officer pulling his sidearm clear and pointing it at Dierka. With a shout, I drew my own sidearm and shot him in the chest. Unfortunately, he wasn't the only one pulling weapons, and soon Dierka and I were ducked behind a console, exchanging fire with his own men.

One of them, a human, vaulted over the console and ducked beside us. I nearly shot him before I realized his gun was pointed back at those who were trying to kill me. Dierka laughed and nodded at him. The human traded looks with me, then turned to fire at the others.

As he ducked back down, an instinct warned me to move, and I did – just as his hand slammed into the space I had occupied seconds before and blew a hole in the console's base. More from reflex than choice, I shot him. As he collapsed, I noticed the weapon in his hand – and when I say *in*, I mean *in*. "Son of a bitch," I breathed.

His weapon was a *shol'kaar*, an implant that channeled energy through conduits in the palm. I'd tried to get that implant before I left the service, but it was tightly controlled, and available only to highly placed intelligence agents. And I'd never seen a human with one.

"Dierka," I said, as the last of the traitors hit the floor. "This guy is Imperial Intelligence." I looked up at him. "How long has he been with you?"

He shook his head. "About a month."

My blood ran cold. That was about the time since Daav's death. "They knew I'd come here," I said. "We were never safe here, and neither were you. Dierka, I need to go. Come with us – this place isn't safe."

He thought, indecisive for too many seconds, and I began to think I'd lost him. "I should die here, *draka*. This is my place." He looked around, then grinned at me. "But I get the feeling you're walking into something that promises a better death than this. Let's go."

We turned and ran from the bridge. I activated my comms implants as I ran. "*Dream*, this is Hunt. Warm the ship up, we're blasting out as soon as I get there!"

Kiri's voice came back, "We're already warmed up. We'll undock as soon as you're aboard."

"Neg!" I shouted. "Do *not* undock. I'll take the con, that's an order!"

As I reached the bazaar, the station shook as the first shots from the Zhen fleet began to hit. The marginally orderly evacuation dissolved into chaos. I fought my way through a sea of people from four different races. I crashed through the corridors and the speakers announced a short lull while the Zhen waited for me and my crew to surrender.

I entered the hatch that led to the *Dream of Earth*, flipped off the artificial gravity in the tube and launched myself down, toward the airlock. The crew had left the lock open for me. When Dierka and I landed hard in the airlock's artificial gravity, the outer door closed and the lock began to cycle. I kept hitting my hand on the door frame, muttering, "C'mon, c'mon, c'mon!" at it. When it opened, I ran past Katherine and Liam, making my way to the cockpit. I brushed past Kiri and hit the docking release switch even as I buckled in. The ship drifted, and I reached out and tweaked the attitude jets to make the ship look like it was tumbling uncontrolled. I nodded to Katherine while she took the nav console and Dierka squeezed into the cockpit behind her, his bulk nearly filling the remaining space.

"Sorry for the orders," I said to Kiri. She settled into the copilot's couch. "Zhen protocol in a situation like this is clear. They're going to start—" I was interrupted by a flash of plasma when one of the first ships to undock fired its engines. A bolt of bright white fire lanced out from one of the Zhen vessels and destroyed the ship. I nodded. "As soon as anyone tries to leave, they'll be destroyed."

"So what do we do?"

I took a deep breath. "We wait."

"For what?"

"A perfect window."

Kiri shook her head at me. "A window?"

I shrugged. "A…a moment. A— There it is…." A large piece of debris was floating in front of the ship. I undocked and matched vector and velocity with it, drifting. When the angle was right, I slammed the engines into full burn, nosing the debris out of the way and heading toward the jump point, trying my best to ignore the scream of metal on metal over the hull. And dozens of Zhen vessels, each shining like a dagger in the night, began trying to kill me.

I flew like an insane buzzfly, yanking the ship all over the place to try to avoid hits while Kiri kept the electronic countermeasures working to keep the Zhen from getting a weapons lock. Katherine, at the nav station, was frantically calculating a jump as I brought us closer and closer to the jump point – and to the Zhen ships. "Where are we going?" Katherine asked.

"Doesn't matter, just get us out of here. We can calculate a new jump when we've got some breathing room."

"Roger that."

"Fighters off starboard!" Kiri shouted. I rolled my eyes; my tac implants had painted the bogeys on my vision the second they'd moved out of the shadow of their mother ship. "I got 'em," I said, affecting a bored tone. I was, to be honest, scared out of my mind. One little ship against a sizable Zhen task force? What the hell was going on? But I needed Kiri – and the rest of the crew – to think I had it under control. The worst thing a captain can do in a crisis is lose his shit. His crew needs to believe he's getting them through this so they can do their jobs as ably as possible. Later, I'd get Katherine alone and tell her how shit-scared I had been. I activated the plasma cannons and took a shot at the two fighters. My first shot missed but the second clipped the lead fighter hard enough to spin it out of control and into the second. Luckiest shot in the universe. "Now that's skill," I said to Kiri, grinning cockily. She smiled bravely at me, and I yelled to Katherine, "Got the jump set up yet, Katherine?"

"Not quite. Give me two more minutes."

Now that I was out in the open, the Zhen had stopped shooting other fleeing vessels. That maneuver had only been meant to flush me out, anyway. My transponder signal did no good at all in throwing them off my scent; they had too good a description of my ship, not to mention my style, both in flying and fighting – it was a pretty easy bet that it was being painted by several tactical AI systems. I engaged my electronic warfare suite, which would thwart their targeting – for a while, at least.

I maneuvered around a slower-moving tug that was accelerating as hard as it could for the jump point. The speed of my maneuver must have freaked the other pilot out; he jerked his ship out of trajectory so quickly the fighter pursuing me slammed into him. The heavy hull of the tug, designed to withstand hits from asteroids in the mining belts, was damaged but still intact. The fighter, however, broke apart on impact.

I snarled at Katherine, "You do realize we're under fire and on a deadline here, right? I'm good, but there's no way I can keep us in one piece forever!"

"Almost got it…*there*! Go for jump!"

The jump status indicator in the upper right of my visual field flashed green, and I yanked the stick, turning the ship toward the jump point. The *Dream of Earth* may not have been designed for war, but even trading vessels get into trouble out in the deep black, and my dad had modified her heavily. She could turn like nobody's business, and she was better armed and armored than many civilian ships, though that wasn't enough to take out one of the Zhen fighters unless I got lucky; it had been more than a few years since the weapons systems had last been overhauled.

As the ship slewed around, I sprayed some covering fire at my remaining pursuit. I kept dodging incoming fire while I flew. Ahead of me, over a dozen ships were waiting at the jump point for their turn.

If you're out in deep space, a jump drive can work pretty much anywhere. But in planetary systems, the gravitic forces of the primary star interfere with the jump engines, creating unstable jumps. Activate your drive in the wrong place, and you could end up anywhere – or nowhere at all. When I was in the military, my ship had found the remains of a vessel from hundreds of years back that had been forced to jump from too deep in the system. It wasn't pretty – we barely recognized the wreck. The crew's remains had been preserved by the cold of space due to the many hull breaches they'd suffered. It was…well, I didn't like to think of it.

The solution is to use a jump point. These are usually set up at stable points between two stellar bodies where the gravity is effectively zero. The jump points are large enough for multiple small vessels to go through together, but this is a bad idea – if the two ships' jump drives are tuned even a tiny bit differently, the resulting gravitic feedback can cause a wild jump. Wild jumps can end with you coming out of jump anywhere, and considering the nature of slipspace, you could end up so far away that it would take your whole lifetime to get home. And that's the *best* case scenario. Usually, the drives on both ships explode, killing everyone and destabilizing the jump point, making it unusable for a few days.

To prevent that, rules had been developed over centuries that every spacefaring race lived by. Ships went through one at a time. In inhabited systems, the order was managed by the local station, and the actual order depended on seniority, clout, and sometimes even bribery. Corporations paid controllers well to get jump priority, but among those of us with lesser resources, a lot depended on connections. A friend at Jump Control was very useful.

Given the current situation, the ships were going through in the order that had been set up before the Zhen arrived, with new ships joining the back of the queue, a testament to how scary the thought of a wild jump was. Normally, at Akhia, I could count on my friendship with Dierka to give me priority in the line. That wasn't going to be an option now, of course. So I jumped the line, rising above the rest of the ships ahead of me and going at full burn toward the jump point.

I ignored the angry cries from pilots who were panicked and still waiting their turn. Switching my comms to full broadcast, I growled, "Settle down, folks. They're after me, not you. Anyone who doesn't want to explode, stay out of the *kark*ing jump zone!"

I wish they'd all listened.

CHAPTER SIX

I'd only experienced a wild jump once before, when I was serving in the Imperial Navy. It was brutal; the only reason my ship had survived was that I had an amazing pilot on my crew.

I wished he was with me now as I frantically hit the belly thrusters in an attempt to avoid the idiot freighter that was rising up before me, trying to beat me to the jump point. I barely made it; the screaming of my hull when it scraped across his dorsal heat vanes seemed to drill directly into my brain.

I slammed my engines to full. I wasn't going to be able to slow down, so I needed to make damned sure I hit the jump point first. I initiated the jump the moment we hit the point, and we slammed into slipspace with far more than the gentle shudder I was used to – a combination of greater than normal stresses and an exploding freighter below us.

I jerked against the belts of my combat harness as the ship tried to throw me out of my seat. Only years of training kept my mind intact as I fought to keep the *Dream* from spinning out of control.

Normally, a jump is carefully calculated, your course along the cosmic flux chosen by the computer while you're in slipspace. The movement of the ship through slipspace is undetectable – normally.

In a wild jump, you have to fight to keep your ship within very specific parameters, or the jump drift will be even worse than it would be in a badly plotted jump. It's a herculean task, and is the reason why so many pilots who get the bad luck to be involved in a wild jump end up so far off course.

I did the best I could for almost an hour, ignoring the physical pain caused by the combat straps cutting into my chest as I was slammed back and forth by the ship's motions, as well as the excruciating headache caused by my NeuroNet's biofeedback. I chanced a look at the jump timer and cursed when I saw it flashing zeroes. That meant the computer didn't have a clue how long this jump would be. When I could, I glanced at Kiri. She held onto her straps for dear life, her face gone white. Katherine patted her shoulder, but looked pained herself. Only Dierka was enjoying this flight, laughing like a goddamned idiot in the back of the cockpit, his massive arms and legs jammed into the walls and floor to hold him in place.

Just when I was beginning to wonder if it would be so bad to let go of the controls and drift off into the wilds of slipspace, the jump ended with a flash of light and we were back in normal space, tumbling out of control. I swore as I fought my way out of the tumble. I brought the ship to a stop and sat back with a sigh – and then grabbed the controls again with a yelp, fired the thrusters at full burn, and tried to find a path through the madness we'd been dumped into.

Directly ahead of us, a marauder vessel, distinguishable by the paint job as belonging to one of the more vicious clans, was powering up weapons. Before it fired, a strike from another marauder vessel, of a different clan, hit it, and the ship went dark, explosions rocking the vessel. I didn't wait to see if it recovered, but simultaneously shoved my flight stick forward and hit thrusters to full. "Find me a path!" I yelled.

"Here!" Katherine shouted, and a flight path fed itself into my vision, allowing us to get out of the battle without having to fight our way through. It was a tense flight, and we took some hits, but eventually we got far enough away from the fireball that I could safely hit chain drive, instantly accelerating us to an apparent .25 light speed and shooting us off into the black. I accelerated and changed course several times, then finally cut out of chain drive in a spot of empty space, maneuvered to a full stop and sat back from the controls again, flapping my hands to get the feeling back. "Damage checks," I said quietly, both into my intercom and to Kiri and Katherine. "Tell me what's wrong with the ship, if anything, in thirty minutes." I turned to Dierka. "Do me a favor and babysit the bridge, old friend," I said. "Sorry the seats won't fit you, but give me a yell if anything needs my attention."

He laughed that horrible puppy-killing laugh and nodded. "No worries, brood-brother. I will sit watch."

I went to my quarters, stripped out of the shirt I'd drenched in sweat over the last two hours, and sat for a moment on my bed, clean shirt in hand. Without intending to, I fell back, let out a heavy sigh, and dropped into sleep.

★   ★   ★

"It's pretty bad," Katherine told me four hours later, after I'd woken, showered, and rejoined the rest of them in the crew quarters. I'd called Dierka back and he had happily found himself a bench big enough for him to sit on. "Life support is about to fail, and we don't have the parts we need to repair it. And no, we can't print them – the fabricator got hit. It's total junk.

"That's actually not the worst thing, though. The jump drive was destroyed by jump feedback. The entire unit is fried. It'll have to be totally replaced. The portside plasma cannons are gone, totally slagged. We still have chain drive, but the armor over the engine compartment is nearly gone. It got hit bad in that last fight."

"The med-bay is fine," Ben said. "Other than the life support system getting knocked out. Auxiliary kicked in, but we've got maybe a couple of hours before that starts to have problems. It's not designed to work longer than it takes to repair the mains."

"But we can't repair the mains."

Takeshi shook his head, his grim expression signaling bad news. "No – we took a hit to stores. We didn't lose everything we had, but we lost a lot. Ben gave me a list of parts we'd need to maintain life support. We have maybe half of them."

Katherine spoke up again. "What we don't have, I can jury-rig. Won't last more than a few days, but it'll do the trick until we can get to a station and get some real parts."

"Shit," I muttered. One of those repairs would be doable; all of them together would cost a shitload of money we didn't have, even with Kiri's funds. We were right back where I'd started, broke and without a workable ship. Katherine met my eyes – she knew what this meant. It was over.

"It's not over," Kiri said. I looked at her, confused. "Hey, look, it's bad, I know – but I have a lot of money, and I checked the navicomp. We're only a few days out from Shoa'kor Station by chain drive. We can get the jump drive there. Maybe we can get some of the other repairs done too."

"Are you kidding?" I asked. "Shoa'kor is—"

"A hellhole, I know. But it's all there is."

She was right, but I didn't like it. Shoa'kor is basically several million tons of metal wrapped around the worst that humanity, and a few other races, have to offer. There's no law enforcement except for the *shoa'tal*, the enforcers that work for the Families, the criminal syndicate that runs the station. We had jumped, entirely unwillingly, to the ass-end of space.

"Okay," I said. "Doesn't look like we've got much choice. But you—" I looked at Kiri, "—do not leave the ship." She bridled, but I ignored her and turned to Katherine. "You'll come with me. I need your tech skills. Liam, you're on backup. If anything in our vitals goes nuts, we'll need your help."

"You'll have it."

I nodded my thanks. "We'll find a jump drive, get it installed, make repairs, and go. Dierka, I'm holding you in reserve. If we get into trouble, you're the way out of it." He nodded, and I continued. "Now, once we've got a jump drive, where's our next jump taking us?"

Kiri said "We...don't know." She looked to Katherine, who took over.

"We've got the jump coordinate, but it's deep in the Uncharted Zone. No telling what we'll find there."

"Shit," I breathed. The Uncharted Zone was just what it sounded like, a huge zone of space the Zhen hadn't yet gotten around to claiming. Nobody – at least nobody I was aware of – knew what was out there, but the consensus was 'not much'. "Well," I said, "we'll deal with that when we have to." I rose and stretched.

"Taj is right," Liam said.

"Don't call me that," I snapped.

"What was that about?" I heard Ben ask Takeshi. Takeshi said something to him that I couldn't hear, and Ben started laughing.

Feeling left out of the joke, I went back to the bridge to set the course to Shoa'kor.

★　　★　　★

"You're insane," Katherine said to the Tradd in the starship parts bazaar. "That jump unit won't last three jumps. No way am I paying that much!"

The Tradd reared up onto his hind legs and bared his teeth at us. While he made sounds as he talked to us, we heard only about half of the sounds produced; the rest were simply too high or low on the audible spectrum for humans to hear. Our NeuroNets' implants translated for him just fine, though. "The drive is not broken," he said. "It is merely old."

"'Merely old'?" Katherine scoffed, waving at the unit. "Look at it! There's no way this thing will work long. We're done here."

As the Tradd took breath to reply, Katherine held up her hand in a gesture of negation. "*Enough*," she said angrily. The Tradd lowered himself to four legs once more and went silent. We turned and walked away. Katherine shook her head. "The nerve of that guy," she muttered. "That drive probably wouldn't have lasted *one* jump, let alone three."

I nodded in agreement as we turned into a side corridor. "Problem is, we still need a jump unit, and that's the only one we've found in three hours."

"I might be able to help," said a voice behind us. We spun, and the figure behind us ducked when I drew my pistol and leveled it. "Don't shoot!" the girl – at least, I thought it was a girl, judging by the voice – yelled.

I slipped the pistol back into my holster and reached a hand out in a calming gesture. "Hey, whoa – not gonna shoot you, but you really ought to avoid spooking a guy like that."

"Sorry," she said as she rose. "Didn't mean to, just thought I could help."

"For a price," Katherine said.

The girl looked at her like she was an idiot. "Uh…yeah." She looked back at me. "Name's Seeker. I find stuff, and then I find people who want it." She glanced back at the Tradd's stall. "Word is you two want a jump drive."

I smiled. "You're not wrong."

"I know some guys who've got one."

"How much?" Katherine asked.

"Not so fast," she said. "You negotiate with them – but my finder's fee gets paid first."

"How much you want?" I asked.

"Not money," she said. "Passage."

I shook my head. "Not an option."

"Why not?"

"Where we're going isn't in civilized space."

"You think *this place* is civilized? I've been living here for years. I can handle anything you've got coming to ya."

I shook my head. "Look, kid – *Seeker* – I don't doubt you're able, but I'm not talking about going to some shithole planet. I don't actually *know* what's waiting for us, but believe me when I tell you that you want no piece of it."

"And? My parents died here and I've been on my own since I was ten years old. I don't care where you're going. I want to come."

"On your own since ten? You don't sound like it."

"Oh, sorry, am I not playing the part of tough girl to your satisfaction now? I said I've been on my own. I never said I was stupid."

"Fair enough." I sighed. "Fine, we'll take you with us."

"Excuse me," Katherine said. "I think you may have forgotten something."

"Yes? Oh." I drew closer to her. "Look," I said quietly, "the kid's not going to budge, I think we can both see that."

"Sure," she said.

"So we take her with us. We have the space."

"Not arguing that. But like you said, we're not going on a sunshine cruise. I have an idea – we can take her, but we don't take her all the way with us. We drop her off on the safest place we can find for her, and let her make her own way from there."

"She's just a kid."

She looked at me almost with pity. "I know you have a hard time letting go of your knight complex, but she's no more a kid than I am, not really."

I conceded that point with a nod, feeling the flush of my skin as I reddened in embarrassment at being called out. I turned back to Seeker. "Okay, kid, here's the deal – we'll take you with us, but you're a passenger, not crew, and as soon as we find a place you can make your own way, you're off."

She shrugged. "Fine with me."

"Then we've got a deal. Now, where's this jump drive?"

"In Quince's repair bay."

I stopped cold. "You're kidding me."

"What?"

"Quince? Jeremy Quince?"

"I think that's his name, yeah."

I sighed and met Katherine's eyes. "Well...shit."

Katherine raised an eyebrow. "Didn't you say he was out in the Enka Expanse?"

"I did. Guess things changed."

Seeker seemed confused. "You know the guy?"

I nodded. "Yeah, I know him. And there's no way in hell he'll sell me even a broken drive unit, let alone a good one."

Katherine nodded. "Probably doesn't like me much either."

"You got that right," came a familiar voice from behind us.

I stopped and turned. "Hello, Quince," I said as pleasantly as I could – which, I admit, wasn't much.

"Save it," he snapped. "What the hell are you two doing together?"

I shrugged. "Not that it's your business, but we're running a ship together."

"How's that work?"

"Pretty well, actually. I tried to make her my executive officer, but cocaptain has a better ring to it."

"You're not in the service anymore, Hunt. Don't you mean 'first mate'?"

I feigned thought. "Right, I always get that mixed up. It's like my dad always said, 'A difference that makes no difference is no difference.'"

"What?"

"Never mind. Look, Quince. You don't like me. I can respect that. I don't like you either. But as much as it might make you happy in the short term to dick me around, believe me, in the long term it's a bad call. I got trouble following me, and you don't want it here."

He rolled his eyes. "Oooh, the big hero's in trouble? Good. I'll enjoy the show." He turned and sauntered away, whistling happily to himself.

I started to go after him, but Katherine grabbed my elbow. "No," she said. "Remember what he's like. The more you tell him, the deeper the grave you're digging for yourself."

I thought about my options, my NeuroNet's tactical program highlighting several factors in the immediate vicinity.

I could shoot him down now, but he had at least three bodyguards nearby that I identified, and two others who were probably undercover, based on the way they were watching the both of us. It would lead to a gunfight here, and even if Katherine and I could take them all out, there were too many civilians around. I couldn't risk it.

I could chase him down and tell him everything, but as Katherine had reminded me, Quince was a contrary son of a bitch. Even if he hated the Zhen, he'd keep me here, waiting for them to get here, just so he could see me hurt. And then a lot of innocents would die.

I had a limited amount of time to get out of this station before the Zhen tracked me down. So it was time to stop acting like a big damn hero, and time to start acting like what the Zhen had made me.

"Let's go," I said.

★   ★   ★

"Ladies and gentlemen," I said to the assembled crew as we sipped our tea, "we're fucked." I gestured at the hologram hovering over the table, highlighting the station and all the security Quince had around his shop. "There's too much organic security. Short of an all-out assault with an army we don't have, the chances of pulling this off are nearly nonexistent."

Nobody argued. We'd gone over seven different plans in the last two days, and we were all feeling the pinch; it was only a matter of time before the Zhen tracked us down again. We were all being incredibly careful to keep our NeuroNets shut down, not connecting to the networks on the station. Any query, even of local databases, was likely to get us caught eventually. So we'd relied on Seeker to find information for us through her connections.

Now she grinned at us. "I have an idea."

I frowned at her. "Something we haven't thought of?"

"Sort of. It's simple: buy it from him."

I rolled my eyes. "Yeah, we tried that, remember? He won't sell to us."

"Not for money, no. But there are more important, more valuable, things than money. When money won't work, which around here is pretty much all the time, you have to ask yourself – what does he want? And I know the answer to that."

"Which is?" I asked impatiently.

She grinned. "You guys with your fancy brain computers. All it takes is a little asking around. He wants the Galaxy Star."

We all stared at her. Finally, Kiri broke the silence. "That's not useful. The Galaxy Star disappeared from Zhen:da centuries ago," she said in what even I thought was an overly patronizing tone. "Nobody knows where it is, or if it even exists anymore."

Seeker stared at Kiri. "I may not have been educated at the finest schools in the Empire, missy," she said, "but I'm not stupid." She grinned impishly. "I know where it is."

"Let me guess," Katherine said. "It's here on Shoa'kor."

"Yep. More specifically, it's in the private collection of Gordon Simms."

"And who's he when he's at home?"

She shrugged. "A crime boss here on station. Not sure how he came to possess the Star, but he's got it, and I can get us into his house."

"How?"

"Well, he's got a party coming up – a recruitment drive for mercs. And I have an invitation for me and one more."

"How did you come by an invitation?"

"I'm his niece," she said with a shrug.

"Wait a second," I said. "You told me you were an orphan."

"I am. My parents died when I was ten."

"But you said you've been on your own."

"And I was telling the truth. Simms hasn't done much for me – though he probably did, behind the scenes – but the important thing is he's trying to get me inside his organization now."

"Any idea why?"

"He's always wanted an heir, but he can't have one, so he wants to make me into one."

"I…see."

"Anyway, I got the invitation a few days ago, and this morning I did some snooping, and found out that Quince wants the Star. He seems to have discovered that Simms has it, so he's going to be going in there after it, soon. But he's planning an assault. We can do it cleaner and beat him to it."

"So, you and I could go in and—"

"Nope."

"But—"

"Tajen, you'll be there, but you're not with me. I want someone who can handle the tech *and* my uncle. I want her," she said, pointing to Kiri.

"What?"

"If I tell you any more than that, you're not going to let her go. And I really do need her. I promise, I'll get her out safely."

I was about to argue when Kiri spoke up. "It isn't his choice, anyway," she said. "I'm an adult, I can make my own choices. I'll go."

I thought about arguing with her too, but Katherine met my eyes from across the table, and Liam, sitting beside me, touched my wrist lightly. I had to admit, she was right. As much as I wanted to protect her and treat her like the little girl she'd been, that was fifteen years ago. I nodded. "You're right," I said. "You're an adult, you can make your own decisions."

"Good!" Seeker chirped. "Now – Kiri and I will go in first. Tajen and Liam will come in after, and play up the 'rich idiot' vibe. You two will get all the attention while Kiri and I do it all quiet-like. Takeshi and Katherine will be our outside guys, handling comms and standing by for transport when we all exit. Now—"

"Hey!" I said, cutting her off. "This is my ship. I'm the captain – well," I said, looking to Katherine, "the cocaptain. Katherine and I make the plans, okay?"

"Okay. Sorry," she said, in a tone that easily conveyed her utter and complete lack of contrition. I stared at her a moment, then traded a look with Katherine, and said, "Okay. We'll go with your plan." I shrugged. "It's a good plan."

She rolled her eyes, then turned to the map. We continued planning, fine-tuning her original idea into a tightly plotted plan that was sure to go pear-shaped the moment we all got in position.

Hey, what can I say? I'm a realist.

★   ★   ★

"We're inside," Kiri whispered. I heard her through the old-fashioned audio plug in my ear. We'd chosen to use old-fashioned tech for two reasons. First, we were still trying to keep from accessing the slipnet unless we had to; and second, it was less likely that Simms would be scanning those frequencies. I reached up and double-tapped the plug to signal acknowledgement.

Liam and I were listening to Kiri and Seeker from up the corridor, dressed in our best and waiting for our entrance. Katherine and Takeshi monitored everything from a maintenance shuttle we'd, well, let's say 'borrowed', from the station's technical pool. We were parked across from the gates to Simms' estate, while Katherine and Takeshi posed as maintenance workers, 'fixing' a malfunction that only existed because a technician who owed Seeker several favors told it to.

Katherine's voice came over the audio. "They're in. Go."

Liam and I immediately linked arms, strolling down the corridor laughing like idiots. As we got to the entrance, I slipped the guard my invitation card. The card, a near-copy of the one Seeker had gotten from Simms, had been the most expensive piece of tech we'd bought for this caper. It was encoded with our background identities as a pair of mercenaries, and our bio-prints, but getting them made had meant bribing the man who'd made the invitations for Simms in the first place, and it hadn't been cheap.

The guard slipped the invitation into his reader, then glanced at my face to verify I was who I was supposed to be, just as Liam leaned close and whispered in my ear while giving the guard a significantly long look from head to toe and back. The guard smiled slightly, blushing. He cleared his throat nervously, finished with the card, and slipped it into a slot in his console. "Go on in, sirs," he said, his voice catching slightly.

As the door closed behind us, I smacked Liam's side lightly. "That wasn't nice."

"What?"

"Teasing him like that."

"Who's teasing?"

"Liam!"

"What? I like sex," he said.

"Liam, you're exasperating."

"Because I like sex?"

"No, because—" I tried to keep my face light, as we were already drawing attention. "Because we're on the clock here. Now stop it, we're getting some attention."

"Well, of course we are," he said, looking around the room. "We're clearly the best-looking men in the place."

"I don't know, that guy's pretty good-looking," I said, indicating a human in the uniform of a mercenary captain.

"No. Gach, no. He'll be full-on ugly up close. You'll see."

I rolled my eyes as the guy caught our attention and came sauntering over to us. He moved with the put-on walk of a man who has to work to make people think he's tough. When he came closer, Liam straightened up, putting a more serious look on his face.

"Hey," the guard said. "I know you two?"

"Not at all," I said, holding out my right hand in the traditional manner. He clasped my forearm briefly, then Liam's. "I'm Jason Steele. This is my partner, Malcolm Long."

"I'm Brett Sarkin," he said. "With the Starlancers, out of Kieli System."

"Kieli," I said. "I wasn't aware there was a human presence there at all, much less a mercenary unit."

He shrugged. "There isn't. Most of the Starlancers are Tchakk, but Simms is a well-known human-centrist. The boss figured it was better to send me."

I raised an eyebrow. "Do the Starlancers need a contract that badly?"

He narrowed his eyes at the borderline rude question. "No," he said shortly. "But we want the guns he's got on offer tonight."

"Ah," I said.

"If you'll excuse me," he said stiffly. He nodded to Liam, and walked away.

When he was out of earshot, I turned to Liam. "Okay, you were right. Not pretty at all."

He nodded, and together we studiously ignored Kiri and Seeker as they walked by us. Kiri looked over her shoulder at Liam, giving him a long look, and he pretended not to notice.

"I think my niece's friend likes you, Mr. Long," a voice behind us said.

We turned. Simms was shorter than I'd thought from the flatpics Seeker had shown me. He looked comfortably rumpled in his expensive suit, bodyguards trying their best to look scary but unobtrusive behind him. "Mr. Simms," I said. "I'm—"

"Jason Steele, of the Black Suns Company." He pointed at me with the hand that held his drink. "I don't remember inviting you."

"Odd," I said. "But not unexpected, given the number of guests in attendance."

"True enough," he said. "To be honest, I don't remember inviting more than half these people. I handed most of that off to my assistant. 'Get me guests with money,' I said. I guess your company qualifies. How's your commander, Helena?"

"*Yelena*," I corrected, and noted his slight nod. He'd been testing me. "She got smashed up pretty badly in a fight with some marauders, but she's almost up to one hundred per cent with the prosthetic arm. She'll be fine."

"Glad to hear it," he said. "And you, Malcolm? Enjoying my hospitality?"

"Very much," Liam drawled, as if he'd been to parties like this a hundred times. "I am wondering, though...."

"Yes?"

"When do we get to the good parts?"

Simms smiled and raised his glass. "Tell you what. How'd you like a preview of the main attraction?"

"Really?"

"Sure, why not? I owe Yelena a favor. Might as well pay it back a little. Come on." He led us through the party. It was a fairly sedate affair, by Shoa'kor standards.

I surreptitiously looked around as we moved through the place, trying to find Kiri in the room, but she was nowhere to be seen. "Kiri," I subvocalized, "we're on the move. Where are you?"

There was no reply. I didn't like that at all.

Simms stopped before a wooden double door with a keypad mounted beside it. He entered the code manually, then gestured at the keypad. "The code changes every day," he said. "I've got a program in my 'Net that keeps track of the code and gives it to me when I need it." He grinned. "There's no excuse for bad security," he said. He opened the door, gesturing us in before him.

I took a few steps into the room, until I realized it was empty, aside from the desk in the center, and the two girls — Kiri and Seeker — who were tied to chairs against the right wall. I spun, reaching for the small blaster I was wearing under my jacket. I stopped when the six men who'd been waiting behind the doors raised their own, pointing directly at my head. I slowly moved my hands away from my body.

"You'd be surprised how loyal some of my people are," Simms said. "For example, Jackson. Even with the hefty bribe he took from you to make that invitation, he felt the need to inform me about it."

I shrugged as one of the guards removed my blaster and another took Liam's. "Is that loyalty, or greed?" I asked. "I mean, I assume he got some kind of reward for ratting us out."

Simms shrugged. "To be honest with you, at the end of the day I really don't give a shit." He walked carefully around me, staying just out of reach, and stopped behind Seeker. "What I do care about is this little bitch here," he said, grabbing her shoulders and squeezing until she cried out. "My own blood, and she turns against me." He let go of her and shrugged. "Well, like father, like daughter, I suppose." He leaned down and pulled her head around to look her in the eyes. "And we all know how *his* betrayal worked out, don't we?" He laughed at the horror on her face. "Oh, come on. You didn't know? Well, I guess you're dumber than I thought."

"I'm going to kill you," she said.

"No, you're not," he said. "Frankly, my dear, you'll be lucky to get out of this with both eyes." He sighed theatrically. "It's a pity, really. I had planned to bring you into the business – but this is too egregious to forgive, really." He was getting into the swing of his tirade, now. "I mean, seriously, stealing from me? I could maybe forgive that. But bringing outsiders into my *home*? What kind of family does that? No, don't answer, I'll tell you: the soon-to-be-dead kind."

Liam glanced sidelong at me and sighed. "You know, I'd pay good money for you to shut him up."

"Why me?" I asked. "You're the infantryman. I'm just a pilot." I shrugged. "*You* do it."

"Excuse me," Simms said. "I'm standing right here, asshole."

"He is," I said.

"True," Liam said. "I can fix that, though."

Simms pulled a blaster pistol from his jacket and shoved it into Liam's face, the muzzle pressing into his cheek. "Do you want to know why you're not dead yet?"

Liam *tsk*ed. "Because the safety's on?" he asked.

In the moment when Simms forgot himself – amateur – and looked at his safety, Liam moved with implant-boosted speed, snapping the pistol out of Simms' hand. He grabbed the bastard's neck with one hand, and spun around behind him, holding his mouth shut with one arm with his pistol jammed into Simms' temple. "Guns down, *now!*" he snapped at the guards. "Or you all start looking for work."

Had we been dealing with professional guards practically anywhere else, we'd have been dead less than a minute later. But we were dealing with the kind of low-rent scum who worked for the cheapest asshole in the darkest ass-end of the Empire. They dropped their guns immediately and stepped back, on the theory that if Liam killed their boss, they'd end up working for someone even cheaper.

Morons.

I grabbed their guns and stepped back. Liam and I looked at each other, nodded, and shot all four guards in the knees. They dropped, and all four of them began screaming in agony.

"Look," I said calmly and rationally, "we could easily have shot you all in the head. But we're trying to be good guys. So do me a favor and *shut the hell up!*" I brandished the pistol, and all four of them tried to stop screaming, with only moderate success. I couldn't really blame them; getting shot in the knee hurts like hell.

I turned back and untied the girls. I grabbed Kiri in an embrace, holding her so tightly she yelped. This once, I didn't care if she was ready, or I was ready. I just held her. She was surprised, but after a moment her arms wrapped just as tightly around me. We stood there for a moment as Seeker took a pistol and held it on Simms while Liam shoved him into a chair and began tying him up, then Kiri disengaged with a little smile before going to the desk and activating the computer. A holographic interface opened, and she began searching.

"What the hell are you here for, anyway?" Simms asked.

"Found it!" Kiri said. She did something else with the computer, and smiled as the holoscreen faded. "And I wiped this moron's computer," she said. "He's going to find it difficult to track the debts he owes, or his operations."

"You mean his successor is," Seeker said, and shot Simms in the face. She stared at the body a moment, then turned to me, and the look on her face dared me to say anything. "I told him I'd kill him."

★   ★   ★

We gathered the crew. I sent most of them back to the ship, while Katherine and I headed to station control. We were greeted by exactly the kind of brainless bureaucrat I'd expect Quince to hire. He took one look at us and said, "Good evening, Mr. Hunt. I'm afraid Administrator Quince is not available. If you'd like to make an appointment, he can see you sometime in the next week."

I rolled my eyes. "Listen, just tell Quince we've got the Galaxy Star, and we're willing to trade it. Now I'm leaving the station. He can speak to me whenever he wants – tell him I'll be monitoring all frequencies while I wait for his call." I gestured to Katherine, and we turned as nonchalantly as we could and walked away.

"Wait!" came Quince's voice. "William, send them in."

"Yes, sir," William said into his comms. He gestured to the office.

When we entered, Quince was sitting behind a bare desk. As soon as the door closed, he said, "Let's see it."

"Quince," I said, "come on. You don't think I'm stupid enough to have brought it here with me, do you?"

"Well, yes, actually."

I gave him a hurt look. "Oh, that's just mean." I turned to Katherine. "Isn't that mean?"

"It's mean," she agreed.

"Dammit, Hunt, I've played this game with you too often. What do you want?"

I stared at him. "And you thought *I* was dumb? We want the same thing we wanted before – we want that jump drive. We want it so bad we're willing to trade you the single most valuable gem in the Empire for it."

"And what am I supposed to do with that?"

"Oh, for the love—" I stopped, breathed once, and continued. "Quince, we know you've been trying to get hold of it. We did it for you. We even dealt with the guy who had it – well, one of my partners did. You're the station administrator. You can easily say you figured out a crime lord here got it, you recovered it, and go back to the Empire's heart a hero."

"And you just want a jump drive."

"Yep. All I need."

He considered it. "What's going on, Hunt?"

"Sorry, Quince. Need to know. You don't."

He narrowed his eyes at me. "I do, or there's no deal." He gestured to a seat. "See, I don't trust you any more than you trust me. And unless you tell me why you'd rather have a jump engine than lay your hands on the most valuable gem in history, I'm not selling you shit."

I shrugged. "What can I say? I like to travel, and my own drive is shot."

"C'mon, Hunt." He looked worried, and for some reason, that shifted things in my brain. Quince was an asshole, and sometimes an idiot, but he was human, and right now he looked like he knew more than he was letting on. Maybe giving him some information would help me in the long run.

"Okay, Quince. There's something out there I'm looking for. The Zhen don't want me to find it. They're trying to stop me." I saw Katherine stiffen beside me, and I gave her a placating gesture.

He chewed on that for a moment. "Any idea why they don't want it found?"

I shook my head. "Nothing definite – but my brother thought he'd found a route to Earth. The Zhen I talked to as much as admitted it was real." I told him everything, from the message Daav had left me to the running chase we'd been involved in since we left Zhen:da.

He looked stunned. His gaze went to the wall behind me, and I stiffened in my seat and turned, then relaxed when I realized he was just looking at a hologram. Then I whipped my head around again and gaped as I realized the hologram was Earth. I turned slowly back to Quince, incredulous. "No," I said.

He nodded, then took a deep breath, held it a moment, and let it go slowly. "Look, Hunt," he said, "despite what you think, I'm not an idiot. I know why you and I never got along." To Katherine, he said, "I was a jackass to you back then. I'm still kind of an asshole, to be honest. I'm a shitty pilot and a barely tolerable human being. The only thing I'm really good at is running this station. But I'm human, same as you.

"All my life, I've wondered where Earth was. When I was a kid I used to write stories where I found it." He laughed. "They were *awful*. Worse than my flying ever was, worse than anything else I've ever done. But man, I loved writing those things." He smiled, then reached out and hit a switch. "William, tell the shop to get that jump drive in bay seven kitted out and deliver it to Hunt's ship. Drop everything else in the queue and do a full repair on the *Dream of Earth*." He sighed. "Now get moving. Get that thing installed and get out of my space before the Zhen find you here."

We rose, and I nodded to him – but he'd already turned away. I couldn't think of anything worth saying, so I did something uncharacteristic, and gave him the last word.

★   ★   ★

Six hours of listening to Katherine bitch at the drive unit later, we were ready to go. As I was doing my final check, Seeker found me.

"Ready to leave?" I asked.

"About that," she said.

"Yes?"

"I've decided to stay here. For now, anyway."

I stopped and turned to face her. "Why?"

She fidgeted a little. "Turns out, killing my uncle opened a door. He hadn't changed his will. I got everything legal, and I'm taking the rest of it too."

"So, what, you're a crime lord now?"

She shrugged. "Sort of. Quince made me an offer. He'll support me if I clean the organization up, get rid of the worst business and focus on the smuggling. In return for his support, he gets a safer station and better terms than Simms gave him."

I frowned. "Any idea why he didn't just take the business for himself?"

She grinned. "I asked him that too. He said he tried. My uncle's right-hand man rebuffed him and threatened all-out war if he tried again." She smiled. "Turns out that right-hand man was an old friend of my father. He's going to teach me how to run things, but also help me clean it up, and stand up to the other Families."

"You really want to do this?"

"Yeah," she said. "I really do. I want to make it better here."

I grinned at her. "A worthwhile goal. Good luck, Seeker."

"My real name's Jette. Next time you come here, look me up. Things'll be different."

She flashed me a grin before leaving in the company of an older man who had the look of an old soldier. A few minutes later I got the all clear signal from Katherine, and a moment after that, she and Kiri joined me in the cockpit and took their positions. "Ready to go, Tajen," Katherine said. "The drive is spun up and ready."

We undocked and, for once, made the journey to the jump point without incident. "Here goes nothing," I said, and initiated jump. Once we'd made the transition to slipspace, I relaxed. I turned to Katherine. "Good work."

"Thanks. Kiri helped a lot, or there'd have been a lot more cursing."

"The best thing is," Kiri piped up, "I learned a whole lot of new curses."

"Great," I said, my eyes widening. "What happened to my sweet little niece?"

"Whatever do you mean?" Kiri asked.

"You used to be so sweet."

"I was two!" she cried, laughing. "I had to grow up eventually."

"Damn, I hate when that happens. All right, I need a shower. I'll see you all later. Katherine, you've got watch." I ruffled Kiri's hair as I passed; she hit me to show her displeasure.

"Good idea," Katherine said. "You smell like T'chakk shit."

"I'm not going to dignify that."

CHAPTER SEVEN

The next ship's 'morning' I got dressed and headed to the cockpit. On my way there I ran into Liam.

"Hey, boss," he said cheerfully.

I gave him the bleary eye and kept walking. He followed. "Something you want, Liam?"

"Just wanted to make sure you're okay," he said.

"I'm fine."

"Great. Any idea how much longer we'll be in transit?"

I climbed into the pilot's chair, checked the board, and shrugged. "Days? Hours?"

"Helpful," he chuckled.

I shrugged. "You know how weird slipspace is."

He nodded and slid into the copilot's station. "I once spent three days going between Terra and Zhen:da on a merchanter crew. The next time it took a week."

"How long between?"

"About three months. Best theory our engineer had was that a badly tuned drive had fouled up the slipspace currents."

I looked askance at him. "Seriously? Kind of a crackpot theory."

"True, but that guy could detect a problem just by listening to the ship. Sometimes he'd find stuff before the ship's computers even noticed a problem developing."

"Sounds like a great engineer."

"Yeah, he was. Until he got caught skimming profits. The captain...." He paused, looking out the viewport, and sighed. "The captain didn't treat him kindly."

There was something there, hidden behind his eyes. "You guys were close?"

He nodded, but said nothing. I rose from my seat and fetched a bottle and two glasses from a small cupboard behind the pilot station. I poured a finger of the amber liquid into each glass and handed one to him. "Here," I said.

He smiled in appreciation and took a sip. His eyes widened. "This from Terra?"

"Yep." I smiled smugly. "One hundred years old, from the Burns Distillery in Speyside." The place names meant little to me, but they'd been given to the colony by the original colonists, people only a few years removed from Earth, and missing it terribly.

"Nice," he breathed, inhaling the scent of the whisky in his glass. "Must have cost a pretty penny. Thanks for sharing it with me."

"Well, you know, nothing nice should be hoarded from one's crew."

He was quiet a moment, then he asked, "Why do you do that?"

"Do what?"

"Distance yourself from us." As I opened my mouth to reply, he said, "And if you give me any of that 'distance of command' guff, I'll smack you. That crap may fly in the navy, but we're not navy here."

"Is it different in the ground forces?"

"No, not really. But that's not the point, and you're evading the question."

He wasn't wrong. He hadn't asked anything I hadn't asked myself a hundred times since we began this quest. When I first met Katherine and her crew, I felt an immediate need to hire them, not because they were amazing, which of course I now knew they were, but because they had something I wanted to be a part of. They weren't just friends, they were family. Something in me had said this was my last chance to find that kind of feeling again. And I'd been so lonely, for so long, that I'd leapt for it.

But ever since that night, I'd gone back and forth between treating them like family, and keeping them at arm's length. We had the camaraderie, but when it came time to be a person, and not just a job on the ship, I was putting the shields I was so used to having between me and other people back up, except with Liam. And I still wasn't sure how he'd slammed his way through those shields.

I considered bullshitting him, the way I'd done it to people over the years who'd tried to break through my wall. But I couldn't do it. So I sighed, took a drink, and shrugged. "To be honest, I think it's just because I'm bad at being friends with people."

"How so? You seem good enough at it to me."

"It's easy with you. But the rest of the crew? Not so easy. I have a hard time opening up to people. Usually people think I'm kind of an asshole."

He snorted. "Newsflash, Taj, you're not wrong there. You treat us all pretty well, and you're friendly enough that every one of us likes you. But you spend a lot of time in your quarters, or locked up here – you and I both know you don't actually have to be here when we're in slipspace. When do you get to be human?"

I held out my hand and said, "I'm human, Liam."

"Yeah, on the outside. And you act human sometimes, when you relax. But when you're in that seat," he said, pointing to the pilot's couch on which I sat, "you become very Zhen. Listen, I know what it's like to be a human in the Zhen forces – and I can only imagine how much worse it was for you, because they don't let many of us join the space forces. But you seem to have coped by becoming more and more like them."

I cocked my head at him. "How so?"

He sighed. "Well, you suck at being family, for one thing."

"Excuse me?"

"Your niece is on this ship. And I can see that you love her, clearly. It's right there on your face every time you look at her. So why do you stay away from her?"

I took a steadying breath. "You are on dangerous ground, Liam."

"You asked. Taj, you talk to me more than you do Kiri."

"Get off the bridge," I said through clenched teeth.

Liam stared at me a moment, then nodded and rose from his seat. "I'll go, Taj," he said. "But any time you want to talk, you know where to find me."

I said, "Stop calling me that."

"What?"

"'Taj'. I know it's just a nickname, but it's a Kelvaki word too. It's not what you want to call me."

He nodded, and turned to go. As he reached the hatchway, he

said, "You know I'm fluent in Kelvaki, right?" Then he was gone.

I sat in a silent rage, my scotch in hand, staring out the port, watching the colors of slipspace flow past the ship. I sat there for nearly an hour, fuming. One thought kept running through my head, over and over until I wanted to slam my glass against the bulkhead – not that I'd waste good whisky like that.

Liam was right.

I'd been avoiding Kiri since we'd launched from Shrakan Station, back on Zhen:da. I'd talked to her, but only about 'safe' topics – childhood stories, family background she hadn't gotten from her dad, ship business. But I'd avoided telling her anything about me. About the real reasons I'd stayed away for so long. About Jiraad, and why her mother died.

I wanted to believe that I was going to open up, before the conversation when she made it clear we weren't 'there' yet, but the truth was, even if she'd unloaded on me then, I'd have kept myself back, remained walled off. Because I wasn't ready. I'd simply been alone too long to open up now.

Except to Liam.

Thoughts of the rugged cargo handler made me blush like an idiot. As I said, I'd been alone for a long time, at least for more than the occasional roll in a spacer's bunk. I couldn't deny my interest in him, but I'd assumed it was entirely one-sided. Until he said he spoke Kelvaki, which meant that he knew damned well he was calling me 'sexy' when he used that nickname. And that meant that my interest wasn't entirely one-sided, which was pretty much the best news I'd had in some time.

I was still sitting there, grinning like an idiot, and trying to figure out what to do about it, when the computer started counting down to realspace reversion. I activated the all-ship comms and spoke into the pickup. "All hands, slipspace exit in five minutes. Five minutes to reversion."

Reversion is usually pretty smooth; this time was no different. The colors of slipspace disappeared with a flash, the ship gave a small shake, and we were in back in realspace. Given what we discovered there, the transition should have been harder.

So. Much. Harder.

★   ★   ★

The *Dream of Earth* floated in the outer system, motionless relative to the asteroid off our starboard side.

"Ten planets," Liam said. "Eight primary, over a dozen dwarf planets…several hundred smaller bodies. There's an asteroid field." He was all business, not mentioning our earlier conversation, but when he looked at me, there was a twinkle in his eye that promised we weren't done with that topic yet.

I smiled at him. "How dense?" I asked.

He glanced over his shoulder as Katherine, Kiri, Takeshi, and Ben entered the bridge, with Dierka standing in the back. He turned back to his board and frowned. "Looks like a standard *tlin* distribution. Lots of room in between, but I've got a few clumps. Including one that…huh."

"What is it?"

"Judging by the sensor return patterns, there are a lot of metal-rich asteroids in the belt, but I'm reading what looks like high concentrations of metal in one of the clumps. Might be artificial."

"Give me a course," I said. He worked it up and flicked it over to my station. When it came over, I locked the course in and engaged the chain drive. Ten minutes later, I cut to thrusters, maneuvering at a crawl the last distance. It took some time, but we reached the 'clump', as Liam called it, and, to a man, we simply stared at the scene revealed by the floodlights.

Ahead of us drifted a couple of dozen starships ranging in size from tiny one- or two-man ships to a hulk that looked as big as one of the smaller Zhen capital ships. They were long dead, all dark and motionless in the black. The ships were of a type we'd never seen before, huge bulbous engine pods attached to what looked to be crew and weapon pods.

"How are they still together?" I whispered.

Liam made a sound of discovery and gestured, and several small areas were highlighted by my NeuroNet. "Tethers," he said. "They link all the smaller ships to the big one."

"Salvage lines?"

He shrugged. "Or the survivors linked their ships together before they died."

Takeshi reached forward to smack his shoulder. "Cheery thought, thanks for the nightmares I'll have for the next week."

Liam snorted and played the lights around the hulks. Many of the ships had obviously been destroyed by energy beams, judging by the dark holes surrounded by melted metal edges.

"It's a battlefield," Takeshi said.

"It's a graveyard," I said. "The ships all look pretty similar. So either they were just obliterated and didn't manage to take out a single enemy, or someone cleaned up the enemy ships, and left these here for a reason."

"Or it was a civil war, and these are from both sides."

I nodded as we all watched the searchlights play over the wreckage. "What are they?" Katherine asked.

"Ships," Takeshi said in an attempt at humor.

She rolled her eyes. "I mean, who did they belong to?"

They were unfamiliar, bulky ships with oversized engines, nothing like the sleekly aggressive Zhen ships I had been flying for so long. "No idea," I said. "Let's find out."

Takeshi looked at me. "Tell me you're kidding."

"Most of the wrecks are in pieces," Liam said, "but I've got one on scanners that looks relatively intact." He flicked the bearing to my station. "Looks like three hundred meters long. It's the biggest ship I can see in one piece."

I eased the ship in that direction, going slowly to avoid slamming into debris. I pulled up to within one hundred meters and brought the ship to a full stop. "Liam, Kiri, and I will go over," I said. There were groans and protests, which stopped when I held up a hand. Liam was looking pointedly at the hand, and I realized I had used a Zhen gesture of negation. "Sorry," I muttered. "Look, we can't all go. I need someone here, and I'd prefer a pilot." With a shrug of apology, I said to Dierka, "One that can fit in the pilot's seat, I mean."

He chuckled. "No worries, *draka*."

"Ben, there's no telling what we'll find over there, and it could be dangerous. Get sickbay ready."

"Will do," he said. "I'll rig up an analyzer too, in case you find any bio samples." He called over his shoulder as he left the bridge, "Takeshi, with me."

Takeshi closed his eyes and took a breath. "Dammit, I hate dealing with bio stuff," he said under his breath. He nodded to me and followed after Ben, and I could hear them arguing their way down the corridor, though I couldn't hear what they were saying.

Kiri was practically vibrating as Liam grabbed her arm and led her off to find her an exo-suit. When I rose from my seat and turned to leave the bridge, Katherine slid into the copilot's seat, then reached out and grabbed my elbow. "Hey, be careful over there," she said.

"Of course," I said. "Remember who you're talking to."

She rolled her eyes. "That's why I said it."

★   ★   ★

Kiri, Liam, and I stood in the port airlock. Kiri was wearing a standard spacesuit. It didn't have the armor or the sensor capabilities of Liam's or my suit, but it would keep her alive. I reminded myself that I'd need to try to find some gravitic induction modules to plug into my crews' suits the next time we were on a station, and mentally smacked myself for not looking for any on Shoa'kor. Ah well, events there had gotten out of hand pretty quickly; I could probably forgive myself.

We were too far from the hulk to fire a guide-cable, and I wasn't sure I wanted to risk it, anyway. We had no idea what was out here, and I didn't want to get caught unawares while tethered to an ancient wreck if it turned out we weren't alone. So while Liam used his grab-nodes to head over to the ship for a quick reconnoiter, I stayed behind to ferry Kiri, who was standing in the airlock's outer doorway.

"You ready?" I asked her.

"Honestly?" she said. "No, no way in hell am I ready to do this."

I grinned at her. "It's not as hard as you think. Just focus on the target, and remember that I've got you."

"Right, I've got that. It doesn't help."

"Kiri, I'm wearing a Zhen-designed spacesuit with gravitic maneuvering nodes. Even if you somehow drifted away from me, I'd be able to get to you before anything happened. It's going to be all right."

"Okay," she said. I could tell she wasn't yet convinced. So I did the only thing I could think of to prove she was in no danger. Which is to say, I shoved her out the airlock.

Okay, maybe that wasn't the best idea I'd ever had. She screamed, somersaulting away with her arms and legs flailing out of control.

"You know, Tajen," Katherine said over comms, "sometimes you're kind of an asshole."

I thought of my discussion with Liam and grinned. "It's true. Kiri, activate your suit's maneuvering jets. They won't get you far, but they can stop your spin."

I watched her spin for a few moments longer, then slow and stop spinning, facing away from me. I activated the gravity nodes on my suit and began to 'fall' toward Kiri. Long years of doing this had left me with a knack for maneuvering in this suit; I practically flew, swooping around Kiri and coming up to her from her other side, so she could see my approach. As I closed, I lowered the field intensity, then switched it behind me to slow me down. I drifted up to her, matching speeds, and grasped her arm. "I've got you," I said. "Liam," I called on open comms, "I'm going to look around a moment. Can you hold?"

"All quiet here, I'm fine," he said.

Kiri and I looped around the ship, looking for markings that might tell us where she came from. The closest we got was what looked like writing on the side, but it had been too damaged by energy weapons and I couldn't even recognize individual marks.

Eventually, I returned to the hole we'd decided to use as an entrance. We alighted on the deck beside Liam, Kiri's boots making a solid *thunk* as the magnetic seals engaged with the metal decking. As she walked slowly toward Liam, her magnetic boots slowing her down, I walked over to him completely normally, as my suit created a personal gravity field for me. "Any movement?"

"None," he said. "Place is quiet."

Kiri breathed deeply for a moment and said, "Uncle Tajen?"

"You just called me 'Uncle'."

"Uh-huh. Two things. First, that was awesome." She looked at me and grinned. "Second, that said, I am going to punch the shit out of you when I get out of this suit."

I grinned back, though she couldn't see it through my suit. "Duly noted." I detached my blaster from the holster on my right thigh and held it in a ready position. We moved forward, toward the bow of the ship. I figured the bridge would be near there; it usually was on Zhen, Kelvaki, and Tchakk vessels I'd seen.

"Whoever owned this ship was humanoid," Kiri observed. "The tech is all set up for a form similar to ours."

"I'd say you're right," Liam said, pointing.

I looked. There was a humanoid, bipedal form floating in a corner of the room. I couldn't tell, at this distance, what the being had looked like. I moved closer, releasing the gravitic node keeping me on the floor and floating over to the body. I reached out and gently turned it around, blinking when I saw its face. "Holy shit," I said.

It was human.

The vacuum of space had sucked all the moisture from the body and killed the bacteria in the environment, so it was fairly well preserved. It had been a man of about my height and build. His skin had been bleached pale by the loss of his bodily fluids, but his hair remained black. "Think this means we're on the right track?" I asked, turning the body so the others could see.

"Well, either that or we hit an even bigger coincidence," Kiri said.

"Weird," I said. "The controls don't look anything like ours." I noticed Kiri staring at me through the transparent faceshield of her suit. "What?"

"You do realize we don't have any purely human tech in the Empire, right?"

I nodded, chastened. "Oh. Right." All human tech, even the stuff we'd developed ourselves, was based on Zhen technology. Nothing the colony ship had held had been salvageable in the long term, considering the damage the ship's systems had suffered in the Accident. Even our control interfaces were largely adapted from Zhen originals.

"I wonder if the computer's memory storage is intact," Kiri said.

"Think we can read it?" I asked.

Kiri nodded. "If it's intact, I can read it. The trick will be engineering a way to access it."

I looked around. The ship had clearly been in battle; even if she'd been alone when we found her, the damage to the hull made it obvious. Things weren't much better in here. The room was littered with the floating remains of hand tools and small bits I didn't want to look at too closely.

"Well, let's find the bridge, and—" I was cut off by my comms beeping with an URGENT code flashing in my vision. "Hold on," I said, and switched my comms, including them in the loop. "What's up, Katherine?"

"We've got something on scopes," she said. "A whole lot of somethings, actually. And they're looking for something."

"Any idea who they are?"

"The computer's dissecting the jump trace now. I think you guys should— They're Zhen."

I cursed. "How many?"

"Judging by the number of jump signatures, at least ten ships. It looks like a battle group."

"We're on our way back," I said. "Don't move, don't power up. And by all the gods, do not use active scanners."

"Tajen—"

"I know," I interrupted, as I gathered Kiri to me and activated my suit's gravitic nodes. "We're on our way."

★   ★   ★

I strapped into my seat a few rather tense minutes later, taking back control of the ship with a nod to Katherine. "Everyone get strapped in," I called. "Bet Dierka's glad we got that Kelvaki couch installed in the lounge," I said to Katherine.

"Considering how big he is, *everyone* is glad. It'd be a hell of a thing to get him thrown into you in the middle of combat." We both dropped into our training, working together almost seamlessly, flicking data points and displays back and forth as we prepared for contact. Halfway through, Liam and Kiri arrived, taking seats at the empty consoles. Katherine nodded to them and began assigning secondary functions to their stations.

Ready lights signaled that Takeshi, Ben, and Dierka were all strapped securely into their couches. "All right, folks," I said. "Apologies to you three in the back, but we're going silent. No transmissions of any kind, including NeuroNet, unless necessary. And keep your voices down. Zhen ships can use laser scanners to read voices through the hull." I shut off the intraship comms and said quietly, "What are we looking at?"

Liam answered, just as quietly, "So far it looks like a carrier group. One carrier, three supply ships, six frigates, and a hell of a lot of small fighters."

"Have they moved?"

"They're spreading out." He examined his plot for a moment, and said, "Looks like a pretty standard search pattern."

I nodded and switched maneuvering from gravitics to cold-gas thrusters. It'd be slow, but it would help us avoid detection. "Find me somewhere to hide," I said.

A lot of holovids show ships that can find other ships just by looking at their sensors. But in real life, space is damned big, and even dreadnoughts are pretty small, relatively speaking. Absent some kind of energy output or transmission, it's possible to be in a star system and not even know someone else is out there. Even if you know someone's out there, knowing where they are is also next to impossible unless they're using FTL comms relays or broadcasting some kind of signal. The best you can get is a best-guess heading, but what you know is always old news, and it's almost impossible to know how things have changed since you got that information. Once you get close enough that you can find people visually, or with short-range sensors, things get hairy fast. Most starship combat is long periods of tense searching, punctuated by short, intense close-range firefights.

Which was why, as we searched for a hiding place, the Zhen were spreading across local space. While their smaller ships spread out, they'd be linking their sensor feeds, all funneling into the carrier at their center. They'd also be sending out unmanned probes to widen their net. If any of the ships detected anything that might be me, they'd automatically compare notes with the rest of the network of ships and probes. The data analysts on the carrier would correlate all the data, and tactical officers would relay commands back down the chain.

The easiest way to remain hidden was to be quiet, in all senses of the word. Quiet helped calm the nerves, and helped avoid panicked and stupid decisions. I had already killed all exterior lights; now I shut down the overheads on the bridge, which was now dark, the only displays 'projected' into our brains by our implants.

Liam flicked a set of coordinates over to me, and I hit the gas jets, moving us toward the parking spot he'd designated. It took nearly half a nerve-wracking hour to make the move, which ended with the *Dream of Earth* tucked up under the largest dead ship, mere yards away from it, as if we'd drifted there over decades. "There," I said softly. "All tucked away like the harmless debris we are."

"Of course," Kiri murmured, "if they look too closely, we're fucked."

I sighed. "Always the ray of sunshine, aren't you?"

She shrugged. "Dad said I was just like you."

I looked over my shoulder at her. As I turned, I caught Liam's smirk. I threw him a look, and then turned back to Kiri to say something suitably snarky, but the breath left me as I saw her wink out of existence. "Kiri!" I shouted. I turned back to Liam, but he and Katherine were gone too.

A cultured voice spoke behind me. "I thought it best we speak alone." I stood swiftly and faced the Zhen who stood several yards away, the sun behind her left shoulder, making her difficult to see clearly.

Wait. The sun? The Zhen?

I realized I was standing in a *charkal*, the ritual fighting ring of the Zhen art of *kartoran*. At least, it seemed I was. It didn't take long for me to realize I was in a virtuality. But I wasn't anywhere near a network, which meant that the lead vessel had a better-than-normal communications capability. More to the point, I hadn't consented to my reality being overwritten, and yet the Zhen before me had done it. "How are you doing this?" I asked the Zhen.

Her crest extended, then folded back across her head, a clear sign of irritation. "I am Salanaa shin Kor shin Telerei shin Kata shin Foori," she said, as if I hadn't spoken. "I seek parlay with you under the rules of *Zhen ka tar.*"

Dammit. She'd said the words, invoking the formal rules of conflict. If I refused, it would be the greatest insult I could offer her, as well as a declaration of open war. Then she stepped forward, and as the sun no longer silhouetted her, I noticed the red skin that signified a member of the ruling caste, the *Zhen:ko*.

Shit. Salanaa wasn't one of the Twenty, and she wasn't the One, but that didn't mean she was powerless. As one of the red Zhen, she could kill any green-skinned Zhen, and the worst she could expect from the decision would be to gain an enemy among the red-skinned that the green worked for. That wasn't much of a problem; she probably had at least a few already. The *Zhen:ko* were constantly scheming, jockeying for position in their internal hierarchy, always aiming for the ultimate prize of being named to the Twenty, and from there, to become the One.

In theory, she had no power over me. Humans had negotiated hard to keep our species out from under the claws of the *Zhen:ko*; it was one reason our taxes were so high. In reality, however, there wasn't much anyone could do if she decided to kill me. And the treaty hadn't saved my brother from the decree of the One.

In other words, this woman held the power of life and death over millions of souls. Including mine, if she wished it. I rarely cursed in English, but... *Fuck.* I stepped forward and said the only thing I could.

"I agree to talk."

Salanaa inclined her head. "Thank you."

I shrugged. "If I may be honest, Honored One, you had me in the conference already. Had I said 'no', would you have released me?"

She gestured *irrelevant disdain.* "Since you agreed, the question is moot."

I sent *acceptance.* "So what do you want, Honored One?"

She hissed a laugh. "I think, under the circumstances, we can dispense with the pleasant titles. Call me Salanaa, Tajen Hunt."

I inclined my head. It was a human gesture, but she understood it. "Call me Tajen."

"Thank you." She took in a deep breath and released it. "I want you to give up this quest before it destroys your race."

I bridled. "And how, exactly, would finding the human homeworld destroy the human race?"

"That's just it, Tajen. Humanity has dreamed of home ever since the Rescue. All of your species, from the Dreamers who actively search for Earth to even the most Zhen-acculturated, who pretend not to care, think about the human world. It is a part of your literature, your entertainment, and even your legends.

"When humanity first joined us on the Kin Peninsula and founded the city of Virginia, there were many among us who assumed you would slowly lose your indigenous culture. Indeed, some factions among us wished to speed the process. Others wanted to slow it — they were concerned we might take from you that which made you interesting." Her tone suggested she thought little of that view. "Instead, you did both — you became an important, some might even say vital, part of the Empire, and yet you also maintained your native legends. Many of you taught the languages your colonists spoke even when it was still illegal — yes, we were aware of it, and we chose to tolerate it despite the law and, when it was judged time, we changed the law to allow it openly. You still teach what literature remains from that written on ancient Earth. Some of your people still follow your ancient mythologies. You see my point?"

"Not even a little," I said. "Okay, we like to dream of Earth. So how will finding it destroy us?"

"We have told you for eight hundred years that we could not locate Earth. The truth is that we found it."

"When?"

"Five hundred years ago."

To say I was angry would be an understatement. "And you never told us?"

She sent *patience*, pacing the ring. "Our psychologists believed that the truth would destroy you as a people, destroy your sense of self." She turned from me, which to a Zhen meant both that she didn't consider me a threat, and that she was displaying reluctance to tell me something. "We had grown by then to care for you too much to let such a thing happen.

"You see, Tajen, your world is dead."

"What do you mean, 'dead'?"

She turned to face me. "I mean that it had been destroyed hundreds of years before we found it. There were no survivors that we could discover." My mind reeled as she continued. "The evidence suggests they destroyed each other in a war using some form of nanotech weapon." Her voice was flat, emotionless. "The destruction of life was total. Nothing living survived."

"Nothing?"

"The planet was scoured of all organic matter. Nothing remained but rock."

She seemed entirely genuine.

She was lying.

"I don't believe you, Salanaa," I said.

The Zhen:ko are not used to hearing 'no' from their lessers. Her crest rose, the spines pointing straight up. "You dare accuse me of lying?"

"Oh, come off it. Of course I'm accusing you of lying. Do you want to know why?"

Her claws flexed, and I idly wondered for a moment if she remembered this was all illusion.

"Because you're lying," I said simply.

Here in virtual space, my NeuroNet didn't provide me the overlay of her body's blood patterns, but I didn't need it to see she was angry. "You *dare* to speak to me in this manner?"

I shrugged. "How else should I speak to you? You're clearly lying to me. Is there some special word I should use?" I smiled sweetly at her. "See, you almost had me. But there's just one little problem. It doesn't make sense. There's simply no reason to have hidden it from us." She opened her mouth to speak, and I barreled right over her. "The Zhen gave us a home, but you have never let us forget it either. So don't try to tell me that the mighty Zhen Empire was so all-fired worried about our delicate human feelings they decided not to tell us our world had been found dead. We'd have become even more beholden to you, even more willing to remain under your claws. It would have been better to tell us than to hide it, and you know it.

"Setting that aside, you Zhen:ko bastards killed my brother. Oh, I know, you had one of your agents do it. But his blood is on the One, and on the rest of you too. So fuck off."

She looked furious for a moment, then grinned. "I told the One it would not work. But she was so eager to leave you alive."

"Why?"

"You have served the Empire well. The One wished to retain that service, to bring you back into the fold." She smiled, that cold Zhen smile that was entirely a threat display. "Instead, I shall kill you."

I grinned at her. "You have to find us, first."

She hissed in amusement. "Stupid little ape," she growled. "Did you forget where we really are?"

My blood ran cold as I realized that *I* had been the one to forget we weren't in a real place, and what it meant that we were connected to each other. I tried to cancel out of the conference. But whatever computer was facilitating the connection wouldn't accept my command. She stalked up to me and reached out a claw, running it down my cheek. The virtual reality routines in my NeuroNet let me feel it, a knifepoint sliding across my skin, just barely light enough to avoid cutting me. I couldn't be cut, of course – feeling it in the virtuality didn't make it real – but that didn't make it any less scary.

She leaned in, my NeuroNet creating the sensation of her breath on my face as she said, very softly, "We have been tracking your NeuroNet since you left the homeworld. We know *exactly* where you are."

★　★　★

I was back in my seat. As soon as I realized that, I started frantically flipping switches and sending mental commands to the ship. "Bring us up to full power," I snapped to Katherine.

"Won't that tell them where we are?"

"They already know," I said.

She didn't waste time asking questions, but simply began powering up systems. "Need weapons?"

"Unless we all want to die," I said.

"I vote no," Kiri said.

"I concur," Liam quipped, as we all began flicking information back and forth. If I'd had the time, I'd have marveled at the way we worked together in a stress-heavy situation so well after so short a time as a single crew, but I only realized that later, when I relived my memories of the fight.

The hulk we were hiding below shuddered, beginning a slight move in our direction – it had been hit by some kind of weapon on the other side. Well, that was good. It meant I had some armor – for a little while, anyway. I matched the movement with thrusters and cringed as the hulk moved toward us faster than I could move without power. "Where are my engines?" I asked testily.

"Coming up!" Katherine said. "Ready…now!"

I slammed the throttle to full and aimed the ship away from the nearest Zhen fighters, already vectoring toward us. Just as we cleared the wreck, a second energy beam hit the drifting hulk, punching through the wreckage and barely missing our starboard weapon pod.

I chose a vector and took off at full thrust, trusting Liam and Katherine to keep up on their own stations. I saw a Zhen fighter arrowing in on an intercept course. Locking him in as my primary target, I took the ship off computer-assisted thrust and turned our nose to him so I could bring all my forward weapons to bear. I fired my last two missiles and two plasma streams on an intercept vector, hoping he wouldn't have time to change course.

Unfortunately for me, the other pilot was good, and he changed course almost as soon as I fired. My weapons missed him by a wide margin. I cursed and flipped back around, changing my own vector slightly to confuse anyone drawing a bead on me.

"Four fighters, closing to CCR," Liam intoned. "Pity we haven't got turrets on this boat."

CCR was Close Combat Range, the point at which pilots reigned supreme. If all of those fighters got that close, we were dead.

Not even my skills were enough to win a contest between a freighter – even a heavily armed one like the *Dream of Earth* – and this many top-of-the-line Zhen starfighters. "The hell with this," I said, and swung the ship onto a vector that would take us away, then initiated the chain drive at maximum field strength. In a matter of seconds, all the Zhen dropped off our scopes. However, we were coming up fast on a planetary body. I cut thrust just in time; we dropped into normal thrust right in front of what appeared to be a small lopsided moon. Well, to be honest, I'm exaggerating. In astronomical terms we were right on top of it, but in actual fact, we had maybe five thousand kilometers between us and certain death. Of course, when you're traveling at nearly sixty per cent of the speed of light, even a magical alien drive unit that somehow cancels out relativity isn't going to keep you from turning into chunky salsa.

I quickly drew as close as I could to the moon, in the shadow between it and the planet below, and placed us into a stable orbit. "Cut everything you can," I said. "Put life support on minimal power." I looked to Kiri. "Kiri, relay this to Ben and Takeshi in person, please: resume silent running. Nobody uses their NeuroNets for anything that could go external. No transmissions, not even to each other." She nodded and removed her safety harness, then left the bridge.

Once she was gone, I turned to the other two. "It's only a matter of time before they find us. Hell, I'm not even sure not using our NeuroNets will help. I wasn't using mine when they locked onto it." I quickly told them what had transpired in my virtual conference.

"Wait," Liam said. "Salanaa?"

"Yeah. You know her?"

"No. But I saw her once, when I was serving – she's bad news."

"How so?"

"Near as I could tell from the conversations I overheard between her and my CO, she doesn't much like humans. I got the sense she thought of us as little more than animals."

"That's rich," Katherine said, "considering how they feel about the Tradd."

"I think it's partially that we're not as worshipful to them as the

Tradd are," Liam said. "She thought we should be 'more grateful' to them and serve the Zhen more directly, like they do."

"Lovely," Katherine said.

"That's interesting," I said, "but it doesn't give us much to work with in this particular situation. Unless you can think of a way that knowing she hates humans will get us out of this."

"I'll tell you one thing it does tell us," Liam said. "It tells us pretty clearly that she can't be trusted."

I conceded that, then glanced at my long-range passive display and cursed to myself. "We don't have a choice, do we? We have to run for it."

"Run where?" Katherine asked. "We don't have a jump destination past here."

"Well, if we sit here, we're dead," I said. "I don't know about you, but I'd like to postpone that particular eventuality. So we're going. Find me a jump point, but in the meantime, I'm heading out."

"Why not just sit tight until I've got it?" Katherine asked.

Liam jolted into action as I fired up the engines. "He's probably moving because of the squad of Zhen fighters on a vector straight for us," he said over his shoulder. "Weapons hot," he added to me.

I was already moving, swinging the ship around to clear orbit. I was clearly not going to get away without a fight; they were simply too close. "Targeting lead ship," I said softly, falling into the old pattern of combat as my NeuroNet bracketed my target in yellow. I watched the range shrink, waiting for the moment when they'd be in range of my weapons. At the moment the brackets turned red, a preset command fired both plasma guns, the bright yellow energy pulses streaking toward the lead fighter. His shields took the hit, fluorescing in waves of bright colors as the shield dissipated the energy.

The Zhen pilot fired at the same moment. His shots impacted on my shield, and seconds later, we flew past each other at high speed. I immediately flipped the ship 180 degrees, firing again until I was out of range. "I'd pay a lot for some more missiles," I muttered. Unfortunately, the space-based missiles used in the Empire weren't something I could acquire without much better connections than

I had. The ones I'd had on the *Lost Cause* had cost me a lot, in money and in social credit, but there hadn't been a way to get them to Zhen:da without being caught. And the *Dream of Earth* had only the two I'd fired already. As the squad scattered, each of them doing their own flip and beginning pursuit, I registered a missile launch, my system identifying seven missiles headed my way.

I flipped back over, reversing my heading, and fired off a set of flares. A thought activated my electronic countermeasures system, my computers doing what they could to end the missiles' lock-on. Sadly, my ECM was thirty years old, and not up to the task. All but two of the missiles impacted on my shields, dropping them down to barely ten per cent of full power. I was in trouble.

Two of the enemy ships dropped onto my tail, firing. My shields dropped, and I changed vector, presenting my dorsal shield to the fighters angling away from my pursuers. They turned to maintain the pursuit, so I changed vector again, cutting my thrust and flying backward while I fired. I pierced one ship's shields, a plasma beam hitting his cockpit. The fighter tumbled out of control, and slammed into the other ship. Both broke apart. I spared the pilots a thought. They were Zhen, but it wasn't their fault they were sent after me.

My sympathy, however, wasn't about to extend so far as letting myself get shot out of space. I dropped in behind the lead fighter on the Zhen side and poured fire into his rear shield. The last of the squad dropped in behind me, firing into my own shield. I could see there was another squad of ships inbound, only a few minutes from joining the fight. "Dammit," I growled, and tagged them as secondary targets.

I stayed on my guy, continuing to fire, trusting in my instincts and the datastream of my tactical system. When the enemy's shield collapsed, I began to think I might actually get through this.

And then my HUD winked out.

"What the *shrak*?" I cried.

"What?" Liam asked.

"My 'Net's out. I'm *kark*ing blind! I've got no tactical!" I was trying not to panic, and failing miserably. Even at fighter range, the distances and speeds involved in starship combat made manual targeting impossible. No matter how good I was, there was no way I could hit a small ship by deadeye reckoning. I had to get away from those ships. As soon as that thought entered my head, I hauled back on the stick until I was angled perpendicular to the Zhen fighters, my ventral thrusters facing the direction I was traveling. I fired the belly thrusters, using them to shed velocity as the main thrusters sent us off on a new vector, skipping off the outer edges of the atmosphere of the planet below, using the drag to shed even more speed.

I pulled the maneuver off beautifully, ending with my nose pointed out into space, and fired my main thrust at full burn, trying to make for the jump line. I didn't dare use the chain drive without my implants to help me navigate. Traveling at near-light speeds is no time to be without computer flight aids.

I was dimly aware of Liam yelling something, but I was too preoccupied trying to figure out what was happening with my NeuroNet. Nothing worked. Not my tac system, not comms, nothing.

I was barely aware when the ship took a series of plasma bolts to the upper and rear shields. The ship shook around me as the shield overloaded and blew. I was quickly overwhelmed as the Zhen pilots swarmed over the ship, firing constantly, each shot chewing into my hull. The ship was shaking so much I couldn't maintain control. I was vaguely aware when Katherine took control of the ship, shouting out to Liam as she tried to get us to the jump point, but I couldn't hear anything she was saying over the sound of the blood pounding in my ears.

And then it all went black.

CHAPTER EIGHT

When I came back to myself, I was lying on my back, staring up at a large sheet of cloth stretched between what looked like two large sticks. Beneath me was hard clay soil, swept clear but baked hard from the midday sun I could see peeking through the rents in the fabric above me. There was a hot wind blowing over me, whipping the fabric above into a frenzy of motion.

I turned my head to the right and saw a small brown-skinned reptile, covered in spines, sitting under a rock, watching me. "Hey," I said – or, rather, I croaked – to it. "Where am I?" It didn't answer, but just stared at me. "Not a talker, huh?" I asked it. "Well, fuck off, then." My voice sounded strange to my ears.

It looked at me for a long moment, then jumped at something and ran off, disappearing under the edge of the tent. I tried to sit up, but that was clearly a mistake, according to my back, and I slumped again, fighting the urge to scream, and failing. Panting with the pain, I tried to take stock of my injuries. There was pain in my left arm, both legs, and my head was pounding like a Kelvaki chieftain was beating war drums behind my eyes. That was about all I could really tell, though I suspected my right leg, at least, was broken. It seemed to have been splinted, but without my NeuroNet I couldn't assess the damage easily.

The flap of the tent was brushed aside and Ben entered, carrying a bundle of something wrapped in a blanket. "You're awake," he said. "That's probably a good thing."

"Probably?"

He shrugged. "Well, you're beat all to shit, frankly. And given our situation, you're going to want to jump back into action, and in case you haven't noticed, you're beat all to shit." He put the bundle down beside me and began unwrapping it. "Not to mention that you're beat all to shit."

I laughed, which pretty much immediately became writhing in pain, because like he said, I was beat all to shit. "How bad am I?" I asked after the pain passed.

"You're pretty bad, but nothing a shower wouldn't cure," he said matter-of-factly. I stared at him. "Oh, you meant medically." He grinned. "Let's put it this way, you won't be walking for a few days yet."

"Days? It feels broken."

"Oh, it is. In three places. But I found this in the wreckage." He held up a medkit. "It's got a full-on nano-surgery unit and it seems to be working. I'll fuse your bones and take care of the rest of your wounds too." He looked me over, and grimaced. "Given the extent of your injuries, it'll take three or four days."

"That won't work. Without a medcomp we can't manage the nanites."

"Tch. I know you military types sometimes had to do it yourself, but you're not in the military anymore. And fortunately for you, you're not the only person with a NeuroNet." He tapped his temple. "Unlike yours, mine's still working. *I'll* manage the nanites."

"You can do that?"

"You can't?"

I shook my head, wincing at the pain it caused. "No."

He looked at me like I was especially stupid. "Must be because you don't have a 'Net with a medical suite." He tapped my forehead. "Maybe I should probe for some brain damage, eh? I didn't think you were this dim."

I grinned at him. "Might be a good idea." I frowned. "You said 'wreckage'. We crashed?"

He nodded. "Katherine managed to land us, but the ship was tossed around pretty bad. It's mostly in one piece, but it's pretty torn up. Liam and Katherine put up a cloak and sensor damper field to hide us from the Zhen, but it's going to take some time to fix."

I spared a thought for the *Dream of Earth*, but the ship wasn't the first thing on my mind. "Where is Liam?"

"Working on the ship with everyone else." He began to unpack the medkit, setting it up around me. "They'll keep working while I fix you up so we can get moving. That sensor damper may not last. Liam decided it was best some of us keep moving, give them a target to follow."

"Good idea. Any sign of the bastards?"

"A shuttle flew over the crash site a few days ago, but nothing since. The cloak field held up, near as we can tell. At least we're not crawling with Zhen yet. Liam thinks they've moved on, but they'll be back."

I cursed. "Damned Zhen. If my NeuroNet was working I'd be more useful."

He looked at me oddly as he placed the nanite package over my leg and activated it. My leg tingled as the nanites in the block began to spread out and surround my leg, working their way through the skin. It was vaguely uncomfortable, but not painful, as they began their work. Ben sat back once the job was underway and sighed. "About your NeuroNet. I might be able to help."

"How?"

"Well. Here's the thing. Kiri already scanned your 'Net, and she was able to reactivate your system. Turns out there's a backdoor code in the NeuroNets – she discovered we all have them – that deactivates the system."

"You're kidding."

"Wish I was."

"How is it nobody's spotted that before?"

He shrugged. "She tried to explain it, but I didn't really understand. So she simplified it – said it would be nearly impossible to see if the whole 'Net was up and running, but it lit up like a floodlight when the rest of the field was dark. Make sense?"

"I think I get the point."

He grunted. "Anyway, she's working on a way to deactivate that node. In the meantime, she told the tech to reactivate your system – but you still can't access it?"

I tried again. Nothing. "No."

He nodded. "Well, as I said, I think I can help with that. One of my specialties was NeuroNet therapy."

"I've heard of that, but never looked closer. Do NeuroNets actually go bad?"

He waggled his hand in a 'sort of' gesture. "Not everyone

tolerates the nanites the same way. It's rare, but sometimes people lose their ability to control the tech, even though it's still there and still wired into their nervous system. Everything's in working order, but they just can't seem to connect. It's somewhere between a technological and a psychological problem. There are ways to deal with it, though – therapies that allow the user to interact with the tech and work through the interface."

"Are you saying I'm insane?"

He grinned at me. "Has that ever really been a question?"

I smiled and changed the subject before I had to think on that too much. "How are we for supplies?"

He grunted. "A lot of our stuff got banged around in the crash. This is the best I've found so far."

He placed the pile of stuff next to me. The feeling in my leg was changing from 'tingling' to 'tiny men stabbing my leg', so I distracted myself by opening the blanket and going through the gear. It was a pretty lousy haul.

In addition to mine, which seemed to have come through the crash intact and charged, we had one blaster, which I discovered, with a sense of fatalistic acceptance, was damaged badly enough I'd need a full field kit to fix it, a pack of emergency rations that would last two people about a week, a flashlight, three knives, one of which I'd been wearing during the crash and which was probably responsible for the ridiculously painful bruise on my left hip, and an emergency kit that had broken open in the crash and held only a fire-starter and a flare. "Not the best haul, really," I said.

"At least I found a blaster," Ben said smugly.

"Oh no," I said. "If you try to fire that thing, it's going to explode in your hand. If you're lucky, it'll fire a shot first. But mine checks out."

"Oh." He looked a bit crestfallen.

I grinned, though the grin became a rictus of pain for a moment as some of the nanites started repairing my knee. "Why does tissue repair have to be so damned painful?" I asked.

"It doesn't. But I haven't got any drugs to numb the pain. Sickbay was hit bad, a lot of stuff got smashed. And your NeuroNet interface isn't functioning, so it can't block your pain receptors."

"Ah," was all I could manage to say, and I barely kept it from becoming a scream.

"Anyway, relax. Like I said, this'll take a few days."

"Right, because that's going to be so easy."

He stood. "Suit yourself. I need to go get some water. Don't move."

As he moved to the tent flap, I called after him, "Was your bedside manner this lousy when you were practicing on Terra?"

He turned back to me. "Probably not. But I didn't usually have patients who whined as much as you have the past few days."

"I was sleeping!"

"And whining," he added.

"*Shka.*"

"Who's the bigger *shka*, you, or the guy putting your dumb ass back together?" He walked out of the tent before I could reply. I thought about calling through the tent, but I knew he'd probably get the last word, anyway – the way I was feeling, I wasn't up to a battle of wits. *Shka* was about the most witty thing I could think of to say.

I lay back and stared at the small sliver of sky visible through a rip in the tent fabric and meditated on the colossal fuckup everything had become.

If we could avoid the Zhen who were probably still searching for us long enough to make repairs, *if* we could get her back into space without being shot down, and *if* we could work out where we needed to go next, we could finish this.

That was too many ifs. If any one of them turned out to be a 'no', it would end this adventure with prejudice – and the odds were heavy that *at least* one of those things would go wrong, and more likely all of them. I was almost certain we were going to get caught.

I felt guilty. I had let my brother's memory down. His dream of finding the human homeworld, as well as my own of uncovering whatever the Zhen were hiding about Earth, was over.

I sighed, but the sigh turned to a sob, and I choked back a lump in my throat. Because dammit, my leg hurt. That's my story, and I'm sticking to it.

★   ★   ★

Some hours later, the tent flap rose and Liam stepped in, Katherine close behind him. He flopped down beside me, folding his legs under him, while Katherine quietly settled into position. They were filthy, covered in sweat, grease, and grime, and Katherine appeared to have a bruise over half her face. Liam took a rag and wiped his face as he sighed. He gazed deep into my eyes and said, "You never take me anywhere nice."

I suppressed a laugh. "Well," I said, "I wanted to take you to Earth, but the Zhen had other ideas." I shrugged an apology, then turned to Katherine. "I hear you got us landed."

She rolled her eyes. "If 'landed' is the right word, sure."

"That you got us all down intact was a miracle. Was anyone else injured?"

"Takeshi broke his arm – minor break, Ben's already fixed it. Everyone else activated the crash fields on their couches in time. None of them failed."

I closed my eyes in relief. Good acceleration couches come equipped with crash field generators, installed in an armored compartment. In emergencies, a combination forcefield and stasis field engages to protect the occupant from damage, but you have to get to the couch first. "We got lucky."

Liam nodded. "What happened to you up there? You were doing fine, and then you just...shut down."

"I'm not sure," I said. "I was targeting the fighters, and then my NeuroNet just quit on me."

"A fault?"

"Nothing showed up until that moment. I think...when I was talking to Salanaa, she traced me. I think the Zhen shut me down."

"*Shrak*," he said. We were quiet for a little while, just sitting in companionable silence.

Eventually, Katherine excused herself. "I promised Takeshi I'd help him cook dinner," she said. She got up and left with a smile..

Eventually, Liam cleared his throat. "Tajen," he said, "about that conversation we had."

"You mean the one where you said you speak Kelvaki?"

"Yeah, that one. So, I have this bad habit."

"Yes?" I asked warily.

"Sometimes I get my desires mixed up with what other people might be thinking. And I wonder if maybe I misread you."

"You mean you think I'm amazing and you're very much interested in me, but since I haven't said anything, you're afraid that I'm not into you?"

He blinked a moment, then said, "In a word, yes."

"Don't worry about it."

His face fell a little bit, and he nodded. "Okay. Sorry to—"

I had to cut him off. "For Siharen's sake, Liam. You didn't misread me at all."

"Oh!" he said, brightening.

"I'm not interested in you, I'm practically obsessed with you. But I'm the captain. I can't get involved with a crewmate."

"Then I quit," he said.

"What?"

"If you can't be involved with me because I'm on your crew, then I won't be on your crew anymore."

"But—"

"Or you could just get over it, acknowledge that I'm a big boy, and we're not in the military."

"What if it goes sour?" I asked. "My relationships usually do."

He shrugged. "If it does, we'll figure out whether I stay or go. It's your ship. I can't ask you to leave. But I don't think expecting the worst is a good way to begin."

I stared at him for a long time. "I guess, maybe you're right."

"Well, then," he said, and leaned toward me.

The tent flap opened, and I turned to look – and was disappointed when it turned out to be Ben. "Liam, he needs his sleep," Ben said. To me, he said, "Takeshi found some intact drugs. They'll make your recovery less painful."

"No," I said. "If the Zhen come for us, we'll need to move. I'll deal with the pain."

"Very noble of you," Ben said while he pushed Liam gently out. "But give me a *kark*ing break. If we try to move you before the nanites are done, you'll lose at least one of your legs. So shut up and take your damn medicine."

I waved acceptance and tried to relax when he pressed the

ampoule to my arm. A few seconds later, my vision got blurry. "Hey, I wanted to see Kiri," I mumbled.

"She's been busy. I'll tell her you asked for her."

And then there was darkness, and a vague feeling of my hand being held. I still don't know if it was Liam or Kiri. Hell, it could have been Ben or Katherine or Takeshi. I didn't care. It meant someone cared about me. And that was a feeling I'd missed for a long time.

★   ★   ★

When I woke up, I discovered it was Kiri holding my hand. She didn't realize I was awake at first, and I watched her through half-lidded eyes. She looked like she was barely holding it together.

"I'm sorry," I croaked.

She looked up at me and smiled, then quickly wiped her cheeks and helped me sip some water. When I was done, she said, "For what? Sleeping all day while we're working our butts off?"

I laughed, which hurt. "Getting you into this."

She cocked her head at me. "Tajen, I'm fine. I mean, don't quote me on this, but despite everything? I'm having fun. We could die at any moment, and I'm actually enjoying it. Is that wrong?"

"No. It's just a sign that you're a Hunt. But if you're having fun, why are you crying?"

She sighed. "You were talking in your sleep, about Mom, and Jiraad."

I froze. "Did I say anything important?"

"Nothing I didn't already know. Which brings me to my question. Are you an idiot?"

"I don't...think so?"

"So why didn't you realize that I'd have looked up the Battle of Jiraad oh, I don't know, *as soon as I could use the slipnet*? I mean, my mom *died* there." She looked angry, but also confused. "I looked up the whole thing years ago. I've known how it happened since I was nine years old, and I've known you were the commander in charge for even longer. I've read your reports. Hell, I ran the simulation based on your ship's flight recorder. I know how the whole thing unfolded.

"And I know that it wasn't your fault. You made a mistake, okay, but you didn't *allow* the Tabran fleet in, and it isn't your fault they beat you. My mother's death is on the Tabrans, not you." She pursed her lips. "The only thing you bear the responsibility for is the way you've acted since we left Zhen. Avoiding me, I mean. Do me a favor?"

"Name it."

Her voice became hard and implacable as stone. "Knock it off."

I looked at her, and I wondered if Daav had ever been bothered by how like me his daughter was. "I will," I choked out, trying not to laugh.

She grinned at me, and her voice softened. "I know I've been doing the same thing to you, and I've been trying to figure out how to stop too." She reached out and took my hand. "You're my family. The only one I've got left, if we're being honest. And it's starting to look like we're going to be stuck together for a long time. Or the rest of our lives, anyway – however long that is. So, we're just going to have to find a way to be a family for real, and not just in name." She grinned at me, her green eyes twinkling. "Deal?"

"Deal."

We smiled, and stayed like that until Takeshi and the others arrived with dinner. Liam built a fire, and they arranged themselves around it. As Takeshi passed out the food, he asked, "Has anyone figured out how they keep finding us?"

"I looked all over the ship," Katherine said. "I can't find a tracker anywhere."

"I can't either," Kiri added. "I also changed the transponder codes after Akhia Station, so they're not tracking us that way."

"They're tracking me," I said. "Salanaa told me they've been tracking my NeuroNet since we began."

"You mean it's true?" Liam exclaimed.

"I guess so," I said. There'd been complaints for years, mostly from humans, but also from some Zhen, that the government could track people through their NeuroNets, and calls for stricter controls. The Empire had always denied it was ever done. "And it's not like they don't know my system's network identifications."

"They can find ours too," Kiri said nervously. "That's got to be in our records."

"Well, we're safe now, right?" Takeshi said. "Tajen's system is down, and we're not near a slipnet beacon anymore. I can't get a signal at all."

Ben grunted. "Then how did they find Tajen? There was no beacon when we arrived here."

I sighed. "It's my system."

"What do you mean?" Ben asked.

"You all have civilian models, right?" They all nodded. "Katherine got hers downgraded when she left the Space Force. I didn't. Mine still has military specs."

Liam whistled. "How'd you manage that?"

"Bribery. Not really important right now. Anyway, when I was a commander in the Space Force, they pulled some of the logs about Jiraad directly from my head." I paused, looking nervously at Kiri. "If any of you ever played the simulation that was made available, it came direct from my brain."

"Sure," Takeshi said. "But you downloaded it, right?"

"Nope." I grinned at the shock on their faces. "C'mon, people. Big autocratic empire, and you're shocked they pull stuff from our heads without permission?" I sighed. "Hell, I used to access my navigators' feeds all the time, to make sure they did their job right. To the Zhen, it's their tech, and the officers are serving the Empire – so it's the Empire's right to look inside. It's not supposed to work with civilians, but—"

"But they got in Dad's head," Kiri interrupted.

"Exactly."

"*Shaak*," Liam said. "What the hell else can they do?"

Katherine's voice was quiet. "They can alter our perceptions." We all waited for her to continue. "When I was in the Force, there was an incident. I was in the mess, and suddenly a Zhen just... died."

"Of what?" I asked.

"Of a dagger in her eye," she said.

"Wait a second," Liam said. "How do you 'just' die of a dagger shoved in your eye?"

"There was nobody there except the five of us," she said. "And then, suddenly, there was a dagger sticking out of her eye. None of us were missing time, it just…happened. The scuttlebutt was, the Special Executive have the ability to alter the information our NeuroNets process – to the point where they can be invisible by telling our brains not to see them."

We all stared at her. "Is that possible?" I asked Ben.

"I think so," he said. "Once we get the NeuroNets installed, they have access to our brain. Controlling what we see is necessary for information to show up in our visual field."

"Well, that's…." Liam began, and trailed off.

"It's insane," Kiri said.

"Insanely scary," Takeshi added.

We sat silently for a moment, trying not to believe that we were surrounded by Zhen we couldn't see.

★   ★   ★

A little less than three days later, I was on my feet, though still moving around a bit gingerly. We packed up the tent and what gear we had and began searching for some sign of life. Katherine said she'd seen some sign of habitation briefly before we hit atmosphere and entered sensor blackout. When the ship recovered, she had other things on her mind, like keeping the ship together long enough to hit the ground.

Kiri had found a computer in the wreckage. It was banged up, but functioning – a testament to the intelligence of my policy of buying military-grade hardware whenever possible. She'd wanted to get started on hacking my implants immediately, but I vetoed it. As eager as I was to get my system reconnected to my brain, I was also anxious to get away from this camp and lead the Zhen on a wild goose chase before they found our ship. I wasn't about to believe they'd stopped looking for us, even if we hadn't seen them in a while.

Liam, Ben, Takeshi, and Kiri would go with me, creating sensor blips every few days and hiding with a cloak field as much as we could. Katherine and Dierka would remain with the ship, doing repairs.

Katherine showed me where they'd already searched, sketching a rough map of the region they'd explored in the hard clay. "This here," she said, pointing in the direction from which the sun rose, "drops into a canyon. No sign of anything sentient down there."

I stood and looked to my left, in that direction. We were on what appeared to be a mesa. To the east, the ground fell away into a wide canyon, the other side rising to more mesa, continuing on as far as I could see. To the west, the land seemed fire-ravaged; thin sticks that used to be trees thrust out of the ground like a graveyard for a lost forest. In the distance I could see trees that somehow escaped the fire. The difference between the two zones was stark – in one, burned trees and dead ground, in the other, short, bristly trees, not entirely unlike the *yorsha* trees in the Muhaak Desert back on Zhen:da.

"We'll go west," I said.

She nodded. "Good luck."

Though I could walk, Ben and Liam insisted on carrying most of the gear while I recuperated. I felt guilty about not carrying my share. There wasn't much of it, so it wasn't really necessary. Still, I appreciated it.

I'd spent the last three days mostly unconscious, so that I wouldn't thrash around and make the nanites' work harder. Ben had declared me fit to get up late last night, but we'd decided to wait until morning to set out. We'd thought about traveling in the night and staying in shade during the day, but we didn't have night vision gear, or even lights. So we'd do the best we could.

We'd risen with the sun and eaten a breakfast of cold emergency rations and some kind of supplement Ben insisted was good for us, but which tasted like fermented shit. Liam had declared it to be even more disgusting than *toka*, a Kelvaki dish that had been known to make humans lose their lunch even before they ate it.

The landscape, so far as we could see, was mostly hard-packed dirt and rocks. The sun, already fierce, beat down on us and reflected off the rocks, making us feel like we were walking through an oven. What vegetation there was gave no shade; it was all short, hardy shrubs. We hadn't found a water source, though there were signs of a streambed long since gone dry.

Over the two hours we'd been walking across this desert, Ben and I had gone from mostly joking insults to more serious conversation. "So, last night," Ben said now, "you were talking about serving with the Imperial Navy. How long did you serve?"

I noticed Katherine and Liam give each other a look, as if they were worried, but neither said or hinted anything to me. I shrugged. "I went in at eighteen. Left when I was thirty-two. So, fourteen years."

"How far up the ranks did you go?"

The question confused me. I was pretty well-known in the Empire; after Jiraad, my face was broadcast on every slipnet commentary program, especially on the human world, where my failure to save the colony was even more keenly felt than elsewhere. And it wasn't like there were very many humans named Tajen. "You don't know?"

He stopped, and looked at me calmly. "Pretend I don't."

That told me what was going on. This mattered to Ben, more than I'd realized. I saw the pain in his eyes, and I wondered how that pain was going to express itself. Although the board of inquiry had acquitted me of any wrongdoing, not everyone saw it that way. I'd been spit on, shouted at, and attacked more times than I could recall. Someone had even dumped a jar of piss on me once. It was yet another of the many reasons I'd gone back into space as soon as I got out of the service, rather than settle on Zhen:da or Terra. I took a deep breath, and looked him in the eye. "I was a commander. My last posting was as the commanding officer of the defense force at Jiraad."

He looked me in the eye for a long time. "Yeah," he said, his deep voice rumbling. He turned back in the direction we'd been going, squinting against the bright sun. "Let's keep moving," he said, and walked on, picking his way gingerly down the side of a short scree.

I followed, sliding sideways down the scree, and nearly fell when my knee threatened to go out from under me. When I caught up, I walked silently beside him for a moment, then asked softly, "Who did you lose?"

"My daughter." He didn't stop, didn't look at me.

"I'm sorry," I said. "I know it's not enough, but—"

He cut me off with a wave of his hand. "Don't," he said calmly. I stopped talking, and walked in silence with him for a while. Just before the silence got uncomfortable, he waved a hand at me.

"Don't take her death on your soul, Tajen," he said. "I forgave you a long time ago."

"But—"

He turned and put his hand on my chest, stopping me. "I wanted to blame you for a long time. I *did* blame you. But I read the Imperial investigator's report on the battle. I watched the trial, and heard your testimony, and that of your crew and the captains under you. Do you remember the bridge recording that was played during the court-martial?" He didn't wait for me to answer. "I do. I remember what you were doing as you watched the Tabran fleet destroying Jiraad. Your men were frantically trying to fix your engines, get your ships moving again. And you were working right alongside them.

"When the Tabran fleet began the bombardment, you were horrified. I watched you, and I saw you crying. Now, here's my question for you." He was calm, collected, but intense. "Tajen, *why* were you crying?"

I'd been asked the same question several times since the battle. I'd given a variety of answers, from the truth I gave the board of inquiry to the half-truth I gave a reporter who wouldn't leave well enough alone.

I decided Ben deserved the truth. "The moment they started firing, I knew there wouldn't be anyone left on Jiraad afterward. The Tabrans never take prisoners." I looked away from him. "I had a visual feed from downtown New Belfast. I saw the explosions and the death and the—" I stopped talking and took several deep breaths as the memories surfaced. Even without my implants working, I saw the scene again, in crystal clarity. "They killed – *everyone*," I said, softly. "Men. Women. *Children*, Ben. Children who'd done nothing wrong, just because they existed on a world the Tabrans wanted." I was getting angry.

"But it wasn't your fault."

I said hotly, "Then whose fault was it, Ben? I was in command."

"And who put you in command?" He turned, and beckoned me to continue walking. "Who allowed the colony to proceed, even though it was obvious as hell the Tabrans wouldn't like it? Who placed your force in Jiraadi space, instead of agreeing to remove the colonists when they were asked to?"

I didn't have to tell him. Of course it was the Imperial Colonial Ministry. The Tabrans had made their claim known. We knew, from long experience, what they were like. The human government on Terra and the colonial administrative office on Jiraad had requested the Zhen move the colony. The Empire had answered that the colony was too far along to abandon now, and that the Tabrans were unlikely to risk open war over the place. They'd sent my defense force to guard the planet and their investment.

I opened my mouth to answer his question when Ben cut me off. "Tell me what you like about Zhen culture."

I was confused at the change in topic, and my anger evaporated. "Um…well, I like their art. *Ashrati* plays, music."

He chuckled. "That's all you've got? Arts and theater?"

I thought about it. When the *Far Star* was found by the Zhen, most of the data in the ship's computers had been lost, including much of the culture of our homeworld. A few books and pieces of music had survived as copies in various colonists' luggage, but it was a drop in an ocean. We had artists and writers in our colony, and some of them had survived and lived to create human art and literature, but much of what Earth had created over more than fifty thousand years of civilization had been lost.

But what we had lost had been balanced by an era of peace. The records handed down in recovered documents made us aware that Earth had been a fractious planet, and the organization that had sponsored our ship's journey, something called the International Space Agency, was a brand-new organization formed after a period of intense negotiation to amalgamate the space programs of several allied nations, in order to reach space before their rivals, some of whom were threatening war.

Under the Zhen, humanity had existed in peace, and if we hadn't done much to improve the technology of our hosts, we'd added to their literature, their music, and their art. And the gifts they had given us, colony worlds and technology that had revolutionized our society, outweighed what we'd lost by far.

At least, that's what I'd thought, before they killed my brother to keep him from revealing the location of our homeworld, not to mention whatever other secrets they held about the place.

"Well, no. But it's certainly a strength of their civilization."

"Sure. But – hell, you served, maybe you can answer some questions for me."

"Okay," I said, confused as to where he was going.

"Do you remember reading about the Shak Rebellion?"

I thought about it. After a moment, I frowned. "No."

"Not surprising," Ben said, sitting on a large rock and waving me to another next to it. Kiri listened, looking interested. Liam climbed a nearby rock and kept watch. He saw me looking and pointed toward Takeshi, who was foraging, with a shake of his head. I smiled and turned back to Ben as he continued. "It's not in the official history, and you'd be fortunate to find even a trace of it on the slipnet. But someone mentioned it around me once, and I started looking for the storytellers, the people who hand down knowledge through stories, as my people did on Earth." He sighed. "The Zhen:shak were another group, equal to the Zhen:la, the green Zhen. About ten thousand years ago, they outnumbered the Zhen:la by quite a bit. Anyway, they decided the Zhen:ko were full of shit and they'd had enough of being ruled by another tribe. So they rebelled.

"Now, Zhen tech back then wasn't much compared to today, but they're an old culture, so it was way better than anything we had on Earth ten thousand years back. They raised an oceanic fleet and went after the Zhen:ko – but the Zhen:ko had figured out atomic weapons by then. They dropped one on the home region of the Zhen:shak. The rebellion ended as soon as it began, with millions of them dead. That might have decided the issue, but the Zhen:shak weren't entirely united.

"Back then, the formal surrender ceremony required the party delivering the surrender to die so that the rest of his people didn't have to."

"I read about that," Kiri said. "They stopped doing that in the thirteenth year of the reign of Rath, but it's the basis for the Atonement Ceremony."

He nodded. "Damn fool notion. Anyway, one of the Zhen:shak leaders got himself named as the proxy. Only he didn't plan to die alone. When the time came, he detonated a bomb in his clothing. It was powerful enough that it killed all but a few of the Twenty.

In retaliation, the remaining members decided to wipe them out."

"Wipe who out?"

"All of the Zhen:shak."

I stared at him. "You can't be serious. Genocide is unthinkable to the Zhen."

Ben sighed. "It is *now*. Ten thousand years ago, it was quite thinkable. They wiped out every last Zhen:shak there was. Every man, woman, and child was put to the sword, sometimes literally."

I was horrified. "How is this not in the histories?"

Ben laughed, a bitter, cynical laugh. "All history is a fiction, Tajen. The historical narrative depends entirely on who has the power when the narratives are written. And the Zhen:shak are all gone, so who would care to remember?"

I shook my head. "But the Zhen:la were there, why don't they remember?"

"Some do — I learned about it from one of them — but it's not in the histories they learn in school, so it's been forgotten by most. Those who do know keep quiet. I was warned to tell nobody I knew about it." He looked thoughtful. "I've often wondered if people don't sometimes die because they've learned of this. I heard the tale more than thirty years ago. I've never told anyone about what I knew, until today."

"But what's this got to do with Jiraad?" Kiri asked.

Ben shrugged. "Probably just an old man's conspiracy theory, but I wonder if Jiraad wasn't sacrificed for the rest of us."

"I don't follow," I said. He gave me a look that said he knew I was lying. But he didn't call me on it. He simply looked at me and asked, "What happened after the Tabrans killed Jiraad?"

What had happened was called Operation 6447A in the military, but to the rest of the Empire, it was called the Revenge. A joint human/Zhen task force had wiped the Tabrans off Jiraad. Then they'd struck into Tabran space, destroying three colonies. Then a small courier ship had flown straight into their home system, bypassing all their system defenses, and broadcast a message to the Tabrans, in the clear: "For every one, we will destroy four. Do not tempt us to come here again." Then it blew itself up, taking out a nearby orbital shipyard and more Tabran lives.

I'd been told, at the time, that the courier ship was a drone. But drone ships weren't common in the Empire, and there had been rumors that the ship was crewed. I'd never found out which was true, but now that I'd seen how loyal Zhen agents operated, I was pretty convinced it hadn't been a drone at all.

Whatever the truth was, the Empire got what they wanted: the Tabran Regency had immediately sued for peace. In the negotiations they gave up not only Jiraad, but three other planets they'd claimed in the previously contested zone.

The Zhen had established Zhen colonies on all four worlds, claiming they didn't want to put human colonies in jeopardy again. "They played us," I said. "Used us, sacrificed Jiraad, to get the world ceded to them."

Ben nodded.

"That's crazy," Kiri said. But even she didn't sound as if she really believed that.

"Maybe. But maybe it made more sense to the Twenty and the One to sacrifice human lives to settle the issue. They certainly haven't found us a replacement world yet. Fifteen years later, we're still getting told to be patient while they find a suitable world."

I had to admit, as crazy as the idea was, it seemed a lot more plausible than it would have before Daav was killed. Humanity now existed on one world and a peninsula on Zhen:da, while the Zhen had claimed more colony worlds.

We started moving again, picking our way carefully over often-treacherous footing. We all fell several times as we climbed down into a shallow valley, but nobody fell as often as I did.

I was getting damned tired of falling.

This valley was fairly narrow, and we climbed back up the other side just as the sun was passing overhead. We crossed the mesa, which was smaller than the one before. When we got to the edge, Ben looked down and said, "Well, will you look at that."

I leaned over, Ben steadying me. At the bottom of the cliff, fifty or sixty meters down, there was something clearly made by sentients – a crumbling, circular sunken room with what appeared to be a doorway.

Kiri lay down on the edge of the cliff and poked her head over. "What is that?"

I straightened and looked at Ben. "Let's find out."

It took us a few minutes to find a way down. It looked like there had been a path once, but it was long since degraded almost to nonexistence. When we reached the bottom, we turned a corner in the cliff face and found what we'd only seen part of from above. None of us spoke for several minutes.

"I'm...not even sure what I'm looking at," Liam said.

Before us was what appeared to be a small settlement, carved out of the rock. "Looks pre-space," Kiri said. "The bricks are handmade, anyway."

"I'd say that's a safe bet," Ben said to her, running his hand down a brick face. Parts of it crumbled. "This thing is old. Centuries, at least. The cliff's sheltered it from the elements. That must be why it's still in decent shape."

"Is it safe to use?" Katherine asked.

Ben pointed at a nearby section. "Some of it's collapsed, but there's no way to know how long ago that happened," he said. "It's either safe, or it'll crush us. No way to tell, but the odds are that if it's stood this long, it'll last a few more hours."

I walked away, my eyes scanning the ruin. It wouldn't shelter us for long – there was no water nearby, and even the emergency rations wouldn't last forever. We'd need to find water.

But there was something else, too. This place, which I clearly had never seen before, was familiar to me in a way I couldn't put my finger on. As I walked around the site, I got a feeling that there was something I was missing. And suddenly I couldn't deal with not having my full set of tools available.

"Kiri, Ben," I said. "Can you get that computer out? We need to hack my 'Net, *now*."

"Sure," she said, reaching for her pack. "But why so urgent now?"

"Well," I said, "partly because we've moved, and we can shelter here for a time. But mostly because I'm getting a really weird feeling about this planet."

Takeshi and Liam stepped close as Ben helped Kiri set up. "What's going on?" Takeshi asked.

I shook my head. "Wish I could tell you. But something's making me uneasy. It's on the tip of my mind, but I can't get it out. Do me a favor, though – keep a lookout."

"We will," Liam said. "Takeshi, let's set up the cloaking field over there," he said, pointing, and the two of them got to it.

"Tajen? We're ready," Ben called.

I lay down where Kiri told me, and she set up a connection between her computer and my NeuroNet. "Link established and secure," she said, her eyes tracking the data scrolling across her visual field.

Easy for her to say, I thought – I couldn't detect anything, thanks to not being able to access my system.

"Okay, let's see what's what," Kiri said. She tapped some keys, presumably read her own implants' projection of the data, then tapped some more. She continued working like this for some time. Finally, I'd had enough.

"Kiri, please try to remember that I'm a person, who would like to know what's going on in my head?"

"Oh! Sorry, Uncle. The system's still up, but you don't seem to be able to access it."

I counted to five, and took a deep breath. "That much we knew," I said patiently.

"Well, yeah. But what's weird is that the command to shut you down seems to have been coded directly to you. It wasn't just a general system command, or it would have hit the rest of us too. And you've got a *lot* of stuff in here I don't have in my system."

Ben was shocked. "You've gone into your own system?" To hack one's own system was one of the most dangerous things you could do; every year stories came out about young hackers who tried to alter their NeuroNet and ended up as vegetables.

Kiri looked slightly abashed. "Yes," she said. "I didn't change anything, but I looked around in there and mapped the system." She frowned, and said, "*Way* less complicated than this one. Shit, you've got some fancy gear."

I grunted. "Military command system. Can you fix the interface between the tech and the meat?"

"Uh…no."

I sighed. "Great."

"But you can."

I opened my mouth, paused, and closed it again. "What?"

"Ben said he mentioned this to you earlier."

"He mentioned some kind of therapy, but he didn't say much about it."

"Oh. Well, how much do you know about the interface between your brain and the NeuroNet?"

"About as much as the average dirtsider knows about hyperdrive operation."

"Ah. Well, in that case…look, the tech is working. But something's gone wonky in the interface. It's pretty common in cases of head trauma. The brain sort of forgets how to work the tech, because it's too busy working through trauma. There's been some success in hooking patients directly into the interface software. Normally it runs under the surface, mostly subconsciously. If we hook you into the interface, you can work with it, untangle the connections and sort it all out."

Ben nodded. "But the interface is screwy as hell. It's all symbolic."

I blinked at him slowly. "What in the Nine Hells does that mean?"

Ben said, "It's like a waking dream, Tajen. You'll start out somewhere that's important to your self-image. It'll branch out from there."

"What kind of things will I see?"

He grinned and shrugged. "No idea. The software writes the simulation on the fly. Everything that happens in there comes from your own mind, filtered through the neural interface. So everything you experience is symbolic of something, either in the tech, or in you. It could be a walk in the park or a raging space battle. Every obstacle is, hopefully, a symbol for some kind of psychological issue that's getting between you and the tech. You have to find the solution to get past whatever obstacles there are."

"And that'll reactivate my implants?"

"Hopefully, yes. Or it could drive you insane." He gestured with his hands as if he was weighing something. "About a sixty-forty chance, really."

"Leaning toward?"

He shrugged. "You should be okay."

"You fill me with confidence," I said, my voice dripping with all the sarcasm I could muster. "Okay, let's go."

He glanced toward Liam and Takeshi, standing a fair distance away from us, watching the approaches. "Want to say anything to them first?"

I shook my head. "Let's get on with it."

"Your choice," he said, and passed a chip to Kiri.

She slotted it into place, then said, "Good luck."

I started to ask about the interface, but then my vision went insane. Then everything went white.

CHAPTER NINE

Just as I began to think that this was not a good sign, my vision returned.

I pretty much immediately wished it hadn't. Not because I was anywhere particularly scary, but because what I was seeing made very little sense.

I was standing in the Combat Information Center of the *Shir'kaan*, the last ship I had commanded. The crew was bustling around me, but their business was largely an illusion — they were basically running around in circles getting nothing done, slamming into each other, into the consoles, and arguing over how to solve whatever emergency they were dealing with. As far as I could tell, none of them noticed me. I appeared to be completely invisible. But that wasn't what was weird. It was their faces.

They were all me.

"Dammit, the systems won't come up," the version of me sitting at the comms system board said. The me wearing an XO's signifier crossed the CIC to that station and leaned over the tech.

"Have you tried rebooting?"

"Of course I've tried that! But the 'Net's staying down. It reads as if it's been reactivated, but it won't communicate with the captain!"

I turned away from them to the one thing on the bridge that made even less sense than a room full of me. Where the door to the flag office should be, there was instead a plain wooden door. What could I do? That was clearly the way to go, so I went through it.

The moment I stepped through the door, I found myself sitting under my favorite tree in the central quad of my secondary school, reading a somewhat 'sanitized' technical schematic on a *Karnakkar*-class fighter. The transition had the quality of a dream's logic to it, but with a harder edge I couldn't put my finger on. The moment I saw Jaden and Samantha Ndiaye approaching, my brain flashed on the specific memory I was reliving. And of course, since this was my life, it was one of those moments you spend the rest of your life regretting. I was seventeen years old, a year and some before my graduation, and this was the day I lost a friend — and a chance at a lot more.

"Tajen," Jaden laughed, "put down the reader, man. Have some fun for a change!"

"No time," I said.

"Oh, come on. Your fitness test isn't for weeks, you can take one weekend off."

I looked at Jaden, irritated. "No. I can't."

He and his sister sat, one on each side of me, and leaned in. Jaden leaned especially close, and I steeled myself as his breath brushed over my ear. "Please?" he whispered.

I remembered this day. In real life, I'd refused, told him off. I was frustrated, and angry at myself for being too afraid to take what he was really offering, what he'd been offering me for years. I'd yelled at him, accused him of trying to scuttle my chances at the Space Force for his silly crush.

Yeah. I was an idiot.

He'd stared at me for a long moment, then simply turned and walked away. His sister said only, "Damn it, Tajen," and went after him. I saw them both a few times over the next year, but none of us made an effort to talk to each other. What could I say? I'd regretted it ever since.

But here, what could I do? More importantly, what *should* I do? I knew what I wished I'd done, but what if that was the wrong thing?

The hell with it. I turned to Jaden and grabbed his head. "Okay," I said, and kissed him.

In real life the kiss probably would have been sweet, but awkward, as first kisses are supposed to be, according to the vids. But since I was making this up in my own mind, it was every bit as nice and sweet as I'd thought it should have been. It was everything he and I should have had that summer, and maybe the next, put into one long, soft kiss.

Somewhere in the back of my mind, I realized I had restored access to my comms systems.

When I pulled away, we smiled at each other. "Get moving, Hunt!" he shouted. I frowned at him in confusion, and realized it wasn't Jaden that had spoken.

He was gone. I was walking across a hard-packed desert plain under a blazing sun. The heat was oppressive, at the upper limits of human survivability.

I remembered this, too. It was a little more than a year after that day with Jaden. I was in Training Camp Skarak, on the Muhaak Desert Plain on Zhen:da, and I was marching while carrying over two hundred kilograms of gear.

It was way more than human soldiers carried. Hell, it was more than any of the Zhen with me were carrying. But I'd been snarking off about how I could do anything a Zhen soldier could do. That had angered Shish, my training commander, who had decided to test my claim by loading me with the gear of a Burning Star, the Zhen commando division. I was carrying everything a Zhen commando would need for an extended incursion behind enemy lines, from weaponry to shelter.

It was killing me.

I could barely lift one foot after the other. I had been sweating nearly the entire march, and according to my bio-monitor system, I was dangerously dehydrated. All sorts of health warnings were flashing in the periphery of my visual field. My temperature was rising, my tongue was swollen, my heart was palpitating, and I was getting dizzy.

Back in training, I'd soldiered through until I passed out. I'd spent three days in the infirmary, but the Zhen had stopped giving me as much grief. I'd thought they'd accepted me, but hindsight made it clear that I was kidding myself. Oh, they'd stopped giving me grief just for being human, but the truth is, it didn't make them like me or my presence among them any more. No matter how well I did, I was still human – even qualifying for squad command didn't gain me much more than grudging acceptance.

That wasn't universal, of course. There were some among them who treated me with respect. But they did so more out of a respect for the chain of command than anything else. None of them stood with me at the inquiry after Jiraad.

So why did I do it? Why did I try so hard to be Zhen, when it was so incredibly clear to me what a dead end that was?

Well, clearly, the answer was that I did it because I was a fucking idiot. I'd so completely bought into the Zhen narrative of the helpless humans who'd been saved and given a new life by the Zhen that I would do anything I had to do to prove myself worthy of the respect of the Zhen.

Well, fuck that.

I stopped, dropped my gear, and grabbed a water bottle. Ignoring Shish's angry glare, I drank deeply. I called up my comms and sent a signal for emergency retrieval, then turned to Shish.

"Okay, I shouldn't mouth off like I did. I'm an idiot, and I'm human, with all the weaknesses of my race. I admit that, I get it. But you? You're a murderous little *shreka* who would rather risk killing a soldier than give up a little bit of your superior bullshit. So, fuck this. Fuck this desert, fuck this vision, and fuck you, you ugly son of a bitch. Shit, you die in a month anyway, what do I care what you think of me?" I turned away from him, and blanched. I had the feeling I'd restored access to something, but I was too focused on the sight in front of me to give a damn.

I was back on the *Shir'kaan*, but this time everyone had their own faces. It was a memory. And, of course, it was the one I wanted least to relive.

"Sir! Weapon launch detected!"

I turned to the officer. "What?"

"Missile inbound!"

"Confirmed!" the sensor tech said.

"Anti-missile batteries seeking target," the fire-control officer called.

I spun to the tactical display. While everyone's tactical implants could show them the same information in the same space, it simplified matters to have the ship's systems handle it, freeing NeuroNet processing power to do each individual's job. The blinking red dot of the missile was headed toward the heart of my group's formation.

So far, the key in all of these visions had been to do what I should have done, or whatever I'd secretly wanted to do. To reclaim myself from years of trying so hard to be Zhen. If that logic held true, then the same should work here. And I knew just what to do.

I stabbed my finger into the plot at the point where I remembered the Tabran infiltrator to be, even as my NeuroNet inserted the memorized coordinates into the tactical data. "Fire all weapons at this point! Scramble Green Wing to mop up. Move us and *Talshka* group to this point," I said, indicating a point that should take the indicated ships out of the dispersal range of the missile's payload. If my ships failed to take out the missile, then *Talshka*'s vessels could jump while the rest were rebooting.

My executive officer peered at the plot even as the flight liaison relayed the order to the squadron. She turned to me, clearly confused. "Sir?"

"Just a hunch," I said calmly. She nodded and moved to babysit the sensor boards. Jana and I had, over the course of our first cruise together, worked out a system. During combat, she hovered over the sensors and tactical displays, and I stayed near the navigation and fire-control boards. It had worked well in every battle we'd been in, at least until this one. I was determined not to let history repeat in this vision, or simulation, or whatever it was. Even if it wasn't real, I wanted the satisfaction of vindicating myself.

The ship vibrated slightly as we fired all missile tubes. The missiles would take some time to get there, but the lasers and plasma pulses should all hit within a few seconds. Most would miss. We could only aim at where a ship was at a given point in time. Our missiles would re-orient for as long as their maneuvering systems had power, but at this range even that was unlikely to help. But we could get lucky – or, if not, it was possible the missiles would cause the enemy to do something that allowed us to lock on with particle cannons and plasma pulsers, which travelled much faster.

Several tense minutes passed. "Status of the Tabran missile?" I asked. I could check it myself, of course, but my mind was juggling so many different factors I didn't want to risk dropping any of them.

"Fighters closing in three...two...one...missile destroyed."

"My compliments to—"

"Sir!" interrupted one of the sensor techs. "Unknown energy signature detected!"

"Clarify," I called, my heart sinking. It was all happening again.

The tech was frowning at her board. "Not sure, sir. When the missile detonated, it released some form of particle unknown to us in a high-energy discharge. The particles have already penetrated local space, sir."

"Any effect on our ships?"

"None I can— Incoming jump signatures in Jiraad low orbit!"

I'd failed. In the tactical displays, dozens of red dots appeared around Jiraad, taking position over each settlement. "*Talshka*," I snapped. "Jump to low orbit, weapons free!" I turned to my helmsman and said, "Follow them in!"

The dizzy sensation of a jump into slipspace came over us as the *Shir'kaan* made the jump. We transited a few seconds, then dropped out just above a Tabran dreadnought. "Open fire!" I cried, and braced myself even as the tactical officers started calling out incoming enemy fire.

The ship shook. At this range, missiles were less effective, but plasma pulse-fire and particle beams were devastating. Our shields could handle it for a time, but we weren't going to last forever.

"Getting reports from the rest of the fleet, Commander! Their jump drives aren't responding. Estimate ten minutes to get back online."

I acknowledged the report. As my ship shook with enemy fire impacting our shields, and then on our hull, I closed my eyes.

We didn't even last five minutes. I had just enough time to look at Jana as she called out that our fusion reactor was going critical before it all went white.

And then I was standing on the *Shir'kaan*'s bridge again.

"Sir! Weapon launch detected!"

I turned to the officer. "What?"

"Missile inbound!"

"What?" I said, confused.

"Confirmed!" the sensor tech said.

"What?" Now I was angry, as I realized the event was starting over.

"Anti-missile batteries seeking target," the fire-control officer called.

I shook my head at Jana as she began to cross to me. "All ships," I called. "Scatter and regroup in Jiraad low orbit!"

My crew, long used to my style, immediately leapt into action. Amid the bustle, the helmsman's voice called, "Jump drives cycling up. Thirty seconds to jump!"

"Detonation!" called a tactical officer. "Unknown energy signature detected!"

"Jump!" I screamed.

"Twenty-five seconds left!"

"Override! *JUMP!*"

Trying to override jump engines to force a jump before the jump field is stabilized, even in the last few seconds, can have disastrous effects. I had just enough time to realize I'd doomed my ship before the white-hot energy of the destabilized field flashed through the bridge.

Once again I was standing on the bridge. This time I fired all weapons where I was now reasonably certain the Tabran ship was lurking before they had a chance to fire the missile – but the destruction of their ship triggered the particles. I watched the Tabran fleet jump into low orbit and open fire.

The fourth time, I simply fired on their ship, then jumped into low orbit. We were waiting when the fleet arrived. We got lucky and took out four of their cruisers in the first two minutes. Unfortunately, they had thirteen more. We lasted another three minutes before I found myself trying to breathe in a bridge suddenly devoid of oxygen.

I found myself sitting high in the air on a large rock, basking in warm sunlight. Around me the vista of the desert stretched. "Did we fail?" I asked.

"Not yet," a familiar voice said from my right, "but you're going to if you don't get a clue."

I turned to look and damned near fell off the rock. Sitting beside me was Daav, as he'd been when I last saw him. "Hello, Tajen."

"Daav?"

"More or less," he said, as he often did in life. "Well, rather less, actually."

"What's that mean?"

"I'm not real, of course. I'm you. Well, more specifically, I'm your idea of who Daav was."

He certainly talked like Daav. "So, you're in my head?"

"Yes. Best guess? Somewhere in the back of your head, you realized you needed help. And you chose your brother – no surprise there, considering the issues between us. Think of me as your spirit guide, if it helps – like the Tradd and their *pushto*."

"Oh…kay. What's your point?"

"You've tried to stop the Tabrans five times now. Have you figured out what you're doing wrong?"

"No," I said, exasperated. "I've tried everything I can think of. Nothing works."

Daav looked at me and said nothing.

"I can't attack first, I can't get my forces in position first, nothing works. Every other test, I knew how to handle – why can't I handle this?"

"Because you're stupid."

"Great, my spirit guide is a sarcastic smart-ass."

He stared at me for a moment. "I may be the amalgamation of everything you feel and remember about your brother, but I'm also you. Have you met yourself?"

I laughed. Touché.

"Everything you've faced in this vision is a mistake you made in your past. Each of them was something you could have done differently, something that would have made you more human, and when you do that, you move on. Don't ask me why those particular things were chosen – it's your head, you did it, *you* figure it out. But Jiraad…tell me, truthfully, did you really make a mistake at Jiraad? And remember, I'm literally in your head. I already know the answer."

I thought about it, as I had many times over the years. It had become a sort of game I'd play with myself whenever I was suffering a bout of needless self-loathing. I'd hashed out every possible thing I could have done differently, and I'd tried them here. None of them had worked. If I was being honest with myself, I didn't really expect them to. The truth was that I'd done everything I could—

Oh.

Oh no.

"You're saying I have to accept that there was nothing I could do."

"No."

"No?"

"*I'm* not saying it. *You* are."

"I can't...I can't watch that again."

"Tajen," Daav said, and his voice was gentle, soft. "How many times have you seen the attack play out in your mind? How many times has the NeuroNet showed you the whole thing, in perfect clarity?"

"Too many," I said, my voice a whisper.

"And you've never accepted it."

"How can I? You know how many died that day. You lost your wife, the mother of your child."

"The Battle of Jiraad has been with you for a long time, Tajen. You're so messed up over it that your guilt has become wrapped up in your self-image. You cannot conceive of yourself without that self-hate. And that's keeping you from accessing your implants."

"That doesn't really make sense."

"No? You spent fourteen years fighting for the Zhen. You defended them. You *killed* for them. And now you've discovered that the people who you thought were worth serving, the people you wanted to please, are, in fact, complete bastards. They're using your people. And the single most important event in your life, the one you've been running from for sixteen years now, turns out to have been a setup."

"That's Ben's crazy theory."

He cocked his head at me, a habitual gesture I had often found rather irritating. "Which you believe."

He was right. As much as I wanted not to, I did believe it. Somehow, the events of the past few weeks had scattered the pieces of my life, and when they fell back down around me, everything was different.

"Yeah," I said. "I guess I do."

"So you're holding yourself back. You failed, twice."

I nodded.

"Well, so fucking what? Who hasn't? Tajen, it's time."

"For what?"

"You spent ten years of your life serving a bunch of assholes. Then you spent fifteen years *being* an asshole – at least when it comes to letting people into your life. Now it's time to grow up. Stop just muddling through, and take charge. Of yourself, if nothing else."

When I was a teenager, I liked to read what little remained from Earth. In the archives, I'd found a fragmentary bit of text. It said that truth was easy to recognize, that it awakened in you a feeling that this was something you had always known. Daav's words rang with truth.

I had been a fool.

I'd entered the service at eighteen years old. I'd served them for ten years, until, in the aftermath of Jiraad, I'd left the service in disgust, mostly with myself. For the fifteen years since, I'd been running – from my failure, from my humanity, from my family.

From myself.

No more. It was time to face myself. "Thanks, Daav."

He stood. "Don't mention it," he said, and I was back on the bridge of my flagship.

"Sir! Weapon launch detected!"

I turned to the officer. "What?"

"Missile inbound!"

"Confirmed!" the sensor tech said.

"Anti-missile batteries seeking target," the fire-control officer called.

I spun to the tactical display. "Launch Green Wing to intercept missile. Second Talon: spread formation, look for incoming jump signatures. First Talon: hold on station. All ships, spin up jump drives, ready for jump to targets when tagged."

I spent the next several minutes waiting. The worst part of space battles at this kind of range was the waiting. Knowing what was coming didn't make it any easier. So I distracted myself by musing on space combat.

Zhen military doctrine held to three 'ranges' of combat: long range, where we were now, was fought primarily with missile weapons. The good part of that was that it was a lot safer than close-range fighting – even with modern guidance systems, missiles don't often hit their targets. The downside, of course, is when the missile *does* hit, or at least comes close. Modern warheads are capable of taking out a medium-sized cruiser with one or two hits. And since they use small chain drives in the missiles, they move fast.

Closer in, missiles aren't useful; at that close range they don't have time to engage the chain drives before they're on the enemy's scopes. It's fairly easy to pick them off before they get anywhere near you. That's when particle beams come in.

Particle beam cannons scare the piss out of me. Imagine something you can't see, that travels at damned near the speed of light, and hits you with a thousand times the energy of a large aircar slamming into you at two hundred kilometers an hour. One good hit can ruin a ship's day; more than one can tear a ship apart in moments, as your armor liquefies and air goes screaming out the hole until all you can hear is your blood in your ears.

The closest range is close combat. It's all about ships getting up close and personal. That's in relative terms, though; the ships are still kilometers apart, sometimes thousands of kilometers. But close range is when plasma weapons and particle beams work best. Close combat is a fighter pilot's game. It's where I'd been living for the last few years.

In large-scale engagements like this one, the command ships tended to stay at long range, smaller cruisers sometimes got to PBC range, and fighters duked it out in close combat. Usually, it all happened simultaneously. My tactical officers tracked units on both sides and kept me informed of the situation. My job was to direct the overall battle strategy. Even fifteen years out of practice, I was still able to follow everything.

Which meant that I was able to watch the incoming missile while being wholly unable to actually do anything about it. As my fighter screen detached First Talon to the missile, I clenched my fists. I could feel my face tightening. As the blips on the screen converged, the missile blinked out.

"First Talon reports missile destroyed," the tac officer called.

At the same moment, the sensor operator called out, "Unknown energy signature detected! Scanning...unknown particle in high-energy discharge." She started to turn to me, then spun back to her board. "Incoming jump signatures in Jiraad low orbit!" Her fingers danced over the board, and she called out, "Confirmed Tabran fleet taking position over Jiraad Colony One."

"All ships," I said calmly. "Jump to low orbit, weapons free." As the sound of the jump drives spinning up reverberated through the hull, I closed my eyes, opening them again at the same moment they fizzled out. The low thrum through the decks stopped all movement for a moment.

"Engineering, this is CIC," a calm voice beside me said into the pickup. "What's going on?"

"CIC, this is engineering. Jump drives aren't working. They spun up, but once the drive tried to initiate, it failed. We're trying to figure out what happened."

"Understood. Get them back up ASAP."

I looked at my exec and said, pitched only to her ears, "Do what you can to bring up the jump engines." She nodded and left the bridge, and I gave orders directing the science officers to coordinate with engineering to figure out what was going on. I knew none of it would work, but I had to play my part.

"Sir," comms said, "fleet reports widespread jump failures."

"Thank you," I said. "Direct any ships who can jump to hit the Tabrans as hard as they can."

"Yes sir."

For ten minutes we attempted to get the engines working. Or, rather, my crew did. I knew what was happening, but I knew what I had to do. I had to be a witness.

The first time I'd seen this happen, I'd been watching my board and my crew more than what was going on. This time, I settled into my station and flicked my media feeds to Jiraad's broadcasts, watching the information my brain had recorded into my implants' memory core.

I watched as a birthday party for the colonial governor was interrupted by a kinetic strike directly in the middle of the park. Three hundred thousand people died as massive metal rods fell through the sky and slammed into the ground at terminal velocity.

I watched the coastal settlement of New Pacifica as it was destroyed by a tsunami, created by the destruction of the military base on the nearby island of New Hawaii. Another hundred thousand people perished as the wave washed inland, destroying whole habitats and more than a few small homesteads.

The kinetic strikes were only part of the attack. The Tabrans also used particle beams and plasma bursts fired from orbit. They scoured the colony from the face of the planet and poisoned the atmosphere.

When the bombardment finished, the Tabran fleet jumped out. We stood for several long minutes, staring at the destruction on the screens – the ones that hadn't blanked out when the cameras they were tuned to stopped broadcasting – until the commtech said, very quietly, on the edge of tears, "Engineering reports jump drives should function, sir."

In the same quiet tone, I said, "Jump to low orbit. Launch rescue operations across the colony."

"Why bother?" asked a voice that sounded oddly familiar, but wrong – higher pitched and less resonant than it ought to be. I turned, and saw myself standing next to my seat.

"Well," I said to myself, "you're a fairly heavy-handed symbol. Who wrote this shit?"

"I think we did," he said. "So why are you launching a rescue op when you know there won't be any survivors?"

I shrugged. "It's what I did originally."

He sneered at me. "You've played your part in this farce. Let's go," he said. He turned and walked from the bridge. As I rose to follow, I realized that all of my crew, and the planet below, had disappeared.

Visions. They're just weird.

I followed him through the hatch that should have led to the bridge's small armory but opened onto a fighting arena. My double was slipping *Zhen'kak* onto his hands. They're often worn by young Zhen, before their claws begin to grow sharp, and humans who study the Zhen fighting style. The small linked rings fit over his four fingers, with small curved blades of razor-sharp metal extending out from his fists. *Zhen'kak* have incredibly fine edges, and cut like nothing else. He stood, shirtless like a Zhen would be, and went through a short form, moving in the sinuous way of a Zhen fighter. He nodded to a table behind me. "Choose your weapon, meat," he said. Shit, he was even talking like a Zhen. I found myself wondering if I'd ever seemed like this to everyone else.

I looked at the table he'd indicated. There was another pair of *Zhen'kak* there, but also a human sword, almost three feet long, with a double razor-fine edge. I was capable with both weapons, but had used the *Zhen'kak* far more often, as it was a requirement to learn the style when I was in the service. I started to reach for them, but changed my mind mid-motion. When my hand closed on the sword instead, I smiled. I turned to the other me and saluted him with the sword. "Obviously, you're the part of me that's up the Empire's ass," I said. "So let's kick your ass and get on with it."

Well, I *meant* to say that. What I *actually* said was, "Obviously, you're the paaarrgghh!" as he was already on me and had sliced across my torso while I was fucking around trying to be witty. I danced backward, putting the sword between us in a guard stance.

My uniform was torn, and I had a nasty scrape across my chest, but I was still in one piece. Which meant I was lucky. "Everyone's a critic," I said.

He just stared at me, dropping deeper into his stance.

"Okay," I said. "I get it. It's *that* kind of fight." I surged forward, closing on him even as I brought the sword around in a fast strike at his head. Hey, why fuck around? But I have always been better in the cockpit than on the ground, and now was no different. He slapped the blade aside, the sword ringing as it impacted the blades on his hand. The other hand flashed up and backhanded me. I felt the unsharpened back edge of the blades scrape across my cheek as I reeled away from the blow.

The Zhen version of me kept attacking, forcing me to fight defensively. It was all I could do to keep him from gutting me with those claws. He hit me again, and this time I felt the claws cutting into my flesh, leaving deep furrows along my right arm. It was only through sheer determination that I held onto the sword.

I spun away from him, unconsciously cradling the wound with my other hand. When he came at me again, he threw a straight punch, driving the points of the claws at my chest. I fell away from the blow, landing on my back and dropping the sword, and he was upon me, driving me back to the floor when I tried to rise, slashing and punching with his artificial claws. In the middle of being cut to ribbons by my own self, it occurred to me that I was going to die. I wondered if dying in this vision would kill my body, leave me a vegetable, or just be a bad dream. None of those options seemed like a good idea.

That thought led to another, and to another. Have you ever lain awake at night, failing to fall asleep as your brain just keeps cycling from thought to thought, happily dancing down a river of ideas while you go insane and wonder when it will shut up? That's what I felt like. Except, of course, rather than trying to fall asleep, I was trying to focus on the fact that I was being killed by my own fucked-up subconscious mind. Suddenly, I was barely aware of the beating, ignoring the pain and examining myself in minute detail.

Frankly, I wasn't impressed.

I'd served the Zhen faithfully for years, and when I made a mistake that cost lives, I ran. I abandoned my command, two hundred and fifty men and women of four different races, because I couldn't face my failure. I was the Hero of Elkari, the man who'd saved a world. And then I lost one. Millions of people died, including Kiri's mother and, in a roundabout way, her father.

I couldn't face that pain, so I ran. I hid in the relative anonymity of interstellar trading, flying cargo from one end of the Empire to the other. I made as few connections as I could and stayed away from the people I wanted very much to be with.

I was *such* a moron.

I suddenly felt very guilty that I hadn't made more of an effort with Kiri. She was just a kid, and I'd let my fear of rejection and my Zhen-trained reserve get between us. That was over, of course. She deserved an uncle who wasn't afraid of her or her reactions to him and his past – or at least one who *acted* like he wasn't afraid.

And Liam…. I'd been lonely for a long time, and like you do when you haven't been involved with anyone in so long, I'd told myself that it didn't matter. I didn't want more than the occasional romp in a rented room with a rented guy. Sex was just a biological necessity, and romance was overrated.

I'd always known I might meet someone some day, and I told

myself I'd be open to it if I did, but the truth was, I'd probably met people who could have made me happy a hundred times in the last sixteen years. But I was too stubborn, too full of my 'lonely spacer' routine, to actually give anyone a fair chance. I'd picked guys up in dozens of bars in the Empire and beyond, wherever I met someone human. But a partner? No. I'd never come close to that, and I saw, in perfect clarity, that the only reason I hadn't was that I hadn't allowed it.

I hadn't been very open to friends, either. Oh, I had some acquaintances, human and Zhen, and a few others, but the Zhen outlook is so different from human that friendship was never a given even if you'd known one for years. And humans? I had no human friends. I'd been alone since I left Imperial service, and even when I could have afforded a better ship and a crew, I'd chosen to spend the money in other ways, gambling it away or partying with people I pretended were friends. Because when it came down to it, the only way I was going to prevent being hurt like my brother had hurt me was to never let anyone else get close. I became That Guy, the ex-Imperial officer who did his job, drank, gambled, and slept with whomever he wanted – and had nowhere to call home but a raggedy old ship. I hated that life, but I did absolutely nothing to change it.

I had finally begun, in the halting, nearly useless jerking movements of a newborn, building friendships – no, I'd started building a *family* – and I was damned if I was going to let any one of them down.

My right hand fumbled about and closed on the sword. This close, with his hands now choking me, I didn't even have to open my eyes. I thrust the sword into his side, twisted it viciously, and threw him off me.

He lay gasping, blood pouring from the wound I'd opened. I climbed to my feet, stood over him and shook my head. "You're everything I wanted to be," I said. "The pinnacle of hundreds of years of Zhen influence over our people." I raised the sword, grimacing with the pain in my arm. "But becoming you would mean abandoning my humanity. I'm done with you," I said, and drove the sword into his – my – our – throat.

He gurgled and died. And I'll always wonder if he really smiled, or if I was imagining it.

What I didn't imagine was his body as it transmuted into billions of bits of light, rising to form a complex, pulsing geometric shape in the air before me.

Such shapes were often used in training or game programs to denote an information point. So I did what I always had with such things I reached into it, calling the information into my mind.

And oh, the places it went.

I saw that the rumors had been true. I'd always known the NeuroNets and other implants used by Zhen elite operatives were capable of more than mine could do. What I hadn't known was that my own system had many of the same capabilities, but they had been shackled by programming. In defeating my mirror self, I had opened the access panels, so to speak. As I saw what the nanites in my system could do if they were authorized, I marveled at how the Zhen had kept humans hobbled.

We'd been told that human biology couldn't handle the systems involved.

They were partly right about that. Some of the capabilities I saw would be dangerous to try in a human – we lack the regenerative abilities of the Zhen, and we're just not as hardy. So the strength augmentation systems would be stupid to put into use. But I saw that there were things I could use too. I activated those systems, instructing the nanites in my body to create the implants I needed, as well as the nanonic artificial nerve fibers I would need to operate the new systems.

When I was done, I released the program access icon, and as it dissipated, I willed myself to wake up.

Then I opened my eyes, said "Hey, I think this might—"

I was looking up, straight into the barrel of a stun pistol, which was held by a Zhen soldier.

She fired, and all was dark.

CHAPTER TEN

Every time I woke up, someone immediately hit me with another blast of a stun beam. When I finally awoke for real, it took a few hours before I could shake off the aftereffects of the stunner and take stock of my surroundings. It didn't help me feel any better about my situation.

According to my NeuroNet, it had been several days since I'd been captured. I was strapped to an interrogation frame with my wrists and ankles held by the frame's shackles, holding me spread-eagled in the center of the frame. I still had my clothes on, which in Zhen circles meant I was in for questioning, and not torture. Probably. A table against the wall held my weapons and other gear.

My NeuroNet was still active, but operating at a minimal level. I checked the access log and noticed that it had been set by the Zhen who'd captured me to a shutdown state. I brought the system fully back online, but set it to ignore any access from outside. Any attempt by the Zhen to alter my implant system would instead filter through my direct control, and I'd adjust it as necessary. For now I set it to passive mode only.

I was alone in the room. Yelling for my captors wouldn't do any good, so I did the next best thing, and began singing an incredibly dirty song about a space merchant and his many sexual conquests. I was just starting the verse about the spacer having both the Prefect's son and the Minister's daughter when two Zhen entered the room. I stopped singing. "About damned time, boys."

The two Zhen stood before me. One of them, the green-skinned one, ignored me. The Zhen:ko reached his red-hued, muscular arm toward me, and ran his claws down my face, just barely avoiding breaking the skin. I wondered at how often this particular gesture had been used against us. "We are going to ask you some questions, Commander Hunt," he said, using my formal rank. The timbre of his voice actually caused the hair on the back of my neck to stand up, and I was suddenly a lot less sanguine about my position.

Not that I was going to let *that* dictate my behavior. "I'm not a commander anymore," I said. "You really ought to update your records."

"But you *could* be, Commander. Co-operate, and you could be reinstated, given a new command."

I rolled my eyes. "Give me a break. Commander Salanaa already tried, and I'll tell you what I told her: *Fuck off.*"

His crest rose in indignation. "Very well," he said, the subharmonics of his voice descending into a growl. "No more pretense."

I opened my mouth, but he shut it for me with a swift slap, forcing my teeth to bite into my tongue.

I spat out the blood and grinned at him. "I didn't know you cared," I said.

He hit me again and asked, "Why are you here?"

I blinked at him a few times. "Because your goons shot me and dragged my ass in here. Shit, I don't even know where 'here' is. Where are my people?"

He bared his teeth at me . "Salanaa was right. You are too far gone to be brought back into service." He extended his claws and began to reach for my throat, but stopped, calmed himself, and backed away.

"Atta boy," I said. I was confused as hell about why he hadn't hit me – and I realized why just as the door opened and another Zhen walked in.

"Kaaniv," I said with a sneer. Mostly to hide the sudden urge to shit my pants. *If you don't turn over the files, I will hunt you down and kill you myself*, he'd said, and I knew the time had come. One of us was going to die today. And at this moment, I didn't think much of my chances.

"Tajen," he said pleasantly, as he crossed to stand before me. He turned to the red Zhen. "With your permission, my lord?"

The Zhen:ko nodded. "See that he answers our questions, Kaaniv. The One is waiting for my report."

Kaaniv genuflected. "As my lord Qaalto commands."

Qaalto gave me a final glance and left the room, leaving Kaaniv and the soldier alone with me. Kaaniv turned to me. "Shall we begin, Tajen?"

I shrugged as best I could in the stocks. "Sure, fuckface. What are you desperately hoping I'll tell you?"

He ignored my jibe. "What was the clue that led you to Earth?"

I had suspected it, out in the desert. But now I knew.

This was Earth.

This blasted landscape, the empty planet, had once been a thriving world of ten billion of my people.

I reached into the datastream around me, careful to disguise my NeuroNet's activity as the usual background traffic that existed in any Zhen installation, so it wouldn't register to Kaaniv or his adjunct. I skimmed over dispatches, requests for supply, terraforming reports, and a host of other day-to-day business of a Zhen outpost. In the timescale of quantum computers, it took me only seconds to find a single sentence that chilled me: *Last human slaves executed by order of the One, third day of Adra, 10891 I.R.*

I looked at Kaaniv, and for the first time in my entire life, when dealing with one of his kind, I let all the rage that had been building since our last meeting show on my face. "You found our world. And rather than tell us about it – rather than make us happy by handing us back our world, even broken – you hunted down the survivors? Made them slaves? Killed them when their usefulness was over?"

He said nothing, just looked into my eyes as I raged.

"What were you planning to do?" I asked. "What story was going to make the human race accept that the Zhen found our planet and never bothered to tell us about it? What was going to make us ignore that you killed the survivors?"

His crest rippled in the Zhen equivalent of a dismissive wave. "If not for your brother's luck, we never would have told your people anything. Why would we? We, as you well know, have all the power in the Empire." He gestured at the soldier, who nodded and thumbed a device on his wrist. My NeuroNet informed me it was receiving a reactivation code and a connection to another 'Net. I pretended to react as if my visual field had activated, and allowed the input to proceed. "As I promised you at that lunch, I *am* going to have to kill you," Kaaniv said in a mocking tone, "but before you die, allow me to do you a small service, in honor of the years you dedicated to the Empire. Learn the truth about your world."

My surroundings changed as my NeuroNet's entertainment suite switched on, beginning a virtuality playback. I was suddenly standing on the bridge of a Zhen cruiser. The date in my visual field said it was from 10082 Imperial Reckoning, which placed it a century or so before the Rescue. I could maneuver my view around within certain parameters, but I could not act – this wasn't an interactive story, then, but a true historical recording. There was a security code running along the bottom of my visual; it classified this information at a level of security far above what my own clearance had been when I was an active officer. Essentially, this information was restricted to the Twenty and the One, as well as high-level intelligence officers.

Clearly, I didn't have much time left. I quickly crafted some dataprobes, small semi-autonomous search programs, and sent them out into the facility's datastream. Hopefully they'd do their jobs quickly. I returned my attention to the record, but also kept an eye on Kaaniv and the guard, who were superimposed by my altered NeuroNet on the virtuality.

"My lord," the sensor officer said, "ship jumping into the outer system, unknown configuration."

"Plot intercept course. Do not hail them, wait for them to hail us," the commander growled, turning to look behind him at a Kelvaki in an Assembly Scout uniform. "It seems the information you gave us was good, thief," he said.

The Kelvaki gave the Zhen:ko a look of pure hate. "I am no thief, carrion eater!"

The Zhen merely gestured with one red-scaled hand, and the Kelvaki screamed in pain as his NeuroNet was used to activate his pain receptors. It was a favorite trick of Zhen military training cadres, and I'd experienced it myself, many times. Right now the Kelvaki felt as if all his nerve endings were on fire. "Spare me your lies, thief. You were caught stealing Zhen secrets. Your guilt is not in question."

"I am a soldier!" the Kelvaki screamed. "I am owed civil treatment!"

"You are Kelvaki, and are owed nothing but death," the Zhen said, as he pulled his blaster and shot the prisoner. He holstered his gun and motioned to a guard to remove the body. He opened his mouth to speak, but his comms officer interrupted. "We are coming into weapons range, sir. They are hailing us."

"Combat analysis?"

"It appears they use laser energy weapons and missiles. Their energy shields are not sufficient to protect them from our weapons. They appear to be a level six culture, sir."

He nodded. "Let me hear their hail."

A voice came over the system, fed to the crew via the NeuroNets, speaking a language I recognized from my childhood lessons, the language of my people. The accent was odd to my ears, but the words were intelligible. "Attention unknown vessel. This is Captain Nathan Adams of the Earth Cruiser *Xu Fu*. We are a peaceful expedition seeking new life. We greet you and wish to open dialogue between our species. Adams out."

The commander stood motionless, only the rising and falling of his crest showing his anticipation. He flicked one claw out, opening the communications channel with the gesture those early NeuroNets required. Then he said, in a quiet but steely voice, "The history of our people has taught us one thing: there can be no peaceful co-operation between species. One must always rule." Another flick of his fingers closed the channel, and he turned to his gunners. "Open fire."

The Zhen ships made short work of the human vessel. As the wreckage of the ship tumbled and spun in the darkness, ever receding, the picture jumped. I was now watching a recording of a briefing. I didn't know any of the high-ranked officers in the briefing, but that was no surprise; the date code was over a thousand years ago – shortly after the attack on the *Xu Fu*.

The Zhen sitting around the large table were all Zhen:ko. I'd never seen so many in one place, and I counted – there were twenty-one of them. This, then, was the Twenty and the One, the rulers of the Empire. Around them flitted many green-skinned ordinary Zhen, doing various tasks. At the foot of the table stood a Zhen in the uniform of the Special Executive, the intelligence branch that answered directly to the ruling council. Beside him stood a young Zhen, probably barely out of the Academy, in the uniform of an Intelligence Service attaché.

As the superior spoke, graphics and illustrations appeared behind him, covering the wall. "We have located the homeworld of the aliens. They call it *Earth*. There are approximately ten billion humans on the planet, with two million more living on their planet's moon.

"Their spaceflight capabilities are limited, but growing. The *Xu Fu* appears to have been their first FTL-capable interstellar ship. We came across it on its maiden voyage. They are currently rushing the construction of the second such ship to follow after the *Xu Fu* and try to discover why they lost contact with it. As near as we can tell, they are increasing the vessel's armaments."

An elderly Zhen sitting at the head of the table spoke up, her voice strong but reedy. "What is their history like, Commander?"

The soldier nodded to his subordinate, who stepped forward. "Lieutenant Shaan has that report."

Shaan cleared his throat, obviously nervous at speaking to the rulers of the Empire. "The humans are a people who are well versed in war," he said. "There have been numerous wars throughout their history, ranging from small border skirmishes to conflicts that enveloped nearly their entire world."

"You could say the same for our own Empire," one of the councilors said.

"Hush," said the Zhen at the head of the table, as she adjusted her sleeves. "The point is, are they a threat to us?"

Shaan's crest flattened, showing his nervousness. "My best guess, Councilor, is that they are. A running thread throughout their history is that they meet any acts of aggression with overwhelming force. They are not a united world – they are composed of several different nation-states grouped into a relatively few faction alliances. One of the few things that seem to unite them is an attack from apparent outsiders. I am afraid that they will see themselves as a united world, if they learn of our involvement, and we will be their targets."

"And so what if they do?" another council member asked.

"Their weapons and technology are inferior to ours. We will crush them easily."

Another, an older Zhen, spoke up. "And what then, R'kan? Remember what happened with the Shrikk when we crushed their rebellion." The word, presumably a reference to another alien race, meant nothing to me. Apparently they were no more; I had certainly never heard of them.

"Then we should strike," R'kan persisted. "Destroy them now, before they become a threat to the Empire." The others sitting around the table looked to the One, who said only, "Clear the room. The Twenty shall debate this in private." As all the green-skinned Zhen left the room, the recording cut out, and I was staring at Kaaniv again. He said nothing, showed no emotion, as another recording overtook my vision.

The viewpoint changed constantly. One moment I was watching from the skies as Zhen fighters swarmed over the Earth space facilities, the next I was witnessing the destruction of a city. For a short while I watched a human woman wearing some kind of cloth over her hair report on a news program about the destruction of London, the next I was watching a gigantic wall of water rushing into a city, bulldozing homes as it passed.

It was a thousand times worse than watching the destruction of Jiraad. This was the homeworld of my people, the place where thousands of years of human civilization had grown, and over a matter of days, the Zhen wiped humanity from the face of the Earth.

The entire history of my people was predicated on the idea that the Zhen had saved us, that the first contact between our peoples had been the chance discovery of the *Far Star*, the human colony ship that had formed the basis of human life in the Empire. And now I had been shown proof that eight hundred years of human history was based on a lie.

And they were continuing that lie. Salanaa had told me the Zhen had found Earth after rescuing the colony, that they'd found a world destroyed by its own war. But as I'd assumed, that was bullshit. They had killed my brother just for finding the route here, so he wouldn't discover the truth, and now they were going to kill me, and very probably my friends and my niece, the only family I had left.

Rage built within me, igniting my blood. Liam liked to repeat a line from an old Earth story, 'blood calls out to blood'. I knew the truth of that statement now. The dataprobes I'd sent out had returned, and the information they gave me was the spark that ignited the firestorm. I had given my life to the Empire, and they had used me so many times. Enough was enough.

I banished the feed Kaaniv was sending me and locked out his access to my NeuroNet. I raised my head and looked him in the eyes. His confusion shifted to concern as I flexed my hands and the manacles holding them and my feet popped open. I dropped to the floor in a crouch. I straightened slowly as I slipped a command to both Kaaniv's and the guard's NeuroNets to delete me from their visual perception. I was now effectively invisible to the Zhen in the room. Kaaniv's eyes widened and his crest rose, signaling his alarm at my disappearance. He began to look back and forth, his tongue tasting the air as he tried to locate me by scent.

"I see you've learned a new trick," he said, motioning for the guard to pull his gun.

I stepped over to the table and calmly collected my plasma gun. The moment I touched it, the stealth program removed it from Kaaniv's and the guard's sight. A flicker of motion warned me, and I dropped to the floor as Kaaniv fired his weapon. I rolled to the side, pulled my gun, and shot the guard in the head. As he fell, Kaaniv assessed the firing position and swung his gun to cover it, but I had already rolled out of the way and rose to my feet carefully. "Too slow, Kaaniv," I said, using my mind to broadcast directly to his NeuroNet.

He looked worried. "I see you've suppressed the communications links in the area. That function is restricted to Zhen commanders. Who gave you that level of access?"

"I did," I sent.

"Impossible," he stated flatly.

"Not at all," I said. "I'm sure things have changed, but remember that I was one of the first humans to get a military command-grade NeuroNet. Apparently nobody thought to remove the code that governed the permissions for high-level intelligence officer functions. So I ran it and gave myself the update."

"How?"

"Wouldn't you like to know?" I asked him, fading into view. He immediately turned his gun on me and pulled the trigger.

Nothing happened.

"The problem with neural link technology is that it's been integrated into practically everything. So tell me," I said out loud, "how are you going to deal with someone who can control your perceptions and your equipment? I made you unable to see me. Then I turned off your gun. Tell me," I said as I stepped closer to him, "does it scare you as much as you've scared my people?"

"As your people say, Tajen, '*Go to hell*.'"

I sighed and shook my head. "I wish I could say I regret this. But the truth is, we both know you'd kill me in a second if you could." I shot him quickly in both knees. As he fell to the floor, he screamed in rage. "If I had any respect left for you, I'd make this quick," I said. "But fuck that."

"Not only a traitor to the Empire, but a coward!" he spat, pulling himself upright on the edge of the interrogation frame. "You could not face me in honest combat, so you use trickery!"

I shrugged. "Fair fights are for people you respect. And honestly? I want to win. So yes, I tricked you." I walked to the table and picked up the dagger that marked me as a Hero of the Empire. As I slid the blade from the sheath, I looked Kaaniv in the eyes. "Look your death in the face, Kaaniv. Face it as a Zhen would." I darted in, slammed the knife into his throat, and stepped away.

Before his body had even finished falling to the ground, I was out the door. I'd located my crew when I was rooting around in the system. Now it was time to rescue them.

CHAPTER ELEVEN

As I left the interrogation room, I turned left, deeper into the detention center. I saw one guard, but my NeuroNet prevented him from registering my presence. I could have killed him, but it seemed a waste of time to go out of my way to do so. If he got in my way, he was meat. Otherwise, why bother? Even if he was Zhen, I didn't feel right killing him for no reason. He'd at least have to piss me off first.

As I moved down the corridors, I routed a call through a secondary comms relay. "Hunt to *Dream of Earth*. You out there?"

A few seconds later, I heard Katherine's voice. "Tajen, we're here. What's your status? Where've you been for ten days?" She sounded relieved, but anxious. "Is Takeshi all right?"

"The Zhen got us. I've been locked up. Just got out. Takeshi and the others are in different cells, but I'm on my way to them now. What's your status?"

"Repairs are done. She isn't pretty, and she'll need more work before too long, but she's spaceworthy."

"Good. We're getting out of here. Stand by – we're going to need a hot pickup."

"Understood." She logged off.

I came to a holding cell and unlocked the door, using the base's override commands. When I walked in, I looked at Liam, hanging in an interrogation frame just as I had been, and grinned. "I'm sure you're having fun up there, but can we go now?"

He stared at me in shock for a few moments, then seemed to gather his wits. "You're kidding me, right?" he asked. "Let's go yesterday."

I unlocked his restraints and caught him as he fell. "Steady, there," I said.

"Easy for you to say," he replied, standing and stretching his arms and legs. "That sucked." He looked me in the eye. "What is it?"

"Nothing," I said. "Well, a big something, really. But later, we're too exposed here."

"Fair enough," he said, and gestured to the guns I had hanging on my shoulders. "One of those for me?"

I grinned and handed him one of the guns. "Don't shoot anyone unless you have to," I said. "I'm doing my best to keep them from seeing us, but I might not get all of them. No sense making more noise than we need to."

"'Keep them from seeing us'? How does that work?"

"Turns out all NeuroNets have backdoors. The security system isn't designed to keep out anyone with top clearance and authorization to use black ops tricks. I have both now."

"You hacked a higher clearance?"

I smiled. "I managed to override the program locks that kept me from using some of the command functions."

"Fancy."

"I like it," I said. We checked the corridor before heading out.

Once again we worked nearly seamlessly, moving as one through the corridors. We got Kiri out, then Takeshi, and finally Ben. All of them were unguarded, and bypassing the locks was simple, which was starting to make the hair on the back of my neck rise. "Listen up," I said when we had all of them. "Katherine has the ship ready. Once we get out she'll pick us up."

"How'd you find us?" Ben asked.

I tapped my head. "Your therapy worked, and then some." I could tell he was curious, but he didn't want to hold us up.

We moved quickly. So far, we hadn't had to kill anyone, and I was getting cocky. That ended as we turned a corner and ran right into a patrol team on their rounds.

I didn't have time to wonder how I'd missed them. On instinct alone, Liam and I jerked our weapons up and fired just as the guards did. Fortunately for us, Liam and I were sufficiently on edge that we were just a moment faster. The guards didn't have a chance.

"Let's go," I said, handing their guns to Takeshi and Ben. "We need to get off this rock."

"Where are we?" Kiri asked. "Did they take us back to Zhen space?"

I sighed. "Let's not get into that now." Telling them the truth about the Zhen wouldn't do any good right now. "Let's get off this planet first. I've got a lot to tell you all."

Kiri was about to argue, but Liam interrupted her as we reached a corridor junction. "Which way?"

I indicated a direction. "We're headed to the armory."

"How do you plan to get in?"

"Same way I got out of my cell," I said, and began moving down the corridor. Kiri kept up with me, Ben followed her, and Liam brought up the rear . We did pretty well, but that was mostly because the guards weren't particularly thick in this part of the base. Once we left the detention area completely, I thought, it would be a different story.

The detention level was in the top floors of the base, in keeping with Zhen psychology – they'd evolved from subterranean-dwelling reptiles, and many had an aversion to heights despite the high-rises they built just to show how little they feared them. Prisons were often placed on antigrav platforms that floated above uninhabited and inhospitable terrain, or in the case of older prisons, atop mountains or artificial spires. It not only unnerved Zhen prisoners, but made escape that much more difficult. If the antigravs failed or were shut off due to an uprising, the prisoners would all be summarily executed by the fall.

That's the Zhen: smart, powerful, technologically advanced, and still pretty goddamned barbaric. I had often wondered over the years if the humans of Earth were any better. Now, I'd always wonder if we'd have turned out better if the Zhen hadn't taken our civilization away from us.

Bottom line, we'd need to either fight our way down through the building, or find another way out.

As we moved down the corridor, Liam checked his gun and tapped me on the shoulder. "Tajen," he asked, "why the armory? We've got guns."

I answered as we moved from the cellblock to the offices on this level, sealing the door behind us. "Well, two reasons. First, we're going to need better weapons if we have to fight our way out. Also, the armory will have grenades and mines we can protect our back trail with."

Liam passed into a four-way junction, and suddenly said, "We've got incoming!" He fired a shot to the left and ducked back as plasma fire flew through the intersection.

"*Shrak*," I said, and flattened myself against the corner beside Liam. Down the hall to our left was a squad of four Zhen guards. If we tried to cross, we'd be caught in their fire; if we stayed here, we were likely to be cornered before long.

I took a deep breath, then ran toward the guards, my NeuroNet's newly upgraded electronic warfare suite doing its best to mess with their perceptions and comms. As I ran, I shot the two in the lead, hitting one in the face and the other in the throat. I ducked beneath a swing of the third guard's claws, then shot him in the knee as I slid past him on my side. As I came to a stop, I rose to engage the last guard.

This one was smarter than the rest, he'd put on a full combat helmet. As I approached, he backed up, giving himself more room to maneuver. I was having none of that; I advanced with him, keeping myself inside his swing. I shoved my guns into the armor over his abdomen and fired repeatedly, pushing into him, trying to ignore the crushing force of his arms. The plasma chewed through his armor, dropping him. I stood, gasping for breath, as the others joined me.

I looked at the pistols in my hands. They were ruined; the plasma had been too close and both muzzles had begun to melt. I dropped them and picked up the guard's rifle, wincing at the pain in my arm. I signaled the others to come forward. Takeshi and Kiri each grabbed a weapon from the guards. "No," I said, taking the gun from Kiri. She glared at me.

"I get it," I said. "You want to help. But have you ever fired a plasma rifle before?"

"No."

"And I don't—" I stopped, considering. What right did I have to tell her she wasn't allowed to fight alongside us? Wasn't that patronizing attitude the kind of thing I'd been doing wrong? I sighed and handed her the rifle. "Here's the safety," I showed her. "This switch controls the shots — single shot, short bursts, or full auto. My advice is, keep it on single shots or short bursts, it's easier to control that way. Stay down, and only take a shot if you can do it without getting yourself killed, okay?"

She nodded at me. "Got it," she said.

I smiled at her. "Let's go," I said to the others.

"I don't get it," Ben said. "We just had a firefight in a main corridor. Why aren't we swarming with Zhen now?"

I tapped my head. "I suppressed the alarm. Nobody outside this block knows anything happened."

"Neat trick," Takeshi said.

"Thanks," I said. "But it won't last forever. Sooner or later they're going to figure out what I'm doing and find a way to block me out of the system."

We neared the armory, and I signaled for quiet. I looked around the corner for just a moment. There were two guards in front of the armory. Neither saw me before I ducked back and signaled to Liam what I'd seen. He nodded, and I whipped around the corner. I shot the first guard in the face, dropping him, then shot the other in the back of the head before he could react to the first shot. The plasma burned a hole in his skull and the body dropped.

"You really hate their faces, don't you?" Kiri asked.

"Plasma takes too long to burn through armor. Headshots work faster." I ducked into the armory and took inventory. "Oh, hello," I said. The armory had weapons, but it also had something I hadn't thought I'd find. "Well, that'll do."

I picked up a piece of tech that looked like a bulky rifle with a spear tip poking out of the end. "We need a window that looks out on the grounds," I said, checking the device over.

"What is that?" Kiri asked. "Looks nasty."

"This," I said, hefting it with a grin, "is how we're getting out of here."

"But what *is* it?" she asked.

Liam answered her. "It's an infiltration line." He was already gathering the gear we'd need to make use of it.

I held the device up again. "It shoots a high-strength carbon line. We find a window, get it open, fire this thing at the ground, and ride it down."

Liam said, "I hate those things."

I looked at him. "Got a better idea?"

He gave me an unhappy look. "Not saying I do. Just pointing out we'll be sitting ducks while we're on our way down the cable."

Kiri looked nervous. "I don't like the sound of that," she said.

Ben wrapped an arm around her shoulders. "We're in a lot of danger already," he pointed out. "Would this really be much more?"

I looked to each of them in turn. All nodded, ready to follow me.

"Okay," I said. "Let's get the hell out of here."

★   ★   ★

Liam blasted the window open and cleared the sill of glasteel shards while I primed the infiltrator gun. I glanced back at Liam and Ben, who had laid down a pattern of mines nearby that would hopefully keep anyone from getting to the window before we were down.

I held the gun in position and activated it; the automatic systems locked it down and fastened it to the floor and the windowsill.

"Katherine in the air yet?" Liam asked.

"Not yet," I said. I activated my comms again. "*Go!*" I said, sending her our position as I walked to the mines to check our perimeter.

"Got a problem," came her reply.

My eyes widened. "What kind of a problem?"

"Zhen problems! Can you hole up somewhere?"

"Not a chance, at this point," I said. "We'll find our way back to you. Send me your position." She did, and I cut the connection.

The others were staring at me. I joined Takeshi at the window and looked out across the field. I pointed at a sleek atmosphere-only ship at the edge of the field closest to us. "That one," I said.

"Nice. Looks fast."

"Also, to be honest, it's the only thing I see that'll work." Most of the vessels on the field – and there weren't many – were larger ships we couldn't handle with our small group, or small flitters that wouldn't be fast enough.

"Good point," he said. "Oh, and did I forget to say 'I told you so'?"

"We're not done yet," I said. He rolled his eyes and turned to cover the window.

"We ready yet?" Kiri asked.

I finished aiming the infiltrator and said, "Ready. Let's do it." I locked in the target and told the gun to do its thing. It fired, the spearpoint aiming straight for the ground in front of the ship. It hit with a small cloud of dust. The machine hummed a moment as it sent nanotech assemblers out from the spearhead to lock it down, then signaled me that the line was anchored and ready.

I handed each person a harness, a small tube with a carbon-fiber lead that clipped onto the nearly invisible line. "I programmed these to slow you quickly. Once you're going slow enough it'll drop you off the line." When each of us held the tube to our chest, it whipped belts around us and secured us.

"Who's first?" Liam asked.

"I go first – I'll secure the ground end and open the ship. Liam's on anchor." Liam acknowledged the order. I couldn't resist giving him a kiss as I clipped my harness to the line. "For luck," I said, and stepped out of the window jauntily, blowing him another kiss as I went.

What can I say? I'm a showy bastard.

The ride down was less 'exciting' and more 'absolutely terrifying'. My NeuroNet trick could only work on systems I saw coming; I had no way of knowing who might be looking out the window and seeing a human riding a line to the ground.

Just as the thought occurred to me that I probably could have disabled the entire building's alarm system if I hadn't been so busy showing off, the alarm went off. We'd been spotted.

"Damn," I muttered as I slowed and dropped from the line. I swung my rifle back and forth as I ran for the ship, fifteen feet away. I was already accessing its computers, using my fake black ops clearances to open the ship and lock out anyone but me.

Just as I got the hatch open, Kiri hit the ground and came running up to me. "Get in," I said. As she scuttled up the ramp, I turned and fired at two Zhen guards who were heading our way. I dropped one, but the other kept coming. I told the ship to start the engine warm-up sequence, grunting in satisfaction as the engines began humming.

As I was drawing a bead on the Zhen guard, he was hit by a plasma bolt from above and fell dead. Liam dropped from the line a moment later, hit the ground running, and skidded to a stop next to me, pivoting and aiming his rifle toward the base buildings and the guards who were even now running out to kill us. He tossed out two small bundles, which spread out and raised short walls of coruscating energy barriers in front of us as they hit the ground. "Just like old times," he said.

"Maybe for you. I'm more used to space."

"Don't worry, spaceboy. I've got your back."

"What are you doing down here, anyway? I told you to take anchor," I shouted over the fire.

"Kiri overrode you," he said, firing the whole time. "Said she's part owner of the ship and she needed me to keep your showy ass alive!"

"Part owner or not, *I'm* your captain," I said. "Not her."

"True," he said with a wink, "but *I* needed to keep your showy ass alive too. You can fire me later if you want."

I looked up to the window, and saw Takeshi and Ben firing back down the corridor. Then Ben did something with their harnesses, and Takeshi came hurtling out the window and down the line. He never quite recovered his center as he came down, and dropped in a heap when released. He rose and limped his way over to the barrier, dropping behind it. "That old bastard shoved me out first!" he shouted.

We all looked as Ben fired one last time, then dove out the window, trusting his harness to catch him. The guards he was fleeing came to the window, aiming out at Ben's careening body.

I started to bring my rifle up to cover him when a new group of guards arrived on the plascrete, firing at us. I ducked down to avoid their fire, then popped back up and returned fire. "Get your asses aboard!" I shouted as one fell. Ben hit the ground, somehow managing to keep his feet under him as his momentum carried him past me.

Takeshi boarded, with Ben close behind. Liam and I backed up the ramp, firing. Once we were fully aboard, Liam slammed the controls to close the door, and I turned to head to the cockpit.

As I dove into the pilot's couch, I wasted no time, raising the ship on antigravs and slamming the thrusters at full. "Katherine, we're on our way," I called. "Send me your coordinates!"

"Coordinates sent," she said. "Be advised, the Zhen problem is nearby. Be ready to move."

"Roger that," I said. "Be advised we're bringing more Zhen to the party. Keep the engines hot, we're ten minutes out." I could see Zhen ships on the sensor, chasing after us. They weren't fast enough to catch us, but they wouldn't be far behind.

I came in hot and low, slamming the landing thrusters into full blast at pretty much the last second. The ship hit hard and slid, coming to rest about two hundred meters from the *Dream of Earth*'s position under an overhang in the cliff. "Everybody out," I said, grabbing Kiri and heading for the hatch.

As we ran across the space between the ships, some of the pursuing Zhen vessels landed, while others started strafing runs. Katherine ran down the ramp, activating a chest-high force shield and crouching behind it while she laid down covering fire for us.

Liam and I dropped into place beside her, Takeshi joining us a moment later. Kiri and Ben headed straight into the *Dream of Earth*, a squad of Zhen right behind them.

As Ben and Kiri passed us, Liam, Katherine, and I raised our guns and fired into the Zhen group, killing all but three of them, but Takeshi, who was closest, froze when he came face-to-face with a Zhen warrior. In that moment, the Zhen reached out and grabbed him, pulling him over the barrier. Takeshi, the only one of us who wasn't a trained soldier, dropped his gun in shock. Before any of us could react, the Zhen smiled and held Takeshi at arm's reach in front of him, using him as a human shield. He turned Takeshi to face us, reached out with his other hand, and ripped out Takeshi's throat in one smooth motion. As blood spurted from the wound in a gush of thick red, the Zhen licked his claws.

Katherine screamed as Liam and I fired into the Zhen, each of us firing into his torso for several seconds. His body fell to the ground in a smoldering heap. "Let's go!" I yelled. We fell back, dragging

Katherine with us. Liam and I kept firing at the remaining two Zhen, but they had deployed their own energy screens, and our shots splashed uselessly on the barriers.

Dierka surged past me, his massive frame filling the field of fire. He took shots from both Zhen, but they were glancing blows that skittered off his armor – even Zhen soldiers had trouble drawing a bead on a raging Kelvaki. He grabbed the first guard, whipping him around and slamming him like a club into the other guard. The sounds made by the impact caused me a pang of sympathy for the Zhen, which lasted exactly as long as it took me to look at poor Takeshi's body lying on the ground.

Katherine threw herself on him, searching for signs of life, but it was obvious he was gone.

"Katherine," I said, "we need to get moving."

"I can't leave him," she said through her sobs. "I can't let those bastards have him."

Liam folded Katherine into his arms. "He's gone. He's not there anymore. And he wouldn't want you to die mourning him."

Dierka picked up Takeshi's body gingerly, cradling it in his arms. "Let's go, honored sister," he said to Katherine.

She stood. The look on her face was a mask of anger and determination. "Let's go." There was no expression on her face, no grief in her eyes. I knew from bitter experience that those would come later. But right now she was in survival mode, and she'd stay there until it was safe to grieve.

My NeuroNet alerted me to incoming flyers. "It has to be now," I said. "There are more Zhen on the way." We ran to the ship, Liam keeping careful hold on Katherine.

As the hatch slammed shut, I ran to the pilot's seat. The engines were ready. "Everyone strap in," I yelled, and lifted off from the desert. I swung the ship's nose around and accelerated as fast as I could, heading away from the base.

Katherine arrived in the cockpit and slid into the copilot's seat. I looked at her. "Everyone settled?"

She shook her head. "Not everyone," she said.

I cursed at myself. "I'm sorry," I said. I could see rage behind her eyes, but it didn't seem to be aimed at me.

"Promise me something, Tajen," she said, her voice deceptively calm.

"Yeah?"

"We'll make them pay, right?"

The blue sky faded to black as we broke through the atmosphere. I set us on a course for the jump limit and scanned the boards for any pursuit. There were four fighters on our tail, approaching the boundary of space right behind us. "Dearly," I said. "But right now we have to get out of here."

She nodded. "I put Liam on the upper turret. Dierka will take the lower; it's big enough."

I activated the chain drive and aimed for the jump limit. "Where's Kiri?"

"Right here," Kiri said from behind me. She slid into the navigator's seat. "Where are we going?"

"Somewhere we can hide and repair," I said. "Use your discretion. But hurry, we've got four fighters nearly at firing range."

"On it." She worked for a few moments. Just as we passed the jump limit, she announced, "Jump locked in."

I hit the jump, and we left Earth, the birthplace and the graveyard of our people, behind.

CHAPTER TWELVE

During the first day in transit, I explained to the others what I'd learned about Earth.

Katherine swore. "Well, now we know what that Tchakk writing meant."

"What Tchakk?" Kiri asked.

I said, "Back when I saved Katherine's ship at Kintar, we were scrounging in the marauder ships. A marauder had written on the wall before she died: 'Death to the dogs and their lying masters'. At the time we didn't understand, but looking back on it, she clearly meant the Zhen."

"How much time do you need to scrub the computer system?" Katherine asked Kiri.

"Two, maybe three days," Kiri said.

Katherine nodded, then got up and left the room without another word.

We spent two days hanging in the middle of nowhere while Kiri went over the ship's computer system, looking for any backdoor codes the Zhen could use to locate us or take over the ship. Then we docked at a backwater station in Kelvaki space for three weeks, where Dierka called in some favors to get the ship repaired and repainted. He also arranged for our weaponry to be upgraded.

For the first two weeks, Katherine mostly stayed in her quarters, coming out only to grab food once a day. If she was needed during the overhaul, she did what was necessary and then went back to her cabin.

During the third week, she walked into the mess room late one night while the rest of us were drinking and cursing our lives. She took the glass of whisky out of Liam's hand, threw it back, and stood silently for a little while before smiling at us all and saying, "I'm back."

"If you need more time—" I began.

"No! No, thank you. I'm okay. I mean, I'm not, but I can function. And Takeshi wouldn't want me to sit in there forever. We've got work to do, I'm thinking." She looked at me. "What's our move, Captain?"

"I thought we were cocaptains?"

She blew out a breath. "We were. But things have gone further than we expected, and frankly...I'm a merchant, Tajen. I served, but I was never a combat pilot, and I wasn't on the command track. Besides, I'm compromised right now. If we ever go back to being traders, I'll be glad to take up the mantle with you again, but as long as we're going to be up against the Empire, I think you need to act as captain for all of us. I'm happy to be 'just' your XO – for now."

I looked around the room. Everyone signaled agreement.

"Okay," I said. "As long as it's understood that as soon as this is all over, or you're ready to pick it up again, you're back to being cocaptain." She nodded. "All right. Here's what's next." I took a deep breath and told them what I wanted to do.

"You're insane," Liam said when I finished.

"Probably," I said. "But it's necessary."

"Why?" Kiri asked. "We already know the Zhen destroyed Earth. What more do we need to know?"

"We know it's probably true," I said. "What we don't know is why." I looked at each of them. "Look, unless the stuff Kaaniv showed me was him screwing with me for some other purpose – and we have to admit that's possible, though unlikely – we know the Zhen wiped out Earth. What we don't know is where *we* came from. Are we descended from prisoners? Is the colony ship story true? Are we the only ones they've done this to?"

"No," Dierka growled.

We all looked at him. He shrugged. "Have you forgotten the Tradd?"

I frowned. "Didn't the Zhen uplift them?"

He rolled his eyes at me. "Didn't the Zhen rescue humanity?" he asked me pointedly.

Oh. Right. If they lied about Earth, what else had they lied about?

"Dierka, tell me the Kelvaki didn't know about this?"

He chuckled. "I didn't know about it. So I doubt anyone else does. Just stands to reason they lied about the Tradd too. And the wars with our people didn't start out of nowhere – we were attacked. It's our good fortune our tech levels were close to theirs, or we might have ended up like humanity."

"All the more reason to go," I said.

"It's a reason to look for answers, sure," Katherine said. "But do we really need to go to the heart of the Empire for that?"

I thought about it. The only place I could get answers was from someone in the government, and highly connected at that. But going to the Empire's capital world was probably not the safest thing to do. I grinned when I realized what I needed.

"Sometimes I'm an idiot. Kiri, can you set up a blind route through the slipnet to Zhen?"

"You want to do an interstellar call?"

"Yes, and I'd really like to avoid the Zhen finding me through the slipnet."

She took a deep breath, then let it out slowly. "I don't think I can stop them completely," she said. "But I can slow them down long enough for you to do what you need to." She rattled off a list of things she'd need, and we started gathering the supplies while she coded the hacks that would hide my net-trail.

While Kiri and Katherine began cobbling together the equipment, Liam and I headed for the market. We were rummaging through a secondhand electronics stall, looking for some parts Kiri had asked for, when Dierka walked up to us. "Tajen," he said deferentially.

"Yes, *draka*?" I asked.

He looked away, his ears flicking in an unconscious gesture I knew meant that he was about to say something he didn't want to. "I am leaving."

"I understand," I said. "Not your fight."

He looked surprised, and a little irritated. "*Draka*, it *is* my fight, because it is yours. But I cannot help you here."

I raised an eyebrow. "And you can help me by being somewhere else?"

His ears flicked again, and he said, "I spoke with my parents over the slipnet this morning." He raised a hand to forestall my outrage. "Don't worry, I used a secret network with encryption the Zhen have not broken."

Liam looked confused. "There's a secret network in Kelvaki space?"

"Yes, used only by our military…and certain high-ranking families."

"How did *you* use it?"

Dierka just looked at Liam for several long moments. Liam looked at me, and I kept my face as neutral as possible. Eventually, he got it. "Who are you related to?" he asked.

I interrupted. "Don't ask, he won't tell you," I said. "I've been working on it for twenty years. All I know is, his family is highly placed in the Kelvaki Assembly."

Dierka said, "At any rate, my circumstances have changed. I must return home."

I'd spent enough time with the Kelvaki to know he didn't really want to go, but his body language told me it was important. "We'll miss you, big guy," I said, offering my arm to him, the fist raised and my forearm at an angle.

He placed his own arm against mine, crossed, and smiled. "Stay alive, my brother," he said.

"You too," I said. "I'll see you again before this is through."

Liam saluted Dierka, who chuckled that horrible sound of puppies being stomped, and said to me, "Count on it." He returned Liam's salute, then turned and walked away.

I returned my attention to Liam, who held a small chunk of electronics out to me. "Is this it?"

I took the device, scanned it, and compared it to the specs Kiri had uploaded to my NeuroNet. "Not even close," I told him. "Keep looking."

★   ★   ★

"Who are you going to call?" Katherine asked.

"A prefectural governor, Jaata. He and I worked together on some reforms a while back. He's very open to human concerns. He's also a military historian, and somewhat connected in government. If anyone can get us answers, he can."

"Will he help you?" Kiri asked.

"I think so," I said. "We've worked together, and he knows me – he's one of the few Zhen I think of as a friend."

"May I remind you," Liam said, "that you said the same thing about Kaaniv once."

I frowned at him. "Thanks, I needed that reminder. But that's why I asked Kiri to route this all over hell and back."

"At absolute best," Kiri said, "you'll have about twenty minutes of real time before they figure out where we are." We were hanging in space at the outer edge of the Shik System. From here we could reach the system's slipnet access point, a small space station in orbit around Shik I, a minor colony with no military presence. "Figure on a little wiggle room, but not much," she continued. "Realistically, maybe ten minutes."

"Won't matter. Even if they send a ship immediately, it could take weeks to get here."

"True, but they can get to Jaata's office much faster. And who's to say they don't have someone close we don't know about? If I was in their place, I'd have ships stationed in deep space all over the Empire, waiting for the call to action."

"Those are very good points," I said. "Katherine, I want you in the pilot's seat. Liam, you're on guns." They moved to their stations. "Katherine, the moment you get anything suspicious on sensors, jump."

"Any preference on where?"

"No – and don't tell me. If I don't know, I can't reveal it if I'm wrong about Jaata and he tries to rip it from my head." I looked at Kiri. "You can't stop that, can you?"

She shook her head. "No, sorry. If they use Neural Rip tech, there's nothing I've got that'll stop it. Good news is, I purged the backdoor code from your system, so they'll have to do it the hard way. But your specs are military. That ought to help."

I grimaced. "Less than you'd think. All right, let's get this done." I leaned back on the lounge and initiated the call.

My reality aboard the *Dream of Earth* faded away, and a nicely appointed office in a tower on Zhen:da appeared around me. I'd been in the real office often enough to know the simulation was perfect. A Zhen stood behind his desk, wrapped in the ceremonial garb of a prefectural governor.

"Jaata," I said.

He inclined his head and gestured me to a chair in the conversation area in the corner, which commanded a panoramic view of the Imperial City. "Please, be comfortable." He came around the desk and approached the chairs. "How can I help you?"

I chose a chair, sat, and leveled my best death glare at him. "I need answers," I said.

"About?"

"Earth."

His crest flattened, the only indication he was taken aback. His hand moved in the gesture one makes when telling another something they already know. "We have been searching for it for centuries, Tajen, you know that."

"Jaata. I've seen it. I've walked on it."

His crest rose in alarm. "You have been to Earth?"

"Yes," I said. I held a hand up, palm facing him. "Don't bother calling for help. I'm nowhere near Zhen:da, and you won't find me easily. I want answers, Jaata."

He regarded me, his crest quivering with obvious worry. Finally, he gave the Zhen equivalent of a shrug and sat down. "Ask your questions."

"Why did the Empire go after Earth?"

Jaata sighed. "How much do you know about the origins of the Empire?"

"The official history."

He made a gesture of amusement. "Then you know very little. Have you ever heard of the Kinj Heresy?"

"Yes, it's the legend that your species got spaceflight by destroying a first contact team from another race called the Kinj. It's ridiculous, no trace of the Kinj has ever been found."

"And do you know what happened to the Zhen who first made this claim?"

"No, I never looked into it."

"He was killed on the order of the One. Do you know why?"

I gestured *negative*.

"Because he more or less got it right."

"Seriously?" Even with the things I'd learned recently, I had a hard time believing him. "An entire Empire got its start by killing a first contact team?"

"More or less. It wasn't a first contact team, though." He sat back in his chair. "The Kinj arrived on Zhen more than twenty thousand years ago. At the time, the Zhen tribes had just begun creating crude computer networks. We took to the technology of the Kinj quickly.

"Over a period of centuries, we learned from them. But we also suffered under them. The Kinj ostensibly came in peace, but they tried to change us. They tried to change our culture, to 'civilize' us." He hesitated. "Their methods were not peaceful. Theirs was a rule of harsh laws and unjust punishments. Eventually, we rebelled, in a bloody war that raged for more than a hundred years.

"We destroyed the Kinj presence on Zhen. But – we didn't stop there. The more of them we killed, the more of their equipment we assimilated, the further we went. What began as a planetary insurrection became a genocide." He looked uncomfortable. "As the war progressed, our people became more and more vicious. We did not merely subjugate the Kinj. We destroyed them utterly, without mercy. They had created terrible weapons, and we used them eagerly. When we were done with their homeworld, we destroyed their colonies. Fifty-seven worlds, some with billions of inhabitants."

It was mind-boggling. I'd seen what the Zhen could do in war, but to hear Jaata's tale threw everything I thought I knew about how vicious our masters could be and multiplied it beyond reason.

Fifty-seven worlds, he'd said. Suddenly Earth seemed like an afterthought. "You didn't stop there, did you?"

He shook his head. "When the Kinj were gone, we continued to learn from what they had left behind, and we realized there were more races out there. Our leaders decided that they could not risk ever coming under the heel of another species again. They believed that the universe gave all species two choices: be crushed, or be dominators. We chose the latter. We became a conquering storm that washed across this galaxy, and many worlds fell before us. Only the Kelvaki held us off for any reasonable time. Eventually the cost of subjugating them was too high, and we sued for peace."

Before the current peace between the Empire and the Kelvaki Assembly, they had been at war off and on for several millennia. Only the Assembly's technological parity with the Empire kept the Zhen away from their homeworld. I stared at him. "I trust you see the irony in that story."

He nodded. "We have become what we fought against. Yes."

"So how does Earth enter this?"

"A little over a thousand years ago, we received intelligence from a Kelvaki agent who had been caught in Zhen space. He bargained for his life by tipping the Empire off to a new race that had just begun to enter the galactic arena – your people."

"I've seen this part. The Zhen commander destroyed the human ship, then the Twenty One—" he winced as I used the human, irreverent version of the group's name, "—decided that humans were a threat to the mighty Zhen Empire, and they wiped out our world. That's not what I'm here to ask about. What I want to know is, where did the humans in the Empire today come from?"

Jaata sighed. "The thing you need to understand about the Empire is that we *have* gotten better, over the centuries. In the beginning, we simply wiped out all species we regarded as a threat to us. Later, we began a sort of triage. If a species was a threat to our stability, we destroyed them. If they were not, then we subjugated them. Only the Kelvaki Assembly ever managed to stave us off for long, and that war lasted for millennia.

"The destruction of Earth was a turning point. It was the first annihilation in over a thousand years, and it struck at us. After that, even the Twenty and the One were not willing to do such a thing again. We were horrified, as a people, at what we had done."

I rolled my eyes. "After all those millennia of death, what about my people could possibly have changed the mighty Zhen Empire?"

Jaata was irritated by my sarcasm. "The change was not instant. As I said, it had been many centuries since the last time we had acted against a species like that. Some in the fleet spoke out at what they saw on your world, and over time their numbers grew. Over the next few centuries, we softened aspects of our approach to other races. We sought peace with the Kelvaki Assembly, and we began easing restrictions on behavior throughout the Empire.

"And then we found the *Far Star*."

I cocked my head. Now we were getting to the point. "So that part of our history is true?"

Jaata's hand moved in a gesture of ambiguity. "More or less. One of our scouts found your ancestors' ship – which had not been damaged – a little over three hundred years after the destruction of Earth. We determined that it had been launched about a hundred years before our first meeting with the *Xu Fu*. What to do with the ship was a subject of debate in the *Talnera* for well over a year. There were some who wanted to destroy the ship and pretend we'd never found it. Others wanted to let the ship continue on its way, hoping it passed through Zhen space entirely.

"In the end, they decided to rescue your people. The *Far Star* and the remaining colonists aboard were 'stored' for another two hundred years while the truth about Earth, as well as all the other worlds and species we destroyed, was removed from our archives and history. After all, control what history is taught, and you control what is known. The Twenty and the One hoped to change the Empire by changing what the Empire knew about itself." He sighed. "Foolish, if noble in purpose."

"Wait a moment – you said the ship was undamaged."

"It was, at first. There *was* an accident – but of our making. An overzealous young gunner fired on the ship before he could be stopped. The remaining crew were rescued, and your people were folded into the Empire and given a place among us."

"Give me a break," I scoffed. "We've been second-class citizens since we were thawed out."

"Well, yes," he conceded. "I admit it was not easy to overcome the prejudices of centuries. Still, it has gotten better since the beginning."

He wasn't wrong. The Empire had improved things for us slowly over the last couple of hundred years. But we were still spit on, and overtaxed, and we were still forbidden from being elected to the *Talnera* or even appointed to high office on our own colony world.

"Why not tell us the truth about all this?" I asked.

He made a gesture one would normally make over an especially slow child. "Tajen. Would you have told a species you destroyed that you were the ones who killed their homeworld? We could not admit what we had done. It would have made it impossible to fold your people into the Empire. And then there was the state of Earth."

"What happened there?"

He sighed. "When the Zhen fleet finished with Earth, there was nearly nothing left alive. The Empire claimed the world as a forward operating base. My understanding is that they hunted the last survivors down." He looked disgusted.

"You don't approve?"

"No, of course not!" he spat. "It's utterly barbaric. When have I ever given you reason to think I would support such a thing, Tajen?"

"You haven't," I said. "But now what happens?"

"Are you asking for advice, or information?"

"Both," I said.

He sat for a moment, considering, and when he spoke, he seemed reluctant. "First, the information: five seconds after you disconnect from this conference, I will contact Zhen security and inform them that we spoke. I'd rather not, but if they discover we spoke without my reporting it, I am dead. We both know what the Special Executive is like.

"As for advice. Tell your people – tell *everyone* – the truth."

"Are you kidding me? Have you any idea the chaos that would create in the Empire?"

"Yes," he said, as if it was obvious, which of course it was. "But this secret is a dark stain on the collective Imperial soul. We will never get out from under the shadow until everyone knows what was done in our name. And…there are other considerations."

"Such as?"

He looked nervous. "Forces are moving in the Empire that have not moved in many years. Ancient laws nobody has enforced for centuries are being quietly put back into force – atrocities committed against both my people and yours." He looked haunted, and it seemed almost as if he wasn't even aware of me anymore. "There are whispers spreading, of dark deeds done in the shadows, ordered by someone among the Twenty. I fear we are about to reverse course once more. Perhaps, if the people were told what has been done, they will move to stop it from happening again." He snapped back to the here and now. "Tell them, Tajen."

"How would I prove it?" He looked uncomfortable. "Come on, Jaata. If I can't prove what I say, people will just ignore me. I'll end up dead and nothing will change."

His crest moved in a gesture that meant *careful deliberation*, and his eyes tracked to the window. "How much do you know about the Imperial Intelligence DataNet?"

"Not much. It's supposed to be separate from the main DataNet."

"Yes. It's also *accessed* separately. Access to the IntNet requires hardcoded keys that are kept in secured locations around the Empire. Their locations are changed regularly, but I have located one of them."

"Where is it?"

He looked pained. He was giving me something he'd hoped to use himself someday. "It's on the Garden Moon of Parzan III." He sent me the details via NeuroNet.

I nodded. "Thank you," I said. "I'll remember your help."

He grinned. "Just don't broadcast it too loudly, my friend," he said. "In fact, I'd rather you forgot it. I'd hate to be remembered as a traitor."

"I'll remember that." I stood, and just before I disconnected, a thought occurred to me. "Jaata, how did you find out about all this? I know you're a historian, but if this was removed from the archives, how did you get hold of it?"

He smiled at me. "Someday, I'll tell you. But not today."

"Fair enough," I said, and disconnected the conference.

★   ★   ★

Liam stared at me. "That's the stupidest thing I've ever heard!"

I knew the feeling. We were on the outskirts of an uninhabited system on the edge of the Inner Suns region, the more central locations of the Empire. The ship was hanging dark and powered down to minimum. We'd gathered in the lounge to talk about what I'd learned.

Katherine smiled at Liam's outburst. "Be that as it may," she said, "what do we do now?"

I shrugged. "Personally, I think we should do what Jaata said. Make it public."

She frowned. "Look, I hate to ask, but do we really want to do that?"

"What do you mean?" I asked.

"Tajen, look. The Empire has its problems, and yeah, we humans pretty much get the shit end of the stick in Zhen space. But this is going to cause problems if everyone finds out what they did."

"And that's not good?"

"Well, maybe. As I see it," she said, looking at all of us and ticking her ideas off on her fingers, "there are three possibilities: the human race blows up over this and goes into rebellion, the human race doesn't care and we just made ourselves outlaws for no reason—"

"We're already outlaws," Liam pointed out.

"Well, granted. But things would get worse if we raid a Special Executive data access node." He conceded that point with a gesture, and she continued. "Or it goes halfway – some of us don't care, and some of us want to rebel. And where do we go then?"

Kiri answered, in a low voice. "It would tear us apart."

Katherine agreed. "And there aren't enough of us left to risk that. What are we, a few million? Can we afford to divide our entire species?"

"What about the Zhen?" Liam asked. "How would they react?"

Kiri crossed her arms. "The possibilities are nearly the same. Either the Zhen shrug and accept what their rulers did to humanity, or it tears them apart too."

"It's more complicated than that," I said. "If the information Jaata's been hearing is real, then something is going on besides what we saw on Earth. Someone wants to wake up the old Empire."

Liam whistled. "Guys, allow me to say what we're all thinking: if we do this, we could start a civil war among *both* races."

"Okay, that's a risk," I said. "But do we have a choice? How many times have you been ignored while a Zhen dockmaster handles the ten ships that came in after yours? How many times have you been treated like shit just because you weren't Zhen?

"More importantly, how many humans have been threatened, or beaten to death, or imprisoned unfairly because they're human? It was illegal to teach Terran literature for three hundred years. It was illegal to speak any human languages. Hell, a hundred years ago we couldn't even go to the same bars."

"But it's legal now," Katherine pointed out.

I waved that point off. "Yeah, but they don't get points for correcting their mistakes when it took three centuries. The bottom line is, I don't want my people living like this. And beyond that," I said, my voice hardening with anger, "they didn't just bomb us into the Stone Age. They practically *annihilated* our world. They hunted down the survivors like animals. And now they've turned our homeworld into a military base for their forces, and they killed my brother to stop us from finding out.

"For good or ill, this is one truth that needs to come out. Humans deserve a chance to decide our own fate, and we shouldn't have to wait three hundred more years. Our people deserve the right to choose their path for themselves. And the only way we're going to get that is if we reveal the truth."

I looked each of them in the eye. One by one, they agreed to my plan.

"Okay, then," Liam said. "Where is this node?"

CHAPTER THIRTEEN

"This is going to be a tricky one," Liam said. "Of all the places I'd ever thought I might go, this planet was pretty much last on the list."

"No doubt," I said wryly. "Can you see the office?"

"Not easily," he replied. "But we've got a problem."

"What's that?"

"These overalls itch."

I rolled my eyes at him, and he grinned like an idiot. I wanted to be annoyed with him, joking at a time like this, but one look at his eyes and I just grinned right back at him.

Besides, he wasn't wrong; they itched quite a bit. They were also necessary. The Garden Moon of Parzan III was off-limits to humans – unless they were part of the staff of one of the many resorts the moon offered to rich and powerful Zhen families. We were currently dressed as menial laborers in one of the specialist hotels.

The Imperial Arms Resort catered to particularly decadent Zhen who had a hankering for the 'grand old days of the Empire'. Where other resorts had robots to clean and maintain the grounds, deliver luggage, and various other tasks, the Imperial Arms had humans and other beings, all either past or present client states to the mighty Zhen Empire. Liam and I were posing as window washers, making a show of getting the antigrav skiff ready and gathering our gear to wash the hotel tower's windows. The office that hid the place we were looking for was across the street.

We boarded the skiff and sent it over the edge of the building. We worked our way down the banks of windows, cleaning them. Most of the rooms were empty, but a few had occupants. As we came down a level, I glanced in the window just in time to see a human staff member being knocked across the room by a Zhen guest. My hand curled as I reached for my blaster. Fortunately for our mission, it wasn't there.

Liam's voice came from beside me, soft. "Taj, you've seen this before. We need to finish the mission. Focus."

I forced myself to grab the window-cleaning machine as I watched the human limp to the door, the Zhen chasing him threateningly. I turned the machine on and moved the emitters across the glass, pretending to be interested in the sonics scouring the dirt from the window. The Zhen sauntered out of his room. "We're clear," I ground out.

As I continued to clean, Liam aimed a small scanner at the office across the street. The device fed the information to both his and my NeuroNets.

The Imperial Special Executive, though whispered about throughout the Empire, is actually fairly good at keeping itself and its operations secret. There was no sign on the office that proclaimed what it was; in fact, it did business every day as a small-time 'Net-ware shop. "No guards," Liam muttered. "Three employees, all Zhen. Looks like there are automatic defenses in place, but they all appear to be pretty standard for that kind of shop."

"The ISE depends on secrecy for its security," I said. "Anything better than a 'Net shop needs would be a dead giveaway to their enemies."

"Who are their enemies?" Liam asked.

"Everyone who isn't one of them. Especially us, idiot."

"Oh. Right." He looked at me sheepishly, then put the scanner away and picked up a cleaning wand. As he began working beside me, he said, "So, normal defenses then?"

"Looks like it. That said, of course, if we count on that, we'll probably end up dead. So assume they've got better than it appears. Also, assume there will be actual guards in place after they close."

"So how do we get this done?"

"Well, for one thing, we don't bother with stealth. And we don't wait for night."

★　★　★

Liam and I burst into the office, each of us brandishing a blaster. I pointed mine at the nearest 'clerk' and shouted "Back up!" When he rose from his seat and reached behind him, I fired, dropping him. I kicked the gun he'd drawn away from him as Liam shot another agent disguised as a clerk in the middle of grabbing for his blaster. "Clear," I said, and Liam repeated.

Kiri entered as I turned my gun to the lone civilian in the room. "Relax," I said. "Take a seat. We're not here to hurt you." The civilian crouched down and slunk into a corner, her crest quivering with her nervousness.

Liam pointed Kiri to the open vault, which held a Koresav Alpha mainframe, a small black box secured to the countertop. "Here's your target, Kiri."

She frowned at me. "Thanks for the help, but if *I* was a member of a big, Empire-wide intelligence service, I wouldn't be so obvious; would you?" She headed straight to the small computer that sat, unsecured, on the manager's desk. "Besides, Zhen psychology is weird. They trust subterfuge over obvious security." As she looked over the computer, she muttered, "Never thought I'd be glad I took those xenopsych classes." She located the computer's access port and plugged a device into it.

"What's that?" I asked her.

Her fingers flicked as she manipulated controls only she could see. "Access buffer and data storage," she said. "If they've got security on this thing – and they almost certainly do – it'll give me some lead time to deal with it before my brain gets fried."

"Kiri, you never said anything about brains getting fried. Is that a likely danger?"

"Yes. If I'm going to minimize that chance, then I need to concentrate, so shut up."

I gave her a 'We'll discuss this later' look, then glanced at Liam. We took up positions in the shop to cover the entrance as Kiri began accessing the system. I guarded the door while Liam monitored local and slipnet communications. I kept looking at the time display in my visual field. We only had a short while before the ISE would be alerted to our presence here. Even if we'd managed to kill the agents before they could raise the alarm, the office was sure to have automatic systems that would alert a response team.

After several long minutes of wishing I'd used the bathroom before we began, Kiri said, "I'm through the security and on their internal network. Looking for the files now."

"Incoming," Liam said softly, from beside me. "I'm reading four security teams on the way. They're talking about an ISE team expected in-system in about fifteen minutes."

"Kiri," I said, louder, "time limit – seven minutes."

"Working here," she said. "Please shut up."

Liam laughed. "She's definitely related to you," he said. "Nobody else is so sarcastic when facing certain death."

"Found the data," Kiri said. "Downloading it to my cache now."

"You get that patch loaded into the system for me?"

Her eyes remained focused on her screens as she said absently, "No, I forgot to do my job. You'd better not take me on your next raid. Also, remember when I said to shut up? Please do that."

"Everyone's sarcastic today. What is that?"

Liam grinned. "Breeding will tell."

"C'mon," I said. "I'm sure there are lots of people as sarcastic as I am."

"Probably not, Tajen Hunt," said the Zhen customer. I jerked my head around to look at her. I noticed two things immediately: first, there was no way I could turn my gun to shoot her before she killed me with the pistol in her hand, and second, she wasn't at all nervous anymore. In fact, she seemed downright predatory.

"I'm almost certain," I said, "that I didn't kick any guns anywhere near you."

"You are not incorrect," she said.

"Which means you're ISE too."

Her crest rose, a sign of excitement. "You were expected," she said, that Zhen smile-that-wasn't-a-smile growing slowly.

I felt almost sick as I realized how they'd known. "You got to Jaata, didn't you?"

"Almost as soon as you finished your conversation."

"Is he dead?"

She opened her mouth to answer, but whatever she said was interrupted by the sound of a blaster firing – and the whopping great hole that opened in her chest. I turned to see Kiri leveling a guard's blaster. She stood there for a moment, then calmly placed the blaster down and returned to the computer.

"Hey, I was talking to her!"

Kiri didn't even glance at me. "She was going to kill you. And I've lost enough family this year."

I exchanged a glance with Liam. He nodded and I left the door, going to Kiri's side. "You okay?"

She didn't look at me. "Yeah, I'm fine."

"Kiri—"

"Tajen," she interrupted me, her face a blank mask. "Look, I just shot someone for the first time. I took enough psychology courses in school to know that's going to hit me really hard once I start thinking about it. But I'm really quite busy right now. The system is trying to stop my download and kick me out, and I need to stay on top of it to keep that from happening. So I don't particularly feel like falling apart just now. Let's table this conversation for a more appropriate time."

I stared at her a moment, then smiled reassuringly – I hoped. "All right," I said. "How long until the download is complete?"

"About six minutes, unless this thing slows me down."

"Don't let it."

She gave me a hard look, and I backed away, resuming my position by the door. "How we doing?" I asked Liam.

"Well, the security teams are almost here and we're trapped with no good exit and a snarky teenager." He grinned. "I'd say we're fucked."

"You didn't used to be this defeatist."

"That was before you made my life get all complicated."

"When wasn't your life complicated?"

"Don't confuse me with reality, Hunt."

At that moment, my NeuroNet alerted me that the sensors I'd placed were registering armed individuals, all Zhen. I accessed one of the visual sensors and saw they were all red-skinned Zhen:ko. "Oh, great," I said.

"What is it?" Liam asked.

"The assault squads are all Zhen:ko."

He grimaced. "That mean what I think it means?"

"Most likely. They want us dead, there's no chance they're going to take us alive." We heard the thump of the mines we'd placed in the corridor going off. A few seconds later, the sound of plasma fire impacting the blast door told us we hadn't gotten them all with the mines.

"Got it!" Kiri called.

"Finally," I said. Liam and I left our place by the door and joined Kiri. I told the inner door to close, and then scrambled the codes with the patch Kiri had loaded into the system earlier. I grabbed her wrist and pulled her down behind the counter. I instructed my NeuroNet to call Katherine. "Katherine, exit strategy three."

"Got it."

"Clock's running! Go!" Even as I said the words, my NeuroNet went insane as it registered targeting data from my own ship converging on my location. At the same time, energy fire started impacting on the closed inner door. The Zhen were trying to burn through with concentrated plasma fire.

We all flinched as the outside wall disintegrated when one of the ship's towing harpoons slammed through the wall and spread out, then jerked back, taking most of the wall with it, opening onto a drop of fifteen stories. The moment the firing stopped, I heard Katherine's voice in my head. "I'm in position! Go!"

"Now!" I said, and dragged Kiri up. The three of us ran for the new gaping hole in the wall. When we reached it, the *Dream of Earth* swung into view below the opening. Kiri yelped as I pushed her out of the ragged hole, landing on the upper hull of the ship. Liam dropped down beside her and pulled her to the upper airlock access hatch.

I was readying myself to jump when the door to the corridor fell from the frame with a crash. I didn't think, I just turned and started firing my blaster on full automatic. The Zhen:ko at the door dropped, and so did the one immediately behind him, both with blaster holes burned through their armor and chests.

"Tajen!" Liam yelled. "We're in! Let's go, let's go!"

The Zhen were beginning to sort themselves out. I grabbed a plasma grenade from my belt, thumbed the activation switch, and tossed it in their direction. I jumped out of the hole in the wall. While

I was falling, Katherine pulled up and began flying away, causing me to hit the hull and slide over the edge of the ship's upper surface.

I cursed and grabbed a mechanic's handhold on the way down, wrenching my left arm. I lost my grip on the plasma rifle, which tumbled off the ship and fell. I spared a moment to hope it fell on an ISE agent's head while I grabbed for the handhold with my other hand.

I managed to gain my feet, and the ship rose under me and banked to the side. I bit back a curse and grabbed for the handhold again and missed it. "Katherine!" I cried, sliding toward the edge of the ship. The ship twisted under me, beginning to move away from the building, and I caught another handhold and began working my way to the hatch.

"Sorry!" Katherine called. "They fired a missile at us. Can you get inside?" She sounded worried.

"I think so," I said, climbing back onto the top of the ship. "Just try to keep the damned ship steady for ten seconds, okay?"

"I'll try," she said, "but you'd better hurry; they're trying to lock on."

I staggered back to the access hatch and dropped inside. Immediately after I hit the deck, Liam slammed the button to shut the hatch. "He's in!" he yelled. "Burn for space!" The ship accelerated nearly instantly, and I heard Kiri, in the crew lounge next door, yelp.

Liam helped me to my feet and flashed me his best grin. "That was fun," he said.

I took a deep breath and made my way to the cockpit. Katherine was in the copilot's seat. I climbed into the pilot's chair and strapped in. "Got that course plotted?"

"It's locked in," she replied. "Ready to give you control when you're ready."

"Ready."

"You have control," she said, and transferred flight control to me even while she turned her controls to the navigation system. "Course is still green," she said. "Jump vector up."

The navigation beacon created by the computer showed up on my HUD. "Got it," I said. "Any sign of pursuit?"

"Negative. I don't think they expected us to get away. They're still scrambling ships. Once we hit orbit, though, I'm sure we'll pick them up."

"That won't be long. Orbit in thirty seconds." I paused. "Good job back there."

"You're kidding, right?" she said. "I almost dropped you."

"But you didn't. Wasn't your fault, anyway."

Liam joined us. "I'm tired of this place," he said. "The food sucks. Let's get out of here."

I turned back to my controls. "Yes, sir," I said.

"Oh, I like it when you take orders."

I rolled my eyes at him. "Don't get used to it," I said.

"Yes, *sir*, Captain *sir*."

I looked up at him. "Sometimes, you are such a child." My console beeped at me, and I looked back at it in time to see the sky outside the viewport deepen into black. "Picking up four fighters," I said. "*Shitakkar*-class. Liam, get to the guns."

"Got it. Kiri, time to put that training to use. Come on!"

As he left at a run, I shook my head. "Seriously? *Shitakkar*-class? That's a little too much, don't you think?"

"Those are brand new, aren't they?"

"Yep. Only the Imperial Guard have them, I thought. But these have ISE codes."

"Well, who else would get the best?"

"True," I sighed. "Those things are supposed to have better range than— Shit."

"Well, the range of shit is pretty low."

I gave her an aggrieved look. "They've got a lock on us. Liam," I called, "are you in the guns yet?"

"Strapped in and locked on," he said.

"We're making the run for the jump point," I said. "Weapons free."

"You always know what to get me," he said. I heard the ship thrum as the guns opened up. So far, nothing had shown up between us and the jump point. I watched the distance to jump tick down as I fed as much power as I could into the engines, ignoring the occasional flashes when shots impacted on the shields as we raced onward. The moment we crossed the jump line, my hand slammed down on the jump controls, and reality twisted around us as we jumped into slipspace.

Twenty minutes into our jump, I shifted flight control back to Katherine. "Be right back," I said. I turned to leave the bridge and ran right into Liam. I barked in surprise and pain, and started to topple over, but Liam grabbed me and we steadied each other. We stood there laughing like idiots for a moment, then our eyes met, and then we were kissing, our arms encircling each other, each of us pulling the other close.

"*Finally!*" Katherine exclaimed. We broke apart, looking sheepish. "Oh, come on," she said. "I've been trying to push you two together since you met. Can't I watch you lock lips a little?"

"No!" Liam said.

"Fine," she sighed. She turned away.

Liam grinned at the back of her head. "Kiri's collating the data," he said, turning back to me. "She says it ought to be ready in about an hour, and that we're not to interrupt her on pain of, and I quote, 'something horrific being shoved in an unpleasant place.'" He shook his head. "Don't know what they're teaching kids these days. How long are we in slipspace?"

I glanced at the countdown in my 'Net's field. "About two days," I said.

"Oh."

Katherine rolled her eyes at us. "We've got *some time*," she said with careful emphasis. "Me, I'm going to go check out the engine room. Then I might visit the galley, make something to eat. And then perhaps I'll come up here and sit a spell." She left the bridge, calling over her shoulder, "Please, boys – for the love of my sanity, don't be here when I get back."

We listened to her footsteps walking away, and looked at each other. An instant later, Liam's hand closed on my jacket's lapel and pulled me down the corridor toward my room.

★   ★   ★

A week of travel, and several days of reconnaissance, later, we were ready. Katherine, Ben, Kiri, and I were on the cramped bridge.

Liam rode in his now-customary place in the main gunnery chair down the corridor. Katherine sat beside me in the copilot's seat, while Kiri was at the flight engineer's station and Ben sat at sensors. The random colors of slipspace slid by the ports. The colors were as beautiful as they were disturbing in their twisty patterns, I knew, but after this many years in space I barely noticed them. My eyes were entirely focused on the display in my visual field, counting down to our reversion to realspace. As the timer approached zero, I spoke. "Everyone, remember your job. Reversion in five, four, three, two – now!" The colors twisted wildly for just a moment, then the reassuring euclidean geometries of realspace snapped into place. We were now on the outskirts of the Fiktosh System, one of the hubs of the Imperial Communications System's slipnet.

With any luck, nobody in-system would notice the brief explosion of color and drive radiation that heralded a ship re-entering the universe. I'd already deactivated all but the most essential systems in an attempt to hide our heat and energy signatures, as well as avoid all the usual sensor pings and handshakes the ship would normally do. "Any sign we've been spotted?"

Ben ran his hands over the sensor boards. "Nothing I can see. Without active sensors, though, our range is limited. I've got passives set to the highest sensitivity."

"Okay, then. Let's get to it." I fired a quick pulse of maneuvering thrusters, sending us slowly toward one of the system's nodes. Unlike the majority of slipnet node-equipped systems, Fiktosh was a communications system hub; it had several nodes, each of them linked to the others in an array that connected Fiktosh to several different systems at once.

We began inching toward the nearest of the linked system nodes. Ben, still monitoring the sensor board, swore softly. "SPC incoming," he said. "Sending vector." Even as he spoke, the system patrol craft's position and vector popped into my visual, as well as everyone else's. We had linked all our NeuroNets before reversion to realspace, allowing us to send back and forth without the usual filter protocols.

I adjusted my course to avoid the incoming system patrol craft, shifting us to a vector that should keep us out of their detection radius. We could see them due to their active sensors, but as we were relying on passive systems only, they had nothing to detect us with unless we entered their active range.

In theory. "Verify stealth routines," I said softly.

Katherine answered, just as softly. "Stealth routines active, emissions at minimum. Your father did a good job with this ship. Her stealth systems are good. You sure he was just a trader?"

"No idea," I said. "How are we, Ben?" I asked.

"Well," he said with a drawl, "I've got a touch of indigestion from Kiri's cooking, but other than that—"

"Ben," I growled.

"Sorry," he said, with a hint of cheek. "We appear to be in the clear. SPC is moving away, no deviations from her course."

"Kiri, is everything ready?"

"Your speech and all the documentation are bundled and ready. Once we're hooked in, and once this turns green," she said, leaning over to indicate a flashing red pulse on my control board, "you hit that switch and it all goes out into the slipnet. It'll take about thirty seconds to upload." She paused. "If you want to make any changes to your introduction, it's too late."

I shook my head. "I said what I needed to."

"All right, then," she said. "I'll get moving."

She slipped from the bridge. A few moments later, my console showed me she was entering the forward airlock.

I brought us to a stop just a few meters from the node. It made me nervous to be this close to anything, but we couldn't risk using even a tight-beam transmitter, as we had to avoid detection for as long as possible, and the closer we were to the node's receiver, the easier it would be to remain hidden long enough to send the entire data packet.

I held my breath for as long as I could, nervous as hell. Ben and Katherine both gave me reassuring looks. Eventually, the connection indicator turned green.

"We're connected. Sending the data."

I couldn't help it: for the thirty seconds it took for the data package to upload into the slipnet, I held my breath, my eyes scanning for any change in the Fiktosh System's activity that would mean we'd been spotted. Nothing happened before Kiri reported, "Upload complete. I'm back aboard."

My NeuroNet informed me that a data packet had been sent to me, high priority, and the file opened automatically. Even though I knew what it was, even though I had tested it seventeen times, I let it continue to play, though I set it to a small inset window so I could fly while it played. I set a course for the outer system, slow and steady to avoid notice.

The file would be popping up all over the Empire very shortly. We had constructed the file very carefully. It would be sent to everyone, human or Zhen, with a NeuroNet – meaning almost every human over seventeen years of age, and all adult Zhen – and would open automatically if they were awake. If they were sleeping, it would first activate their wakeup alarms, and then open once they were conscious. I'd thought about sending it only to humans, but I wanted the Zhen to know what I had found too. They couldn't all be bad, after all.

I tried not to cringe as my head and shoulders appeared in front of me. "Greetings, fellow citizens," it said. "My name is Tajen Hunt. For a time, I was known as the Hero of Elkari, and later, the Man Who Lost Jiraad. I have been a trusted member of the Empire's military establishment, but now I am hunted by that same military.

"The Empire will tell you that I have committed treason by releasing classified Imperial secrets. This is, technically, correct. But the information has a direct bearing on our Empire, especially on the humans who reside within it.

"Humans of the Empire, we have been lied to. The Empire claims that we were rescued after an accident nearly destroyed our colony ship. This is a lie. They claim they do not know the location of Earth. This is also a lie. I know, because I have been there.

"Earth is not lost to time, as they have claimed for eight hundred years. But the Earth as our records show it is long gone." My face was replaced with a picture of Earth as it was now: a wild place, with vegetation covering most of the landmass, thriving in land that had been cities with millions of people a thousand years ago. We also included Zhen records of the planet from orbit, showing the land mass every student had had to memorize in primary education.

"As the records now spooling into your 'Nets prove, the Zhen destroyed all life on Earth three hundred years before they found the *Far Star*. Billions of humans and countless animals died in a matter of days. Three hundred years later, the Zhen found the *Far Star* on its way to a new world, *fully intact*. They nearly destroyed the last humans in the universe – they nearly destroyed *us* – before they changed their minds. And ever since, they have treated us like shit they stepped in by accident.

"Humans are not allowed to own land on Zhen except in the Virginia enclave. We do not elect human representatives to the *Talnera*. We pay twice as much in taxes to the Empire as the Zhen. We have put up with this because we believed they were our saviors. We believed we owed them." My voice hardened as I said, "We. Were. *Wrong*. They are *not* our saviors. We owe them *nothing*. What they gave us was what they *owed* us, atonement for their crime of destroying our civilization.

"I ask you to join with me in demanding an end to the Contract and our status as a client species. Demand that we be given the rights of full citizens in the Empire, and above all, demand that they return our world to us.

"To the Zhen Empire, I will say this: I do not hate you. I accept that these actions were taken a thousand years ago, and you are not your ancestors. But I demand – yes, I *demand* – that you make it right. I don't expect you to coddle us, but I do expect you to stop taxing us at the absurd rates we pay, remove all restrictions on our trade, and above all, give us the option of leaving the Empire. Give us back our homeworld, and allow the population of Terra to decide for itself whether or not it will remain with the Empire.

"The Zhen among you are wondering why they were sent this information. I sent it to all for two reasons. First, because while the actions of the Empire most concern the humans, they should also concern our Zhen neighbors and friends. Second, there is more that is being done in your name, and this you should also know.

"The files attached to this message contain all the relevant information I have on illegal actions undertaken by the Imperial government. They have placed a military base on Earth over what was once a thriving city of millions of my people. They are planning to increase their presence there, showing further disrespect to our people. The data you now hold shows the movement of troops and materiel to this facility, as well as more being planned in the months to come. In short, they are preparing to strike out at our neighbors, the Kelvaki and the Tabrans. They are preparing for a new war, one that will consume worlds and possibly billions of lives. I ask of you one thing: stop them.

"Humanity – as well as the Zhen – has now been armed with the truth. Choose wisely what you will do with it."

As the playback faded, I looked over my shoulder. Ben smiled at me, then jerked his gaze back to the readouts. "Uh-oh," he said. "That SPC is back, and it's headed right for us."

I started us moving again. Katherine activated our exit course, which caused the jump point we needed to show up on my tactical HUD. I swung the ship toward the point.

"They must have caught the upload earlier than I expected," Kiri said.

"You think so?" I said calmly.

"Sorry, Uncle."

"Not a worry, kid, as long as we get— Shit!" I cried as the SPC began firing at us. I dove away from the plasma bolts, pouring power into the engines.

"Detecting missile launch!" Ben said. "Launching counter measures."

"Everyone strapped in? Good!" I said, without bothering to wait for a reply. I snapped the throttle to full and turned hard to starboard. Unfortunately, that put the ship right on our tail, which was less than ideal – but at least there was only one of them. I began to juke randomly as we headed for the jump limit.

"Reading three more ships jumping in-system," Ben said.

"Come on! That's not fair!" I whined.

"New guys are heading right for us. Bastards must have detected us earlier, after all."

"Doesn't matter," I said. "We'll hit the jump point in twenty seconds."

"They're hailing us."

"Let me see it."

A Zhen in a commander's uniform appeared in the comm area of my visual field. "Tajen Hunt," he said, "you are bound by Imperial

Law. Bring your ship to full stop and prepare for boarding."

"Negative, Commander. I will not comply."

"You cannot win, Captain Hunt. We are many, and you are one ship."

"That's true. But you know what's really easy to hide? One little ship. So, as my grandfather used to say, 'go fuck yourself.'"

I hit the jump, and we were gone.

★   ★   ★

We exited slipspace a few days later in a system of no consequence – it had slipnet, but no military presence, and was so unimportant that it had only a number instead of a name. When nothing came after us for a few hours, we relaxed, setting a course for yet another backwater and settling in to watch the Imperial media response to our message.

It was pretty predictable. The Zhen government's immediate response was that the terrorist Tajen Hunt and his confederates had faked the information he had 'leaked' to the public. They maintained that Earth had never been found, and begged all humanity to ignore his 'deplorable lies'.

Some people bought it. This didn't surprise me in the least. People tend to believe whatever will maintain their worldview with the least amount of work. Changing how you look at the world takes energy a lot of us just don't have. It was much easier, for some, to believe that the Zhen were the good guys, and I was a disgraced military officer who, driven into madness by my brother's death, was trying to get revenge on the Zhen for my disgrace.

Some bought that story, but not all. Many were ready to believe the Zhen were not all they had claimed they were. It wasn't just the records I had released. Those, I had to admit, weren't terribly difficult to fake with the technology available to the Empire. It was, in fact, the same factor at work – believing my accusation against the Zhen was all too easy for people who were sick unto death of being treated as the lowest form of life in the Empire.

On Terra, crowds of humans surrounded the Zhen administration complex, holding signs with slogans like SHAME ON ZHEN and GIVE US BACK OUR WORLD. There were also counter-demonstrators, who had signs with things like PUT HUNT IN JAIL or THE EMPIRE IS NOT OUR ENEMY. Things got tense, both between the two human groups, and with the armed Zhen military officers manning the walls, but the human leadership managed to defuse things. There were ongoing demonstrations, but so far, there had not been any violence.

On Zhen itself, though, things weren't going as well. A crowd of several thousand humans who believed us had gathered at the Imperial Palace, and when they hadn't left after three days, the Zhen military surrounded the plaza and ordered them to leave. When they didn't, the military threatened them with arrest or violence. And on the fourth day, they opened fire.

The government news sources reported that a little more than two hundred people died in the square outside the palace, and about one thousand five hundred were arrested. Human demonstrators in Virginia City, however, claimed that closer to two thousand people died, and ten thousand were arrested, many sent to Imperial prisons with no legal way for their families to see them. On Zhen, martial law was declared, and limits placed on human gatherings in public spaces.

The night we saw that report, I went alone to my quarters and got quietly drunk.

Over the next few days, I received several queries through the slipnet from both journalists who wanted a story and humans who wanted to join up with me. I deflected these as best I could; I wasn't forming an army.

Late one night, I was on watch alone when Katherine's voice broke the silence I'd been sitting in. "You're fooling yourself, you know."

I turned to see her. "How so?"

"You keep telling people you're not trying to start a war."

"I'm not."

"Well, you should be."

"I'm not even considering open revolt."

"Really, Tajen?" She slid into the copilot's seat. "Do you really expect all this to end with a nice handshake with the One and a happy Empire? Do you think the Twenty and the One will just smile and hand Earth back to us, lower our taxes, and say they're sorry?"

I sighed. "Well, no. Not really."

"No." She sat for a moment, then said, "They're going to strike at us, and you know it."

"So we stay where they won't find us."

She leaned toward me. "How'd that work out for Tinaari during the Jumari Rebellion?"

I shuddered. "You think, if I don't give them a target, they'll go after my friends?"

"They've done it before."

"Joke's on them, then. All my friends are here."

Her face hardened. "Mine aren't. I have friends and family on Terra."

Oh, shit. I had been so wrapped up in feeling like I'd gotten people killed, I hadn't thought about the fact that my crew had friends and family to worry about. "I'm such an ass, sometimes."

She smiled weakly. "I won't argue with that."

We sat in silence for a moment. "I need to get away from you guys, and become a public target."

Her eyes narrowed. "Can I ask you something, Tajen?"

"Sure."

She turned and leaned toward me. "At what exact second did your brain evaporate?"

I blinked at her. "What?"

"Seriously, that is probably the dumbest thing you've ever said to me. And you've said some pretty stupid things over the time I've known you."

"I don't know how to do this."

"Well, fortunately for you, you don't have to."

"Come on. You can go back to Terra, get clear of all this. Disavow me and have a life."

"Not gonna happen," she said. "Do you remember when we voted on whether or not to pursue your brother's legacy? I voted against it. I was wrong."

"Listen to me—"

"Don't bother," Liam said from behind us. I twisted in my seat to look, and found him standing behind us, Kiri and Ben beside him. "We're not leaving you."

"Guys, there's no reason for you to get—"

Liam cut me off. "Tajen, I love you, but seriously, if you don't shut up *right now*? I'm going to punch you right in the goddamn face." He wasn't kidding around; I could tell he was furious. "For crap's sake, do you think you're the only human on this ship? Do you think you're the only one the Zhen have shit on? Are you the only one who made the decision to do this?"

"Of course not," I said defensively.

"Then knock off the 'noble leader' routine. We all stumbled into this mess together. And we're only getting out of it together."

"We're with you," Katherine said.

"You could die," I said.

"No shit," she said. "But I could have died when you saved us all back in the Kintar System. I could have died at any time in the thirty-six years I lived before that day. Hell, I could have died several times back when I was in the military."

"That's a little different."

"Dead is dead. And I'd be a lot more willing to die trying to fight this nonsense than in a marauder attack."

"Your brother already died because of me. I—"

She rose from her seat, angrier than I'd ever seen her. "Don't you dare! Takeshi didn't die because of you, you arrogant shit!" She took a deep breath. "He died because of the Zhen, and because he *chose* to go with us on this mission. Do not *ever* take that choice away from him."

I let out the breath I'd held when she rose. "I'm sorry," I said.

She sat back down. "Be better, Tajen." She gave me a sad smile. "Or I'll help Liam kick your ass."

"So will I," Kiri said. "I'm already the daughter of a traitor according to the Zhen. There's nowhere for me to go but with you."

I sat for a moment, weighing what to tell them. "The truth is, I was trying to avoid a fight for your sakes. If it was just me, I'd be fighting already."

"Well, that's settled," Ben said. "Let's kick some ass."

"Where do we begin?" Liam asked.

I was about to answer when the console started making an obnoxious sound. Ben grimaced at the noise, but Katherine and I both went pale. I spun to the board as Liam headed for gunnery control without waiting for instructions. "We've got ships incoming," I said. "Reading fifteen vessels."

"Plotting an escape course," Katherine snapped. "Kiri, Ben, strap in!" As she worked, she glanced at me. "Tajen, why aren't we moving?"

I stared at the sensor board. "They're not Zhen," I said, confused. "They're Kelvaki. Fourteen fast-attack craft and a *Kelthar*-class command ship. They're hailing us." I answered the comms, piping the audio to everyone. "Identify yourself," I said.

There was a pause, and then a familiar voice came over the comms. "Is that any way to greet an old friend, *draka*?"

"Dierka?" I laughed.

"Indeed, Tajen. My shuttle is en route to your ship. May we board?"

"I'll meet you at the lock," I said. I shut down the comms and unstrapped, flicking helm control over to Katherine. "Liam," I said over the ship's network, "stay on the guns. Katherine, be ready to bolt if we need to." I left the bridge, Kiri on my tail.

"You don't trust Dierka?" she asked me as we walked.

"I trust Dierka," I said. "I don't necessarily trust anyone he's got with him. That's a lot of ships."

I got to the airlock just seconds before the inner door cycled open. Dierka maneuvered his large frame through the lock, followed by two more Kelvaki. I gestured for them to follow me and led them toward the crew lounge. I frowned at Dierka. "Look, I'm glad to see you, old friend, but – and please forgive my rudeness – how the hell did you find us?"

He looked chagrined – and on a Kelvaki, that look can be unsettling. "Now it is my turn to apologize for rudeness, Tajen. I took the liberty of leaving a slipnet homing beacon on your ship for just this eventuality. I'm almost surprised Kiri didn't find it."

Kiri broke into the discussion. "So am I. I've scanned this ship five times since you left."

"I will give our intelligence community some well-deserved

compliments, then." I glared at him, and he gave me an unrepentant look. "But if you must deactivate it," he said in a conciliatory tone, "it is a disc about two *cro* wide, black with a silver rim. You will find it in the waste-processing bay."

"No wonder I didn't find it," she said, her face wrinkling in disgust.

"Quite. It took days to get the stench out of my nose after I placed it."

When we arrived at the lounge, one of Dierka's soldiers stopped him before he could go through the door. "Your highness," she said, "please allow us to scan for danger."

"I am in no danger here, Sikar," he growled. She didn't budge. He sighed, "But go ahead."

I looked at Dierka. "'Your highness?'"

He made a rolling motion of his ears. "Yes."

"And you never mentioned this because...."

"I was further from the throne then. But when I was summoned home, I discovered that I had come considerably closer."

"How'd that happen?"

"Several of my cousins were killed." He looked at me for a long moment. "I'm supposed to think it was an attack by a marauder clan."

"Who was it, really?"

"Oh, it was marauders. But they were put up to it by someone in the Empire. Near as we can tell, someone high in the military."

Oh, shit. Pieces snapped into place, and I suddenly realized that things were far bigger than I had thought. If the Zhen were already moving against the Assembly after two thousand years of peace, even through proxies, then things were moving faster than I'd realized toward making the Empire more like the 'conquering storm' it used to be. "Dierka, someone in the Empire is trying to return to the old ways. If they're getting to a point where they're willing to reignite the war with your people, then things are further along than I'd expected."

"Which is part of why I'm here. My ships are yours, Tajen."

I stopped in the middle of opening my mouth to speak, and stood there for several seconds. "What?"

"His Majesty, my uncle, has released these ships from their normal assignments. They are mine to use as I see fit. I choose to use them to aid you." He handed me a datapad. "He also asked me to give you this, but insisted that it not be sent via neural link."

"What is it?"

"A copy of our most recent intelligence reports."

Intrigued, I took the pad and began to scan through the report. As I did, an idea began to come to me. "Dierka, can we trust all your people?"

"Of course. They are all blood family, sworn to my cause."

Which, by Kelvaki rules, meant they were also *my* family. I smiled and started to explain my idea, but I was interrupted by a call from the bridge. "Tajen, we've got another ship on comms asking if they can meet up with us."

"Can we trust them?"

"No way to be sure, but I recognize the captain's name. I've worked with her before. And she's using some pretty good encryption."

"Anyone I'd know?"

"Maybe? Elaine Gregory, out of Virginia City."

I recognized the name, and agreed with her assessment. "Good enough." I pulled some coordinates from my memory and sent them to Katherine. "Tell her to meet us there. And send the general call message we discussed – direct responders to the same coordinates."

"Roger that. I'll set a course."

"Copy it to the Kelvaki. They're coming with us."

There was a moment's silence, then, "Will do."

I turned to the Kelvaki prince standing before me. "Dierka, my friend, let's go liberate a planet."

"Excellent."

I led him and his group back to the airlock. He saluted me in the manner of a Kelvaki, and went back through to his shuttle.

As it cycled, I turned to Liam. "You love me?"

Liam turned to me with a twinkle in his eye. "Shut up." He took my hand as we headed for the bridge. "We've got work to do."

CHAPTER FOURTEEN

We burst into normal space already moving at high speed, trailing a long swath of the glittering colors of slipspace. The moment we hit normal space, my weapons started coming online, and Ben, manning the sensors, designated target priorities.

Less than a second after the weapons reached full power, they fired, plasma bolts searing through the dark, slamming into the system's newly installed automated early warning station. The station, shielded only by minimal armor to protect it from wayward micrometeorites, broke under the assault, disintegrating in seconds. "Glad the Kelvaki report told us about that," I remarked. Katherine grunted an assent, and I added, "Now let's hope we killed it before it told them we're here."

As we swept past the remains of the small station, tiny fragments bouncing from my shields in pretty little flares of light, the guns fired once more, precisely aimed shots destroying the mines and other traps the Zhen had installed in the remains of the fleet while the Kelvaki spy team had watched.

We'd been joined at the rendezvous by three human vessels: two traders and a repair ship. Once we'd verified they were all human, they'd been added to the task force that came for Earth. Now, while the Kelvaki and I maintained our heading toward Earth, the three civilian vessels slowed and began nosing their way through the graveyard, looking for a space to hide the repair ship. It was the only ship-repair facility we were likely to have for some time, and I was adamant that it needed to be protected, not least to justify the faith of its crew in joining our little rebellion.

"Hope Dierka's crew got their targets," Kiri said as we angled in toward Earth.

"They did," I said.

"How do you know?" Kiri asked from her seat at the tactical console.

Ben answered her. "If they hadn't, we'd be dead by now." He got the distant look that meant he was paying extra attention to his 'Net's input for a moment, and said, "Looks good. Of course, we'll need to sweep the system later for the rest of the traps."

"Maybe," Kiri said. "Better idea'd be to switch their targeting profiles. Make them work for us."

We reached Earth orbit a few hours later, and found nothing in orbit except our own ships.

Katherine shook her head. "Typical Zhen. We announced we want our planet back, and they didn't put a guard on it, just some mines."

"Isn't that good?" Kiri asked.

"Maybe," Katherine said. "It could mean they don't think we have the ability to take it. Maybe they don't know about our allies."

"Or they plan to let us commit ourselves before jumping in behind us," I said.

"Oh, there's a cheery thought," Kiri said.

"That's me, Mr. Cheery."

"No one has called you that, ever."

Katherine cleared her throat. "If you two are done?"

"Oh, fine, let's blow some more shit up," I said in an aggrieved tone. I quickly verified all our ships were in position, then opened a comms channel. Then I stopped, cocking my head. I'd been planning to warn the Zhen, give them a chance to leave Earth willingly. But after all I'd learned, I couldn't give them that opportunity. Whoever was pulling the strings, this outpost was part of a conspiracy to reawaken a force for chaos and death throughout known space. I closed the channel. "You know what? They didn't warn Earth. Fuck 'em." I switched to the fleet tactical band. "Commence attack sequence alpha."

Fifteen ships began raining plasma fire down on the Zhen base, eliminating the relatively sparse ground defenses. At the same time, Kelvaki dropships from Dierka's command vessel dove for the base in damned near free fall, their thrusters engaging and slowing them down when they were only a few hundred meters above the surface.

The ships all but slammed to the ground, hatches dropped open, and Kelvaki attack squads began pouring from the ships, along with Liam, who had been put in command of the ground assault. His command was a political move, so that a human commanded the retaking of Earth and to keep the Kelvaki, who had all traded their Assembly insignia for that of a known mercenary group, officially neutral; his 'second' was actually the commander of the Kelvaki troops. It was a flimsy lie, but it might be enough to prevent war between the Kelvaki and Zhen governments, at least for a while.

The troops swarmed over the Zhen facility. I heard Liam on the tactical band, calling out targets. In the middle of a command, he was cut off by an explosion, and my heart froze. I waited, dread growing, until I heard him come back on the channel. "That was a close one," he called. "Zeta, take out that gunner." I let out the breath I hadn't realized I was holding.

I'd wanted to be part of the surface attack, but my crew had pointed out what should have been obvious: my training and most of my experience was in space combat. On the surface, I'd be a distraction to the soldiers who would need to keep an eye on me. So I'd taken command of the orbital element of the attack. It rankled that I was essentially backup in taking my own world, but listening to the battle, I realized they'd been right.

My attention was reclaimed by Katherine's alarmed voice. "I'm reading three Zhen couriers leaving Earth's atmosphere," she said, passing the coordinates to me via NeuroNet.

I locked in an intercept course and began moving. "Ships two through five, on me. Six through fifteen, remain in position. Do not let anyone through."

"Confirmed, flight leader."

I flew under full burn to the intercept point. The ships were small attack craft, each capable of carrying two Zhen. Just as they broke out of orbit, I locked missiles on them and fired both missiles and plasma guns. Two ships exploded, but the third managed to elude my weapons and sailed off into the black, firing at me as she passed.

I hauled the ship around and engaged a pursuit course, my Kelvaki allies joining me. They knew better than to fly in a straight line, which was pretty inconsiderate of them, as I was trying to lock weapons on their ship, but at least the maneuvers prevented their using the chain drive to get away even faster. Some people, you just can't trust them to do what you want.

"Can you overtake them?" Kiri asked, anxious.

"Not likely," I said. "They're faster than we are. But we don't need to overtake them. I just need to get a lock."

Katherine swore. "I'm getting a power spike – I think they're powering their jump drive." She glanced sideways at me. "They get away, we're in a world of hurt."

I spared her a very short, but very hard, glance. "I'm doing the best I can here." I adjusted course, trying to keep up with them long enough for my weapons system to get a lock. I took a deep breath and shut down the engine safeties, pouring on the speed. The engines immediately began to whine in protest.

"Oh *shrak*," Katherine said, her hands flying over the controls, trying to keep the power balanced.

The noise of the engines got higher and higher as they redlined, the sound becoming painful. We were going to need a lot of repair when this was over.

The moment my weapons locked on, they fired – and passed harmlessly through the spreading cloud of colors from the courier's transition into slipspace.

I cursed as I pulled back on the throttle, bringing my engine power back into the safe zone.

"That's not good," Kiri said.

"How long do you think we've got?" Ben asked.

I was busy grinding my teeth and feeling sorry for myself, so Katherine answered. "We knew they'd find out eventually, but we thought we'd have more time before they launched a counterattack. Now...factoring the closest Zhen military base, and the time they'd need to get back here...maybe a month."

I hauled the ship around and headed back toward the planet. "We need to get busy," I said. "No way it's going to take a whole month."

*   *   *

"No! Dammit, no!" I slammed my hand down on the console. On the other side of it sat two trainees, one of them a fresh-faced kid, the other a freighter pilot in his forties. "If you do that in combat, you'll *both* be dead! What the hell were you thinking?"

Liam, standing beside me, placed a calming hand on my shoulder, but said nothing. Katherine, on the other side of the room, was trying not to laugh. I shot her a 'don't push me' look, and she sent one back that said 'oh, please'.

The older of them sighed and buried his head in his hands. "Dammit, I can't get this."

I took a deep breath and calmed myself down. While I was at it, I reminded myself that I wasn't Zhen, that I'd hated my Zhen flight instructors, and that I shouldn't be trying to emulate those bastards. "Look," I said. "Up until that maneuver you were doing fine. You got three kills in that engagement before you went boom. So don't beat yourself up." I grinned. "That said – what *were* you thinking?"

"I expected Karen," he said, referring to the woman in the other seat, "to head for the second fighter group."

"Why?"

He shrugged. "It just made sense."

"Tell me, are you psychic?"

He blinked at me, taken aback by the question. "Uh, no," he said in that tone of voice humans use when they're answering a very stupid question – which of course it was.

"So, you can't read her mind?"

"No."

"Can you read mine?"

"No."

"Okay. So you have no idea what would have made sense to her."

"No."

"Good. Now – was she in command during this 'sortie'?"

"No," he said, confused as to where I was going.

"Who was?"

"Uh, I was."

I nodded. "Then why would you just assume that Karen would do what you thought was logical, when you *didn't give her any commands?*"

He stared at me for a few seconds. I could see when he finally got it – he closed his eyes and hung his head. "Man, I'm stupid."

I smiled. "You're not stupid. You're just new to this, and you've got a lot of habits that work great for a merchant in a freighter, but not in a fighter. We'll get you there." I turned and gestured toward the holotank. "Start the playback, Jenny," I said to my tactical officer.

We'd been training anyone with any piloting skill for a little over three weeks now. Human vessels had been appearing in Earth orbit within days of our taking Earth. We were supplementing our ships with the few Zhen fighters that hadn't been destroyed.

I wasn't sure how the word had got out to the human race so fast, but I suspected Dierka had something to do with it.

As the holotank spun up, icons denoting the fleet's disposition in the simulation appeared. Each trainee had been hooked into the TacComm, their implants acting as simulators, while the more experienced pilots, currently on patrol, took turns 'parking' their ships near the station and taking part in the drills, playing the part of Zhen attack ships assaulting the station Dierka's people had built for us in high Earth orbit.

"See, here's where you could have—" I was interrupted by the sound of the alarm klaxon. "What the hell?"

The tall woman working the sensor boards shook her head. "Oh, *shaak*. Sir! Zhen forces jumping in!"

I turned toward the holotank as she switched it from the recorded war-games to the current situation. "How many?"

"I'm counting...." She turned white. "I've got about fifty ships, sir, ranging from frigates to three *Shikasa*-class fighter-carriers."

"Katherine, with me," I snapped, turning on my heel and heading out of the control center.

Liam followed, and I stopped in the corridor and held a hand to his chest. "You're not coming," I said. "You and Jenny have overall command of the fleet."

"Are you insane? You're the one in command, *you* should be here."

I shook my head. "Look, I'm a great pilot, and a decent tactician – but overall strategy isn't something I ever did particularly well.

You've proven that you're brilliant at it. I need you here. You tell me what needs to happen out there, and I'll figure out how to get it done."

He didn't look happy, but he nodded. "Be safe," he said.

"I always am," I said with what I hoped was a disarming grin.

"No you're not," he said. He looked to Katherine. "Keep him from doing anything stupid," he said to her.

"Do my best," she said, "but no promises. You know what he's like."

"Hey, I'm standing right here, you two," I said. "Let's go!"

Katherine and I ran to the docking bay where the *Dream of Earth* was docked. I opened both airlock doors while running down the boarding tube, twisting my body sideways to slide through before it was open all the way. I grabbed the edge of the inner door as it opened, used it to swing myself around to the left, and ran down the corridor to the bridge, rebounding off the corridor wall.

When I reached the bridge I slid into the pilot's couch, reviewing the course the ship's navicomp had suggested based on the sensor readings relayed from station command. "Course locked," I said.

Katherine came in behind me, slapped a shoulder of the crewman at the sensor board, and slipped into the copilot's couch. "Looks like we've got people in the guns. Want to get Smith and Njemi up here to run the sensor boards?"

"No time. We've got who we've got." We had been training someone to man the engineering station, but I had no intention of waiting. "Station command, this is Captain Hunt. Releasing docking clamps." As the ship moved away from the station, the autopilot following the course I'd set, I went to the tactical frequency. "All ships, this is Captain Hunt. Assuming command." A series of confirmations came in.

"Captain," Liam said over comms, "they're just sitting out there. None have moved from their exit points."

"Any idea what they're waiting for?"

"We think they—" His voice was interrupted by a sound I knew only too well. It was a widecast, broadcast on all frequencies at a power level high enough to blanket out everything else. It was a horrifying sound, like a knife sliding along your nerves, designed to get the attention of any sentient who heard it – though I'd heard from some Zhen that it wasn't as unpleasant to them as it was to humans.

"Attention human occupiers of Staaen System. Any ships attempting to leave this system will be destroyed. Any ships coming within one hundred thousand kilometers of Zhen vessels will be destroyed."

Katherine whistled. "Stars be damned, why'd Dierka have to leave last week?"

"His uncle demanded a report in person. I think he needed to assure the Assembly that their heir is sane, after he threw in with us. Well, maybe he can avenge us," I said. I slowed as we rendezvoused with the rest of our ships, spread in a defensive formation around the station. "Whenever they make their move, we're as ready as we'll ever be."

"How ready is that?" Katherine drawled.

I sniffed and glanced back, then pitched my voice for her ears alone. "Not very."

"Maybe they just want to blockade us?"

"Sure. For now. Tell Ben to get the medical center ready for casualties. They're going to move on us eventually. I just wish I knew what they were waiting for."

CHAPTER FIFTEEN

The Zhen vessels continued to hang just off the station, doing nothing, for a week. We increased the ship presence, keeping most of our ships in orbit, but rotating ships back to the station for maintenance and downtime.

Notice I didn't say R&R. There was no rest, and little relaxation, to be had. On- or off-duty, we all remained at high alert, each of us just waiting for the alarms to signal that the Zhen were on the move. I wasn't sure how long my pilots could keep doing this – even with downtime, nerves were starting to fray. We'd had a few fights on the station already, and things were getting more and more tense with every day.

I was no different. When I was in orbit, I was all business, speaking only when necessary to give orders or acknowledge reports. When I was stationside, I was even worse. I practically lived in the command and control center, and when I wasn't there I was hooked in via my implants, reviewing reports and status messages nearly constantly.

Kiri was fed up with me, but Liam was ready to kill me.

"You keep insisting that your pilots rest. Why are you exempt from that?" he asked one night as I stopped into our quarters to shower and change.

"Liam, I'm not just a pilot. You know that. I'm in command of the ship element. I don't stop being in command just because I'm not out there."

"Of course not. But you're not going to do the fleet, or this colony, any good if you ride yourself right into the goddamned sun. And frankly, it would do the rest of the colony good to see you in public *not* looking like you're about to vibrate into another dimension. And in case you've forgotten, *I* am in overall command of this mess. If I have to order you to take some time off, I will."

His voice softened as he added, "They need to see that you're not worried, Tajen – or at least that you're good at faking it."

I sighed, and sagged against the couch. "You're right," I said. I reached out to him, taking his hand and squeezing it. "I'm sorry." We sat in silence for a while before I said, "How's that restaurant working out?"

"Well, the rations are still shit, but Lou thinks he's improving on them. Most of us are letting him believe it – it makes him so happy, nobody has the heart to tell him otherwise. He keeps claiming that this Kelvaki pre-fab space station isn't good for cooking human food. I think he's just a lousy cook."

I laughed. "Want to go out to dinner?"

He grimaced for a moment. "Ah, why not?" he said with a grin. "He's got some good desserts, at least."

"Let me clean up, and then we can *go*. And maybe later we can go."

"Cheeky, aren't you?"

"I've been in space for four days straight. Shouldn't I be?"

I went to the 'fresher and splashed my face with water. I didn't really feel like going out, or even like doing anything other than checking the fleet's status every ten seconds. And maybe sleeping for a few minutes. But Liam was being incredibly patient, and he was just worried about me. So for him, I'd do it.

And, as much as I hated to admit it, he *was* right.

As I came back into the living room, an alert message flashed in my field of view, and an alarm sounded in my ears. "C&C, report!" I snapped.

The OpsTech on duty appeared before me. "We've got an incoming jump, sir. Four vessels, all civilian. Sir, the Zhen are targeting the civilians."

I cursed and looked at Liam. "So much for dinner," I said, already moving to the door.

"Right behind you," he said, following.

As we ran toward C&C, I brought up my comms system and sent a message to my crew. "Alert! We may be going out soon. Get to the ship. If you're altered, tell command you need a replacement." If any of my crew were drunk, there'd be hell to pay later, but right now I just needed useful people on my ship. I sent a similar message to Jenny, who acknowledged it even as we came through the door.

"Nobody's fired yet, but the Zhen have all the civilian ships targeted," she said aloud. "Our own ships are holding fire, but are vectoring to cover the civvies."

"Do we know what the freighters have?"

"Nothing but colonists, according to them. They're screaming that to the Zhen too."

I nodded and opened a comms signal to the Zhen ships. "Attention Zhen task force. You are targeting civilian ships. If you do not cease targeting them, you *will* be fired upon."

A Zhen:ko appeared in my visual field. I immediately started my NeuroNet recording the conversation in full virtuality mode. The slight waver in her form told me she was not physically in the system, but that her image was being relayed via the Zhen command ship's slipnet comms. She was dressed in opulent robes that covered everything but her head. The least valuable gem in her bejeweled headdress, shining silver against her age-faded red scales, would buy an entire fleet of starships – not that she needed another fleet. "Tajen Hunt, I am disappointed in you."

I swallowed the sudden knot of fear in my gut and raised an eyebrow. "You say that as if I were unaware, Empress."

"You are many things," she said drily, "but 'unaware' is not one of them."

Despite my fear, I found myself slipping into the cadences and diction of formal court language. "And yet, there are so many ways I could have disappointed you. Against my better judgment, I must ask – to which do you refer?"

Her face didn't change, but her crest quivered slightly – despite herself, she was amused. "You are too…human."

I cocked my head. "And this is surprising?"

"We saved your people from the brink of death. We welcomed you, gave you a colony world to call your own. And you have turned against us."

I nodded. Using memories of my training to force myself to remain still and calm, I said, "Yes, you did rescue a few of us." I hardened my voice a bit. "But before that, you destroyed our world – our entire civilization. How are we supposed to thank you for saving a few hundred thousand of us when you first destroyed over ten *billion*?"

She waved that off. "Irrelevant. Those actions were taken more than a thousand years ago, by people long since dead. Are we, now, to pay for the mistakes of previous generations?"

"When you are still reaping the benefits of those actions? Yes! You people didn't just destroy our world. You suppressed our culture, our language. You robbed us of our literature, our music, everything that made us who we are."

"And yet you are still yourselves, still *human*," she said, as if the word gave her a bad taste, "still fractious, rebellious. We gave you our language, our technology, our culture. We gave you our *Empire*. And you have wasted it."

"We've wasted *nothing*," I said, feeling my patience slipping. "We are fighting for the soul of our people."

She gestured *tolerant amusement*. "A lofty idea, but foolish. You've no idea what your vaunted Earth was like. Your culture was divided by regional ideologies. Your world was poisoned by your own technology. Many lived in poverty while a few reigned over the rest from on high. It was a disaster of a world," she said with distaste.

"And how is that any different from the Empire? The Zhen:ko are few, compared to the rest of the Zhen, and yet they rule over all. And *all* Zhen are higher than the human race in the eyes of the law."

She gave the Zhen equivalent of a shrug. "My caste has ruled the Zhen for more than twenty thousand years. Are we to reorder our Empire for the convenience of a few humans?"

"We would not ask that. I can almost – *almost* – forgive the destruction of Earth. It was, as you say, a thousand years ago, and those who did it are long dead. But you have done very little to make it up to us. Why subjugate us? Why not just tell us the truth, give us a colony world, and leave us alone? Why make us lick your boots?"

Several emotions played across her face, and she narrowed her eyes at me. Whatever war she waged with herself, her better nature lost as she spat, "Because that is all you are good for."

I blinked. Sure, we were second-class citizens in the Empire, and I'd been called a lot of names by Zhen over the years, but I never expected to hear such raw hatred from the One. "Then why 'save' us?" I asked incredulously.

She inclined her head, and her crest moved in a way that meant *resignation*. "The Zhen of the time felt guilty. But our guilt does not make you better than you are. They felt that only by guiding you could we avoid your vengeance for what had been done. They felt that, in a few thousand years, perhaps you would be a civilized people. *Then* you would be worthy to become our equals. *Then* you would be able to bear the truth." Her face turned grim. "But for that to happen, we must cut out the discontented among you. And so we allowed you to take over this system, to stage your little rebellion. And now that you have gathered those who are like you, it is time to spring the trap. Once we have destroyed you, we will civilize those remaining." She paused. "Molding your race more directly will slow our expansion plans, but in the end, we will have human soldiers who will fight and die at our word."

I tried to think of something, anything I could say, that would stop her. But it was like trying to stop the tides, or the heat of a star. She looked to her side, and said simply, "Begin the attack." She faded from view.

"Oh, hell," I said. "All ships – protect the civilians. Prepare for attack—"

"Zhen firing!" Jenny exclaimed, just as the icons in the battle tank shifted – and one, denoting the lead freighter, flashed orange, indicating damage. "Lead civvie hit. Damaged, but still in one piece."

I was already running for the airlock where the *Dream of Earth* was docked. While I ran, I snapped orders to the crew. I hit the airlock at a run, making my way to the pilot's couch. I turned the final corner; Katherine appeared from another corridor and fell into step.

I careened into the cockpit and slid by the standby operator, Phillip, an inexperienced young man whose job was only to keep the ship running and ready for launch whenever it was on station. "No time for a replacement. Strap in," I said, and tried to ignore the way the blood drained from his face. As the ship's systems interfaced with my implants and the HUD unfolded in my vision, I strapped into my seat, Katherine sliding into her own.

"All hands, prepare for launch on my mark," she said. I nodded, and she hit the release. "Mark."

I moved us away from the lock with maneuvering thrusters, swung the nose around toward the developing combat, and slammed the throttle to full. "Attention Earth forces," I said on the all-comms. "Prime station has battle command. All ships take their orders." The fight had developed into a full-on dogfight before we'd even cleared the station. The computer highlighted targets, automatically prioritizing them for me.

Dozens of small ships were moving in different directions, struggling for firing positions while the capital ships sat in the distance, their gunnery officers no doubt working out their own firing solutions. "Liam, talk to me," I said. "Who needs the most help?"

With our slipnet down, we were using a Kelvaki comms system Kiri and Dierka had installed in our ships, eliminating the communications lag of radio comms. Liam's voice came back mere seconds after I'd asked the question. "The lead freighter, the *Jessalyn*, is limping. She needs protection. I'll update your target list as necessary."

"On it," I said, and set course for the freighter. I activated the chain drive and felt the slight surge of speed that bled through the inertial dampers. Seconds later, I cut the chain drive out and the freighter flickered into view as we dropped into their neighborhood.

Almost immediately, the ship's weapons system locked onto the ships harassing the *Jeremy Lynn*, prioritizing the nearest ship, which had just flipped over, coasting backward as it fired on the freighter. I squeezed the trigger, sending plasma energy coursing from my guns into their rear thrusters. The resulting energy discharge tore the ship apart as the engine blew.

"That's one," Katherine remarked.

"I can count," I said, and changed our vector to pursue the other ship, which had noticed us and was angling to get clear. "Oh no you don't," I said, diverting power to the thrusters.

As we closed on the ship, Katherine started to look nervous. "Tajen, he's going to—"

"I know he is," I said. "In fact, I'm counting on it." I sent a command to the ship, power switching from thrust and my forward shields to the guns. The Zhen ship began to flip backward in an attempt to bring the forward guns to bear on us. "The bonehead maneuver," I said with a grin. "Let's show 'em why it's called that." When they presented their topside shield facing, I fired all my weapons at her. The first shots blasted through the already-weakened shield, the last few shots impacted directly on the ship's hull, and the plasma chewed through the ship's armor. Immediately after I fired, I changed my ship's vector by ninety degrees and performed another instant-long burst of the chain drive, flashing away from where I had been in seconds. Even with the second or two the chain drive takes to initiate, we were well away before we hit him.

When the chain drive quit, I hauled my ship's nose back toward the Zhen just in time to see another of my ships take him out. "Nice flying," I commented to Katherine.

"Should be," she said. "That's James Doyle's kid."

"Seriously?" James had been my first civilian boss, right after I got out of the military. Since then he'd become a rather notorious smuggler, known for flying rings around Zhen patrols.

"Yep. Joined us last week. She said a Zhen interdiction patrol shot her dad out of the sky over Maak just after we found Earth."

My implants highlighted the new targets Liam had prioritized for us, and Katherine set the course as I kept us moving, dodging through the firefight, trying to prevent anyone from drawing a stable lock on us. "They got Doyle?"

She grinned. "Nah. They got his ship, but he'd already launched an escape pod. Way she tells it, she had to fight to keep him from going on a one-man war against the Zhen after your broadcast. But he's on his way – went to get the rest of their family, first. Look out for that fighter!"

"I see it," I said calmly as I shifted vectors. "I look forward to seeing him ag—" I cursed and jerked the controls, barely avoiding a full-on crash with a piece of debris that had sheared off a nearby out-of-control Zhen fighter. It didn't miss me completely, however; the chunk of metal slammed into my portside weapons pod, shearing it off at the hard point. "*Shraak*," I shouted, fighting to control the *Dream of Earth*. "We've lost the port plasma guns. We've got plasma leaking."

"On it," Phillip called. "Repair bots are closing off the plasma conduits."

"Reroute to the remaining weapons," I said, pretending to be calm while I tried to tame the ship. He decided not to inform me he'd already thought of that, which was just one of the several reasons I was going to have him assigned to my crew permanently once this fight was done. The kid was *good*.

I finally managed to get the ship under control and looked around wildly, trying to find the target Liam had assigned me. Belatedly, I cursed under my breath at my stupidity and let my tactical system guide me to the target, a Zhen gunship that was angling for a firing solution on the station.

Katherine swore. "If that ship gets in position...."

"I know," I said, and hit the throttle to max. The ship surged forward. I started to check the repair status when the ship bucked under me, and we were all thrown up against our harnesses. My NeuroNet was sending me so many alarms I was barely able to track them all. I instructed my NeuroNet to shut off all the alarms for systems not at my current station. In the resulting semi-calm, I called "Report!"

"We took a hit topside," Phillip called from his station.

"Yeah, I noticed that," I yelled back. "How bad?"

"It slammed through what was left of our dorsal shields and the armor," he said, his voice falling into a clinical pattern. "We still have power, barely, but guns are down, gravity is down, navigation is down, engines are damaged – still powered, but not enough for movement." He paused a moment, then said, "External comms are down too."

The ventral gunner reported her weapons were powerless. I already knew the main guns were dead. There was no report from the dorsal gunner, and a quick check of the system showed he was gone, his gunnery pod open to space. "We're dead in space," I said, setting a reminder in my 'Net to contact his family when I could.

"Yes, sir."

Katherine and I looked at each other. "The hell with that," she said, unstrapping. She floated out of her seat, and turned to leave the bridge. "Phillip, with me. We're going to fix those engines or die trying."

They headed aft to the engines, and I hooked my NeuroNet into the engineering station and looked over the status board that came up in my visual field. In a nutshell, we were screwed.

The engines were hanging by a thread, with available power barely enough to keep them idling. The system had closed down the links to weapons, life support, and flight systems to conserve energy. Fortunately, the secondary life support system had kicked in, and that would keep the temperature and oxygen going for a couple of days, but eventually the batteries would die, and then so would we, if we didn't get out of this before then.

I checked our inertial monitors and groaned – we were drifting at speed, headed away from the planet. The farther out we got, the more difficult it would be to find us.

"Liam," I whispered. Unless Katherine and Phillip worked a miracle back there, I'd never see him again. Or Kiri, or Ben, or any of the people who had, since we began this crazy campaign, become important to me. I sat there, on the knife-edge between anger and frustrated tears. I was waiting for the other shoe to drop – for some passing Zhen ship to take a potshot at the nearly dead human ship, and send us straight to hell.

"Seriously?" The question came from right beside my head. I jumped, and only the restraints around my torso kept me from flying off in the zero gravity. Standing behind my chair, apparently unruffled in the zero-gravity reality I was sitting in, was Daav.

"What the hell?" I said.

"You tell me," he replied.

I blinked at it. "You're from my vision."

"Yes."

"Am I unconscious?"

"Are you?"

I took stock quickly. "No, it would appear not."

Daav merely cocked his head at me.

"So," I said slowly, "you're not a vision."

"No."

"But you are the Daav *from* my vision."

"Yep."

"I thought you were a manifestation of my self, created by the machine."

"Yes, you did."

"You said it."

He shrugged. "Yep."

"But I'm not hooked up to the machine. Why are you here?"

He sighed. "Tajen, I'm a figment of your imagination summoned up by your subconscious to help you out when you're stressed. You didn't really think you were going to get through all this without a little bit of psychosis, did you? Anyway. All this hello-how-are-you stuff is fine, but you're in a tight spot right now and you need to pull your head out of your ass. Enough of this 'I'm going to die boo hoo' crap. You need to get out of this and take care of your family. And I don't just mean Kiri. Now get moving!"

I sat staring at him for a moment, then shrugged. Even if he was a looming psychotic break, he wasn't wrong. I banished the engineering board; that was Katherine's puzzle to solve. Mine was the battle. I called up a three-dimensional view of the battle as it had been when I got my last update. Things would have changed by now, but the general shape of the battle as it stood a few minutes ago would help me make sense of things.

I started a battle simulator in my NeuroNet, setting up a typical Zhen commander virtual intelligence to run the Zhen side. I tried my best to counter everything it did, but the Zhen simply had too many ships, and too much firepower, for the humans – for us – to win. Try as I might, there was only one outcome.

"We're dead," I said. "How the hell am I going to get out of this?" But my hallucination of an older brother was gone, and my question echoed on the empty bridge.

★ ★ ★

Slightly less than an hour later, full power came up. A second later, a shout of triumph floated up from the engine room.

I brought up the status board and grinned as the lights went green. I told the system to update our position and the tactical simulation.

Just as Katherine entered the bridge and slid into her seat, the comms came live. I accessed the system and found the situation had changed, and not in a good way.

The Zhen were still dominating the system. They hadn't yet managed to get into a bombardment position in orbit, but they were getting closer. The station was still intact, and seemed to be directing human and Kelvaki activity, but the situation was getting increasingly desperate.

The status for chain drive stayed red. "Damn," I said. "No chain drive."

"No," Katherine said. "The drive unit is totally slagged. We've got jump capability, though."

"Great," I said, rolling my eyes. "We can jump. Fat lot of good that is when we're already—" An idea began to form in my head. "Oh."

"I've seen that look before, Tajen. It means you have a plan," Katherine said.

"Oh, I've got one – but you're not going to like it."

"I never do."

I craned my head around to Phillip, who was just starting to strap himself back into his seat. "Phillip, how's our escape pod? Still intact?"

He looked chagrined. "Yeah, but—"

"But?"

"I just got us functional," he said.

"*We* just got us functional, thank you," Katherine said.

"And I thank you both," I said. "Truly. But we're going to need the pod." I outlined my plan.

They both stared at me for a few seconds. Finally, Katherine spoke. "I don't like it."

"Told you," I said.

"It's insane," she cried.

"Of course it is. But if it works—"

"It'll end this battle, and quick," Katherine said. "But if it fails—"

"Then we're dead. But you gotta die of something."

She grinned. "All right, I'm convinced."

"You two get the escape pod ready. I'll prepare things up here."

Katherine nodded, then glanced quickly at her board. "You'd better hurry," she said. "I'm reading two Zhen ships coming this way. They must have realized we're back up."

She and Phillip got out of their seats and floated from the bridge, and I slipped my perception from the reality of the bridge to the ship's computer network. I stood in the datascape, tracing the lines of the ship's control systems. I isolated the control systems for the jump drive. *There we go.*

Before me was a tangle of blue and red lines, each filament of light representing the code that ran the system. I traced my way through the knot, looking for one particular code fragment. It seemed to take forever, but I was working on the scale of milliseconds, here. I'd have been surprised to find I'd been in the datascape for more than a couple of seconds, so far.

Ah, there it is. The node I was looking for pulsed in my vision. I considered just tearing it apart, but I realized that wouldn't work in this case – the safety lock in the system was too well integrated into the drive; if I just destroyed it, it was likely to cause a cascade failure that would leave me without any options at best, and destroy the ship and all four of us left aboard, at worst. I studied the code intently, wishing I'd paid a little more attention in my engineering classes and looking for a way to unravel it without causing drive failure.

Ah – there. I reached out and took hold of the code, pouring my awareness into it, rerouting the system so it wouldn't even recognize what I was going to ask it to do. It was tricky, and I nearly lost the thread several times – but I managed it. With a grin I switched my perceptions back to reality. "All done here!" I called over comms.

Katherine's voice came over my 'Net. "We're ready at the pod. Need us up there?"

"No," I sent back. "Get everyone in the pod. I'm on my way."

I slapped the emergency release on my harness and floated toward the bridge exit. I tried not to think about the sacrifice I was about to make of a ship that had been in my family for more than a hundred years. "I'm sorry," I said to the ship as I headed toward the escape pod, my NeuroNet still in contact with the bridge controls. "I wouldn't do it if I didn't have to." I delegated a subroutine to calculate the coordinates I needed. The program reported a solution just as I reached the pod. "Everybody ready?" I asked.

Phillip nodded from his couch, where he'd already strapped himself in, but Katherine looked at me like I was insane. "I'm not sure anyone can ever be ready for a stunt like this. Are you sure we can get far enough away from the ship in time?"

"Of course," I said, all bluster. I glanced at Phillip, who looked dubious. "Well," I modified, "reasonably sure. Sort of."

She rolled her eyes and began strapping into one of the crew couches. "Let's just get it over with," she said. "We're probably dead either way."

"That's the spirit," I deadpanned, and strapped in to my own seat, taking control of the pod's flight systems as the remaining gunner entered the pod and began to strap herself down across from Phillip. I noticed the two of them give each other a look, and said, "What, you guys don't trust your captain?"

The gunner smiled. "We trust you, Captain," she said, the perspiration glistening on her dark skin, "but this plan of yours? Not so much."

I smiled. When she had finished preparing herself, I shut the door and launched us. "What's your name?" I asked the gunner.

"Tatiana, sir," she said, sounding irritated that I'd forgotten it.

"That's right, from Galileo," I said, naming a city on Terra.

"Yes, sir."

"Well, Tatiana," I said, as the pod crossed the minimum safety margin for a jump, "I hope you're wrong. Here we go." I triggered the jump I'd programmed into the system.

Space warped and twisted itself around the stricken *Dream of Earth*, and the ship disappeared from our NeuroNet's awareness. I switched to the tactical view, still being relayed, thank the Nine, by the station's TacComm.

Everything looked normal for several long seconds, before the readings on the Zhen flagship went insane. The readouts made no sense, but something was going on – and of course I knew just what.

I'd programmed the *Dream of Earth*'s jump drives to jump her to the coordinates in the middle of the flagship – or, rather, to where I expected the flagship to be moments after jump. If what I was seeing on the TacComm was accurate, I'd been off by only a small distance – which meant that my ship had tried to exit jump space inside the flagship, just as intended. I'd aimed for the hangar, but I was probably off by a bit. Still, the resulting energy discharge, not to mention the almost immediate destruction of my own ship's fusion core, would wreak havoc on the larger vessel. Essentially, I'd turned my ship into a fusion bomb.

Normally, of course, the safeties in the jump system would prevent such a thing – but I'd disabled those safeties, which in normal cases was downright suicidal.

The flagship began firing its own escape pods, and moments later, it exploded. We saw the explosion over the TacComm, and we heard the pilots discussing it, and then some time later our pod was buffeted by the shockwave. We rode out the craziness until the pod's computer began to fire the thrusters, bringing our tumble under control.

"What do you know," I said. "It worked."

We stared at each other for several long moments, then we began to laugh in relief at still being alive, in fits and giggles that built in power until, finally, we were doubled over in our harnesses, practically unable to breathe.

And then the pod was hit, and I was slammed against the restraints. A klaxon sounded, the sound fading as the atmosphere vented into space, and we found ourselves truly unable to breathe. *Well, shit*, I thought as spots began to appear before my eyes, *guess I don't get the happy ending*. I looked at Katherine, and yelled, "I'm sorry!" at her, the words swallowed by the vacuum. She gave me a sad smile, then closed her eyes and settled her head back against her headrest, as if she was going to sleep.

I watched in horror as the others lost consciousness one by one, my implant-enhanced metabolism helping me stay awake a few more minutes. I spent them railing at the unfair universe that had led us all to this moment, raging at my failure, and cursing the Zhen, before I, too, fell into darkness.

★   ★   ★

I woke up, which was rather pleasant. I mean, I'd hoped for a rescue, but you never know, right? According to my NeuroNet, I'd been out for two days. I was in a hospital bed, in a semi-reclining position. I took stock and, against my expectations, I seemed to have all my parts. I blinked into the bright white lights overhead and cleared my throat. Well, I tried to. The sound I actually produced was somewhere between a croak and a whimper. I reached up to the sensor on my temple and pulled it off. There, that ought to get someone's attention.

An unfamiliar woman, carrying a box stuffed full of what looked like medical supplies, stepped into my view through the doorway briefly, then she was gone. "He's awake!" I heard her cry.

Moments later, Liam and Kiri arrived at my bedside. "Glad you're back," Liam said. Kiri just hugged me.

"How am I?" I asked.

"Not great," Kiri said. "We got to you before you died, barely, but all of you needed time under nano-surgery. You look pretty awful, but Ben says you'll heal pretty again. You owe Phillip and Tatiana your lives, you know."

"Oh?"

"I've seen the pod's vid feed. While you and Katherine went all 'noble death', Phillip and 'Tiana got off their asses and sealed the breach."

"Oh," I said. "They're good. How's Katherine?"

"She's been up for over twenty-four hours. Phillip and 'Tiana too. We weren't sure you'd wake up."

"I needed the sleep," I said.

"You're an idiot."

"Yes." I smiled at her, which hurt. "Did we win?" I asked Liam.

He looked grim. "We beat them back – your destruction of their flagship totally screwed up their battle planning – but the victory cost us. We lost most of our fighters, and half the larger ships."

"What's the Zhen response?"

Kiri answered. "I got a message from someone I know on Zhen:da. The *Talnera* is in debate over how to handle things. The Virginia

Peninsula is under martial law, and the humans are laying low. But we haven't got much in the way of assets there. For all we know they're marshaling all their remaining ships to come after us."

Liam spoke up. "Dierka's people offered us sanctuary. I tried to order everyone to head for Kelvaki space."

"Tried?"

"They flat-out refused. Said they'd already given up everything to come here, they were damned well not going to give up their rightful world even if it means dying on it."

"What, all of them?"

"Well, a few left. Some to the Kelvaki Assembly, others are going to try to sneak back to Terra. Some of them offered to be our agents in the Assembly or the Empire. But the majority stayed."

I was surprised. I knew a lot of our people had suffered under the Zhen, but to consider death preferable to escape? I didn't understand it at first. But it came to me, eventually – if my people fled to the Kelvaki Assembly, they would be, in a way, trading one alien overlord for another. Maybe the Kelvaki would be more beneficent than the Zhen had been, but why would anyone take that chance, when the Zhen had treated us so utterly badly? If they returned to Zhen space, they'd be suspect, even on Terra. No, far better to take a stand. And if they – miners, and grocers, and ordinary people who had never fought in their lives – could make the decision to stand, here and now, against our oppressors, then how could I not stand with them?

I nodded, and sat up. Kiri handed me some clothes from the chair beside my bed and I nodded thanks at her good thinking, then said to Liam, "We'll stay too, of course. We'll leave the comms system. We can use that, and Kiri put in some backdoor protocols that ought to keep us linked in. We'll need access to intel if we're going to fight." I stood up and gave him my best smile.

"I love you," he said.

"Of course you do. I'm amazing."

"Look, I've got to get back to planning."

"For?"

"Since almost none of our people took up the offer for sanctuary, Dierka's sending us a task group to protect the colony, and some supplies to start us building. I'm working with an advisor from the

Assembly to find a defensible place to put the first settlement. I love you, Taj. See you soon." He winked at Kiri, cocked an eyebrow at me, and left.

Kiri watched him go. "I'm glad you two found each other," she said.

"Me too. But...."

"Yes?"

"I'm sorry, Kiri."

"For what?"

I sighed, and sat down on the edge of the bed. "For getting you involved in this mess. You know we're doomed, right?"

She sat beside me. "I know the odds say that. But I've been watching you and this crew of ours fight the odds, and we win more often than we lose. I'll take my chances."

"You're insane, you know. Smart move is to head for Kelvaki space."

"But you haven't suggested that – and you won't. Right?" she asked, giving me a look that suggested I'd better not.

I smiled, and put my arm around her shoulders. "Not a chance," I said, giving her a squeeze.

"Good. Now. Are you gonna marry Liam?"

"Shut up," I said, embarrassed.

"Not a chance. Get yourself in gear. We need to head down to Earth and help Liam figure out where we're going to put our colony."

"Yes, ma'am."

She looked at me with the same impish grin that had charmed me when she was two. "Goddamn right," she said.

"Did your dad ever tell you you're too much like me?"

"Sometimes he was smiling, sometimes not."

"I miss him."

Katherine appeared in the doorway. "Ready to go?"

"Yeah," I said, taking Kiri's hand for a moment. "Let's go."

EPILOGUE

Three days later, the five of us stood before a bonfire, silent. We had laid the wood according to Terra custom, and placed Takeshi's effects on the bier along with his body. Terra's funereal rites were a mishmash of several Earth customs that the original colonists had passed down, along with some elements adopted from the Zhen and other alien races in the Empire. We stood silently, watching as his body and his few possessions were consumed by the fire. As Takeshi's body was consumed, we moved away to a smaller fire. We sat around this fire, staring into the flames, for quite a while.

Eventually, Katherine cleared her throat. "Takeshi Ryan Lawson," she said. "Born on Terra, died on Earth. The first of his line in over a thousand years to see home." She flung a handful of powder into the fire. It flared, the flames climbing higher for a second, signaling that she had finished speaking.

Liam spoke up. "Takeshi and I met at a difficult time for me. He taught me to laugh again." He threw his powder into the fire.

Ben said, "It took me forever to train him, but he was the best damned nurse I've ever had. I'm going to miss him." The fire flared once more.

Kiri said, "He was my friend. He gave me so much good advice."

I leaned forward. "I only knew him a few months, but he was part of my family," I said. "He was wise far beyond his years, and the best cook I've ever known." I threw my own powder into the fire, then leaned over and grabbed a bottle of whisky one of the recruits had given me when he arrived – "A gift from my mom," he'd said – cracked it open, and passed it around as we told stories of our departed friend.

Ben said, "Takeshi liked to play tricks on people. One year, on his birthday, he got hold of a bottle of *kaltopesh*."

"Tell me he didn't drink it!" I exclaimed. Human and Kelvaki biochemistry is different enough that their food rarely tastes good to humans. Some of it is downright poisonous, but mostly it just tastes bad. *Kaltopesh* is a liquor, and it was particularly foul to human taste, even though it didn't smell bad. I'd never heard of a human managing to actually swallow the stuff – it was that awful. I tried it once, on a dare. Every once in a while, I'd remember the taste and shudder.

"*He* didn't," Ben said. "But he had a problem with a guy who insulted his cooking, so he got hold of a bottle, and poured it into six black stoneware cups, so the guy couldn't see what it was. He took it to the guy's table and spent six minutes concocting this ridiculous 'ancient Japanese ritual of apology'. He gave them each a cup, and kept one for himself – his had water in it – and explained they had to slam it back when he said the word. Then he shouted the word, threw his back, and watched as they all started choking." He chuckled. "They were pissed, but he thought it was the funniest damned thing. And they were so busy choking they couldn't punch him. By the time they'd recovered, security had arrived and made sure they left peacefully."

I shook my head, laughing, and leaned against Liam as Katherine started to tell a story from their childhood. At the end of it, Liam and I were both fighting to breathe through the laughter.

We sat all night telling each other stories until the sun began to rise, at first about Takeshi, but then about ourselves. We shared our lives in ways we hadn't had a lot of time for until now. Then we all went quiet, watched the dawn, and wondered how much time we'd have before the hammer fell. We all knew it was going to fall, sooner or later. But right now? Right now was a time to be grateful what was left of our family was still here.

As the sun cleared the horizon, Liam stood beside me and took my hand. "I get it now," he said quietly, nodding toward the sun as it shone over the green valley spread out before us. I squeezed his hand.

For the first time in over a thousand years, humans were in possession of Earth.

Now we just had to find a way to keep it.

ACKNOWLEDGMENTS

Writing a book may be a solitary endeavor, but publishing one is not. Many people had a hand in getting this story to you. First and foremost, I'd like to thank my editor, Don D'Auria, for taking a chance on me, and further thanks to him and to copy-editor Imogen Howson for helping to make this book better than it was when I first sent it to them.

This is the last of many drafts, and several people read those earlier drafts and helped me improve it. Chief among these were my fellow Science Fiction/Fantasy writers. Devin Singer, Beth Morris Tanner, M.E. Garber, Laurence Raphael Brothers, Paul Starr, C.C.S. Ryan, Jacob Herlitz, and Alex Haist all helped make the story better, as did our VP instructors Elizabeth Bear, James D. Macdonald, Steven Gould, and Patrick Nielsen Hayden. Thanks also go to Teresa Nielsen Hayden, for encouragement and conversation.

Many friends acted as tireless cheerleaders and support during the writing of this book. In no particular order: Miles Cochran, Jerry Kennedy, Brian Gray, Lynne Ruvalcaba, Daniel Gatten, Cricket Kennedy, Jim St. Claire, Laura-Ann St. Clair, and Joseph Harney. If I have forgotten anyone, the fault is mine; *mea culpa*, and I'll catch you in the next book.

Thanks to my wife and fellow writer Elli Johnston, and our daughter, Tegan Johnston, for endless understanding when I'm gone to conferences and deep in writing or editing. Finally, thanks to my aunt and uncle, Karla and John Hillis, for raising and encouraging me.

FLAME TREE PRESS
FICTION WITHOUT FRONTIERS
Award-Winning Authors & Original Voices

Flame Tree Press is the trade fiction imprint of Flame Tree Publishing, focusing on excellent writing in horror and the supernatural, crime and mystery, science fiction and fantasy. Our aim is to explore beyond the boundaries of the everyday, with tales from both award-winning authors and original voices.

•

Other titles available include:

Junction by Daniel M. Bensen

Thirteen Days by Sunset Beach by Ramsey Campbell

Think Yourself Lucky by Ramsey Campbell

The Haunting of Henderson Close by Catherine Cavendish

The House by the Cemetery by John Everson

The Toy Thief by D.W. Gillespie

Black Wings by Megan Hart

The Playing Card Killer by Russell James

The Siren and the Specter by Jonathan Janz

The Sorrows by Jonathan Janz

Savage Species by Jonathan Janz

The Nightmare Girl by Jonathan Janz

Wolf Land by Jonathan Janz

Will Haunt You by Brian Kirk

Kosmos by Adrian Laing

The Sky Woman by J.D. Moyer

Creature by Hunter Shea

The Bad Neighbor by David Tallerman

Ten Thousand Thunders by Brian Trent

Night Shift by Robin Triggs

The Mouth of the Dark by Tim Waggoner

•

Join our mailing list for free short stories, new release details, news about our authors and special promotions:

flametreepress.com